Dawn Grave Book 1

Grave Regret

Chapter 1

Sweat pooled at Dawn's back, despite the hire car air-conditioner blasting at her face. She watched the temperature gauge climb as the ostentatiously painted backpacker van, with politically incorrect slogans sprawled down the side, spluttered and backfired up the steep incline.

This was the only hire vehicle she could organise on short notice. Early spring in tropical Far North Queensland was touristville, and Cairns was full of southerners trying to soak up the warmth before the rainy season kicked in.

Fighting to keep herself awake, Dawn fiddled with the radio. Static fizzled and screeched back at her.

'Damn!'

She was travelling right off the back of a major murder case in the middle of nowhere, with only a few hours' sleep on the plane from Adelaide to Cairns. All to chase up a cryptic message from her sister, in a place she hoped never to see again.

The murder case in desolate Coober Pedy kept her occupied all week and she'd avoided each message Lisa sent her. A tiny shred of guilt knotted in her stomach. As soon as the case was cracked, and her murder suspect in custody, she tried to call Lisa—but there was no answer.

Now, as she drove past the hospital, she was worried something terrible had happened. Shaking her head, she forced the thought from her mind. When Lisa failed to answer her calls, she did what any good detective would do.

She rang the hospital and the local police. She would have rung Lisa's friends, if she knew any of them.

Turning the rusted Toyota HiAce van down the dirt track off Boundary Street, Dawn braced herself for the vibration the tiny tyres and rutted road were sure to produce. Despite her preparation, the wheel jerked in her hands at the first pothole and the van pulled hard to the left. Steering it back, she cursed under her breath.

The dense bushland closed in around her as the road narrowed. It was amazing how the scrub was still so close to town. The new highway from Mossman to Cooktown saw the remote town growing in popularity. It was only a matter of time before these blocks were cut up and more winter holiday homes covered the hillside.

Turning left into the barely visible driveway brought a rush of memories. None of them good. Forcing down bile, she focussed on avoiding the corrugations and stray branches lying at the edge of the winding track.

A gasp caught in her throat as the homestead came into view. Standing tall on stilts, with timber weatherboards hanging loose and crumbling, was her childhood home. The classic square-pane casement windows were ajar across the front of the balcony.

She parked the van in front of the double-sided staircase with tulip cut-outs and slatted balustrading. A curve crept across her lips, despite her clouded memories.

Composing herself, she scanned the yard from inside the van, before finally putting her hand on the door and opening it. As she slid out from behind the wheel, the moist humid air assaulted her. The result—instant sweaty armpits and frizzy hair.

It was spring, but even spring in Far North Queensland was humid.

So damned humid, she thought.

Dawn lifted her tight-fitting tank top away from her already damp skin and pumped it, trying to let some airflow in to cool her. Failing, she slammed the van door closed with a creak and followed the crushed rock path to the left side of the double staircase, where a rusty iron gate hung open.

'Lisa! Are you home?'

She mounted the first rung cautiously and waited. No cheery reply came. Slowly, she stepped up towards the long, wide and airy wrap-around veranda. The wooden stairs creaked with each footfall. Glancing down, she noticed they were grey and weathered.

She stopped herself as she reached for the banister rail. The sage green was faded and flaking. The once-white slats, on close inspection, were cracked and daylight shone where it shouldn't.

Despite not wanting to come here, Dawn found herself fighting back tears. Tears desperate to be shed for a past long forgotten.

'Lisa. It's Dawn. I got your message.'

She reached the landing and opened the fretwork gate, jumping as it fell from the hinge with a thud.

Her heartbeat quickened. The place was derelict.

'Lisa!'

A row of stained-glass wind chimes hung from the veranda, along with a mix of ornaments, including a Native American dreamcatcher and a macramé plant holder featuring a gigantically overgrown asparagus fern.

The swaying chimes tinkled in the light afternoon breeze. The sound did nothing to settle her nerves.

'Lisa! Where are you?' She pulled on the carved wooden screen door. It opened without protest to reveal a timber hallway with flaking polish.

Eerie silence greeted her as she crept down the wide hallway. Her stomach churned, while her mind raced, but she suppressed her fears and forced herself to breathe.

Reaching the kitchen, at the far end, she scanned for any sign of a struggle. Her sister wasn't known for her tidiness, but nothing lay broken on the floor. Clean dishes were piled in disarray on the sink. A frying pan on the stove, empty.

The unvarnished kitchen table was covered with jars of fruit preserve, an overflowing fruit bowl, bottles of vitamins and cut native flowers, with a pair of secateurs and gardening gloves abandoned alongside.

A tingling sensation made Dawn turn, but no one was in the kitchen. Peering down the long central hallway, she found it empty.

Meticulously, she searched from room to room. The tiny classic windows let in very little light, but a soft breeze blew through, making the sheer curtains in the next room she entered billow gently.

An iron bed took centre stage in what was once her parents' bedroom. A picture on the wall told Dawn her sister now slept here. There were no fancy cushions arranged on the high-set bed. In fact, it wasn't made. A mosquito net, tied in a huge knot, hung from the high ceiling.

Dawn checked every room efficiently and found no one. Taking the front stairs two at a time, she rushed back down to check the garage under the house.

The picket-slatted doors weren't locked. Dawn pulled one open and peered into the under storey. There was no car. A rusted bicycle hung from the floor joists above. A long bench with disused tools occupied the right wall.

Her sister still wasn't home. She wasn't answering her calls, and the police had no idea where she was.

Striding towards the van, Dawn jumped when her mobile phone rang in her pocket.

Retrieving it with fumbling fingers, she checked the screen. A local number, but not one she knew. She answered.

'Detective Dawn Grave speaking.'

'Detective. This is Senior Sergeant Martin from Cooktown police.'

Dawn's stomach tightened.

'Yes?'

'You called this morning, asking about your sister, Lisa Grave.'

'That's right.'

She wanted to scream for Sergeant Martin to pull his finger out and get on with it, but she knew he was simply going through standard procedure.

'Lisa's car has been found.'

She waited. Her mind flashing with a crash scene. Just like the young constable's brother back in Coober Pedy, only a few days ago. Was she too going to be visiting the scene of a car accident?

She forced herself into professional mode. It was her go-to when stress threatened to trigger a panic attack.

'Sergeant, where was the car found?'

'Out at Archer Point.'

Her stomach did a flip.

'And my sister?'

'I'm sorry Detective Grave, but your sister wasn't with the vehicle.'

'I'm on my way.'

'Hang on. On your way from Adelaide?'

'No Sergeant. I'm at my sister's house now. She's not home. It's been left unlocked, and something feels wrong.'

‘Leaving the place unlocked isn’t that unusual. Lisa’s house isn’t exactly one you’d trip over unless you knew where to find it.’

The sergeant was right. She’d been living in the city too long. No one ever used to lock their house in Cooktown.

‘I’ll be at Archer Point in half an hour.’

‘Hang about Dawn.’

She said nothing when he used her first name. She didn’t like it, but she couldn’t stop him. Sergeant Martin knew her father, and he’d known her since she was a baby.

‘The road out there is crap at the moment. I’m guessing you’ve got a hire car. Why don’t you come to the station. I’ve got a local ranger here. He found the car. He’ll take you out to meet Constable Jamison on scene.’

‘I’ll be five minutes.’

She hung up, shoved her phone in her pocket and yanked the van door open. Within seconds she had the motor started and was backing the van out. She didn’t bother with her seatbelt as her mind raced with regrets.

Why didn’t I return Lisa’s call sooner?

Chapter 2

The police station, like most buildings in Cooktown, hadn't changed. The height of the palm trees lining the path was the only indication of the passing of twenty years.

The drive into town sparked memories she had spent the past two decades trying to suppress, but then there were some that made her smile. Like her first time sneaking into the RSL for a beer with friends. Swimming in the river and praying a croc wasn't on the hunt. The first time sailing a dinghy in the bay.

But the few happy reminders weren't enough to wipe out everything else. Shaking her head, she forced the turmoil in her stomach to still, before pushing the station door open.

A man in his late fifties waited at the front counter. His eyes warm, his smile unforced.

'Dawn. You haven't changed a bit.'

'You're a good liar Sergeant Martin.'

'Call me Ross. You're not a kid anymore.'

'You were always Constable Martin. Sergeant now. When did that happen?'

'Not long after you left town. Detective, hey?'

His eyebrows lifted.

'Life throws this stuff at you.'

He nodded.

The sound of someone clearing their throat made Dawn turn. Standing with his back against the foyer wall, Akubra held to his chest, was a park ranger whose dark brown eyes studied her.

Sun-bleached blond and red streaks mottled his curly mop of hair and seemed out of place against his dark complexion.

'Michael. This is Dawn Grave. Dawn, this is the ranger I told you about.'

He stepped forward, hand extended, eyes drilling hers, expression unmoving.

His eyebrows lifted. 'Lisa's sister?'

'The very same.' Dawn shook his hand firmly.

'You ready to head out?'

He didn't wait for an answer. Dawn watched his retreating back, turned to Sergeant Martin and shrugged.

'I'll be back later. I want to meet you out at the house. Something's not quite right.'

'See what you find out at Archer first, hey?'

Dawn nodded, then turned to leave. Michael waited by the door, holding it, foot tapping impatiently.

'You're in a rush for a local.'

She couldn't help noticing Ranger Michael didn't seem to have the usual local Indigenous casual approach to life.

'I've got work to do.'

Another anomaly.

She said nothing as he let the door go after she passed through and quickly overtook her on the way to his vehicle.

A white Toyota troop carrier with a turquoise logo on the door featuring a dugong and the words *Yuku Baja Muliku Ranger* wrapped around it, made her stop a moment.

'You're not with National Parks?'

'We contract in the homelands.'

He pressed *unlock* on the keys, lights flashed, and he opened the driver's side door without another word.

Dawn suppressed all the questions running around her mind as she pulled herself up into the passenger's side. It seemed some things were different about Cooktown after all.

'Where exactly was the car when you found it?'

'Parked under the trees at First Beach.'

Michael started the car and backed out, as he pushed the vehicle into first, his eyes scanned Dawn's face.

He was expecting her to ask more questions, but her mind was racing. They'd visited Archer Point a lot as teens. Fishing, swimming, sunbathing, but as far as she knew, neither of them had been back since …

She sighed deeply.

'Everything okay?' Michael watched her from the corner of his eye.

'My sister is missing. How can everything be okay?'

'Sorry. I meant, are you okay?'

Now he decides to make small talk.

'I'll tell you when I see the car.'

The Archer Point Road lived up to the warning. Her campervan would have shaken to pieces on the corrugated, rutted road. The two creek crossings, despite the usually drier time of year, were still too deep to get anything but a four-wheel drive through.

A police vehicle came into view as they turned into the First Beach parking area. A large commercial bin framed the cyclone-wire fenced entrance. Trees hung low over the area, creating shade, but making parking difficult.

A *No Camping* sign caught her attention.

'Since when has camping not been permitted?'

'Since white fellas decided to piss and shit and leave their rubbish in the bush en masse.'

'Understandable then.'

A tall, lean constable in police blues strolled towards the vehicle as Dawn opened the door. Another wave of humidity brought instant perspiration from every pore. She noted the constable's wet armpits and decided her deodorant was going to get a pounding on this trip.

'Ms Grave. I'm Constable Jamison.'

'Call me Dawn.'

She accepted his outstretched hand and shook it firmly.

'This her car?'

She didn't wait for an answer. The mustard-coloured Isuzu was the only vehicle in sight.

'Ah.' The constable followed her. 'I don't think you should touch anything.'

'No! Really?'

She didn't hide her sarcasm. Then thought better of it. Maybe the constable didn't know she worked with the police.

'Sorry. Is there any sign of foul play? A struggle? Was the vehicle broken into?'

The constable frowned.

'I'm with SAPOL. Detective Sergeant Grave.'

'Oh.'

He stood up straighter. Dawn craned her neck to maintain eye contact.

'I only got here twenty minutes before you. I've called the State Emergency Services, so the SES volunteers will help us check the area. The Yuku rangers are getting a boat in the water.'

'You think she went for a swim—out here—alone?'

Dawn circled around her sister's vehicle, eyes scanning as she made sure not to disturb any evidence.

'We don't know. It's not croc or stinger season, but there's a local fella about three and half metres long. Lives in the next beach around, at the creek entrance.'

'My sister has lived here all her life, Jamison. There is no way she would have gone swimming out here alone, anytime of the year. Besides, we've got history here. I don't understand why she came out to this place at all.'

'History?'

Michael's question made her jump. She'd forgotten he was still there.

'Long story.'

Michael waited. His dark bushy eyebrows knitted together. She waved her hand dismissively and turned her attention back to the vehicle.

'Something sinister has happened here Constable, and it's not a swim session gone wrong. My sister left her house in a hurry. Check her phone records. Check CCTV footage. She's been taken from here. Believe me.'

Jamison scuffed his feet in the dirt. 'I'm sorry, Ms Grave.'

'Call the sergeant and stop messing with my crime scene.'

'There's no reception out here.'

'Damn. I forgot.'

In truth, she hadn't known, but it was obvious in hindsight. Last time she was out here, only a handful of people she knew even owned a mobile, and reception in Cooktown was sketchy even on the front veranda of the pub, let alone all the way out here.

If they'd owned a phone last time they were here, they wouldn't have had to drive all the way back to town, shaken and frightened. They wouldn't have needed to describe what they'd seen lying broken and battered on the rocks.

They wouldn't have been prime suspects in a murder investigation, and her brother would still be alive.

Chapter 3

A mix of khaki ranger uniforms and fluoro orange SES surrounded Dawn as she glanced down the line of volunteers searching First Beach. Tension hung in the air as eyes peered at the ground, flicking from left to right.

No one spoke as they spread out across the exposed sand. The tide was out. Fingers of coral reef protruded from the crystal blue water. Dawn returned her eyes to the fine sand, shoving aside visions of the last time she visited this beach.

That day was much like this one. Sunny, warm, sweaty. Her older brother drove their father's rusty Datsun 1600 down the rutted road. Back then, at the age of sixteen, Dawn hadn't been fazed by the rough ride. They were used to it. Four-wheel drives weren't on the roads in plague proportions back then.

Shaking her head, she forced the past back into the box she stored it in. Now wasn't the time to be lost thinking about her brother. Right now, her sister was missing, and Dawn's instincts were telling her it wasn't a case of misadventure.

'Detective!'

She turned towards the familiar voice. Sergeant Martin was speed-walking his way across the sand towards her.

'What's up Sergeant?' Dawn waited for him to catch up. The line of searchers carried on, closing the space she left.

'I don't think you need to be out here.'

'You're kidding, right?'

'Why don't you head into town? You've not even unpacked yet. Leave this to the SES.'

Dawn shook her head. More from disillusion than as a negative response to the sergeant's request.

'My sister is missing. I'm not going anywhere until this area is searched from top to bottom. When, and only when, every square metre of the beach has been scanned, and the dive team comes up empty, will I be going anywhere.'

Sergeant Martin chewed his lip.

'I know this place holds bad memories for you. I was just trying …'

'It holds *terrible* memories, for me and Lisa. That's why I know there is no way she came out here on her own. Or, if she did, it was for a bloody good reason. I'm staying until I find out why her car is here and whether Lisa was in it. Is a forensic team on the way?'

'Detective. This isn't your case.'

Sergeant Martin's tone was firm, but fatherly, something Dawn wasn't used to.

'Just answer the question, Sergeant.'

More lip chewing before Martin straightened, pulled his shoulders back and appeared to decide this wasn't a fight worth having right now.

'Cairns lab has been alerted. A team should be here before dark.'

'Good. In the meantime, I suggest you tape off the vehicle and put a constable on guard to ensure no one goes anywhere near it.'

Sergeant Martin opened his mouth but didn't get a chance to speak.

'Got something,' Michael called across the open ground between Dawn and where the line had carried on searching.

'Don't touch anything,' Dawn called and hurried over, Sergeant Martin two steps behind her.

'You're not running this investigation Detective.'

Dawn ignored the comment as they reached Michael. Constable Jamison joined them a second later.

'You got a pair of gloves on you?'

Dawn eyed the constable who gaped a moment before plunging his hand into a pocket of his utility vest.

'What are you doing Jamison? Don't give her gloves.'

Sergeant Martin stepped up between the constable and Dawn.

'Look Sergeant … Ross …' She reminded herself not to be heavy-handed. It never got her anywhere, rising through the ranks. 'I know I have no jurisdiction here, but my sister could be in danger. We both know what happened last time.'

Martin deflated.

Constable Jamison's eyes flicked between Dawn and his commanding officer.

'That doesn't change the fact that if this is, as you suspect, a case of foul play, then your handling of evidence, when there is a local police officer present, will likely render anything you find inadmissible.'

Sergeant Martin's arms rose to cross over his chest, then slipped back to his sides. But the smug expression didn't leave his face entirely.

It was Dawn's turn to chew her lip. As much as she wanted to run this investigation, as desperate as she was to find her sister, the local police needed to be the ones to collect evidence.

'You know …' All eyes turned to Michael, who scowled at them. 'I don't actually give a stuff who picks up the evidence, as long as one of you bloody well gets on with it sometime soon. We need to carry on searching.'

Dawn scanned the faces of the two SES volunteers standing either side of Michael and blushed.

'You're right Michael. Sorry.'

Sergeant Martin waved his hand towards the half-buried item. 'Constable, if you will.'

Dawn realised she was so busy arguing over who had jurisdiction she hadn't even bothered to see if the evidence was worth collecting.

A torn piece of royal blue fabric protruded from the sand. At first glance, it could easily have been unimportant. A discarded piece of rubbish. Or a beach towel forgotten by a visitor.

Dawn's voice caught in her throat as she tried to speak. She didn't recognise the fabric. It wasn't a particular piece of clothing her sister owned. She couldn't tell if it was a piece of swimwear, stretchy T-shirt or lightweight cotton.

What was unmistakeable was the embroidered insignia of the local school. Dawn's hands grew clammy as she swallowed bile and willed herself not to vomit.

'You alright?' Michael stepped towards her with his hand outstretched, ready to catch her if she fell.

Putting her hand up, she shook her head. He stopped.

'I'm okay.'

'What is it?'

Constable Jamison peered up as he put the fabric in an evidence bag.

Dawn turned to Sergeant Martin, seeing his pale features matching her own.

'It looks like a Cooktown school uniform emblem.' He whispered the words.

A memory flashed into her mind. A scene she'd spent her entire adult life trying to forget now flooded over her like a tidal wave.

'And how does it turn up out here? After all this time?

Chapter 4

Dawn hovered under the hot water, letting it run over her face, through her hair and splash onto the chipped white tiles at her feet.

Visions flashed from the depths of her memory. A blonde girl—bronze skinned. Naked. Her body beaten, bruised and torn—lying on the rocky island surrounded by turquoise blue water. The tide rising fast, creeping through the rocks. The trickling sound as the water covered her delicate hands. The girl's matted hair, rising and floating around her battered face.

Turning off the water, she leant against the wall, palms flat on the tiles, chest heaving as she caught her breath.

She ripped back the shower curtain and stumbled out, groping for a towel. She snatched it from the rail and held it tight to her face. Breathing deeply, she wiped the water away and peered at her reflection in the fogged over mirror, thankful she couldn't see her own features.

Sighing, she wrapped the towel around her torso, reached for another and bound her hair in it. She fought back tears as her eyes found her mobile phone, perched on the corner of the vanity basin. All those calls from Lisa she'd ignored. So many texts left unanswered. Why hadn't she taken her sister's calls?

She knew the answer. It was only her own guilt making her question herself now.

She jumped as the phone vibrated on the porcelain next to her hand. An unknown number appeared on the screen. Her hand hovered as she considered if she should answer.

The last person she wanted to talk to right now was some spammer trying to sell her a new phone plan, but it could be the forensic team. They were still out on site. Maybe they'd found something.

'Detective Dawn Grave speaking.'

'Dawn.' It wasn't anyone she was expecting. Silence hung heavy. 'Are you okay?' The concern in Michael's voice was evident.

'I told you earlier. I'm okay.'

'Yeah. I know you did. Call it instinct, but I don't believe you.'

Dawn grinned despite the tension filling her chest.

'I figure you haven't eaten. I know you missed lunch. I certainly did. Meet me at the Top Pub for a bite to eat.'

Then he was gone.

'I'm too tired for food,' she spoke to her phone's generic factory set screensaver.

He was gone. She sighed as she placed the phone back on the vanity, unwrapped her hair and gently rubbed the excess moisture away. Reaching for her comb, she teased out the knots.

Her phone buzzed. A text popped up on the screen.

You've got ten minutes. Then I'm coming up!

'What the hell!'

How did he know where she was staying? Her first thought was to just let him try. She'd ignore the knocking. He'd go away.

Then what?

She shook her head, left the bathroom and flung open her suitcase. Throwing tops and pants in all directions, she searched for something other than suit pants and her preferred high-neck sleeveless tops.

Finally, she found a pair of green shorts and a rust-coloured cotton blouse, crumpled from travel. At least the sun had set. Hopefully the heat would soon be sucked out of the day by a cool sea breeze.

Frowning, she checked her reflection in the teak-veneer dressing table mirror at the end of her bed.

Wet hair. No make-up. What did it matter? She was back in town for one reason and one reason only. To find her sister.

Dawn reached for her room key. Shoving it into her shoulder bag, she checked her wallet was inside and adjusted her pocket pistol to sit snugly between the partitions. Satisfied, she twisted the antique brass doorhandle, flicked the old-style snib lock and slammed the door closed.

Her footfalls were soundless on the worn olive carpet as she descended the stairs to the bar. Voices drifted up the void. The source—a mixture of backpackers and locals lining up two deep, waiting to order drinks.

Dawn had been tempted to stay somewhere more upmarket. But there was something about the Top Pub that drew her in.

Nostalgia maybe?

Her brother used to work at the pub. Her dad certainly knew his way around the old Queenslander building. He'd slept at the bar regularly, before finally being pushed out onto the street when the owner needed to lock up for the night.

On occasion, the publican would let her dad sleep it off in an upstairs room, if the owner had a spare one and her old man could make it up the stairs.

She gave the publican a wave as she passed the bar. Two fingers touched his forehead in a scout-like salute.

His beard was trimmed shorter than she remembered. Probably because there was more grey than ginger these days.

Still, what he lacked in facial hair, he'd made up for with more tattoos than she recalled.

Returning to this remote, monsoonal North Queensland town was never on her agenda. But her sister needed her.

Michael caught her eye with the raising of his beer glass. She crossed the room and slid onto the wooden bench seat opposite the ranger.

His hair was washed, wet like hers. He was wearing a tight-fitting light blue T-shirt, and she couldn't help but notice his firm chest muscles. The colour contrasted against his dark brown skin. The smell of aftershave wafted on the warm night air.

'Thought I was going to have to come up for a minute.'

It was the first time she'd noticed him smile.

'I really should have ignored you.'

'But you couldn't.' He rose. 'What are you drinking?'

'Tell Ben I'll have a top shelf sav blanc, and don't let him give you a house special.'

Michael's eyebrow rose. 'Sergeant Martin said you were from around here, but I thought it was a long time ago.'

'It was. But not much has changed.'

'I'll be back in a minute.'

Dawn nodded as he stepped over the wooden bench.

She studied the picnic table, which would have been more at home across the road in the park, than in a pub.

As she ran her hand along the paintwork, she realised it hadn't changed either.

A cheer rose from a group of backpackers playing darts behind her. The unmistakable accents of Britain and France drifted her way.

An old man perched on a bar stool frowned at her, before easing from the stool on unsteady legs. His glance didn't waver as he wandered her way, one wobbly step after another.

'You're Fred's daughter, hey?'

She wanted to say *hey what*, but there was no point. Far North Queenslanders ended most questions, even statements, with the word.

'I am. Do I know you?'

'Your old man used to talk about you all the time. He had you …' he belched, refocussed, then continued, 'earmarked for the nineteen ninety-eight Commonwealth Games, hey.'

'He did.'

Michael approached, stopped and waited patiently behind the old man. A smile on his lips told her he was listening.

'What happened?'

'I decided I didn't like swimming anymore.'

'Just like that?'

'Just like that.'

'Excuse me.'

The man staggered sideways at the unexpected voice from over his shoulder. Scanning the room, disorientated for a moment, he finally focussed on Michael.

'You with him?'

The man's tone was icy. His lip curled in a snarl as he hoicked his finger at the ranger.

'Well, he's holding my drink.'

'There was a time when his sort wasn't allowed in here.'

'Yes. And there was a time when old drunk men died early of liver cirrhosis too, but aren't we lucky civilisation has advanced?'

The old man shook his head, as though he were trying to figure out if her response was indeed the insult he thought it was.

Scanning her hard-set features, he seemed to realise the conversation was over. Placing one unsteady foot in front of the other, he tripped and shuffled his way back to his bar stool, now occupied by a tall man with Scandinavian features and long, blond hair tied up in a man bun.

The old man's body language told Dawn he was ready to hurl an insult but changed his direction for the front door instead.

Michael slid the wine across the table and sat down.

'I can't believe you said that.' His grin was wide.

'I can't believe he spoke to you like that, and you just took it,' Dawn countered and Michael shrugged.

'No point arguing with facts. He's right.'

Michael turned his beer glass a quarter turn clockwise on the cardboard coaster as condensation ran down the side.

Dawn gaped. Her mind raced with words ready to fire back at him, but she closed her mouth. What could she say?

Michael glanced up, his eyes sad, his face smiling. 'It is what it is.'

'That's not a solution. That's a cop-out.' The words were out of her mouth before she could stop herself.

'You've been gone nearly twenty years, right.'

It was a statement of fact. She remained silent.

'Not much has changed during those years. You said so yourself.'

Dawn reached for her wine, lifted the glass to her lips to prevent herself from responding. She knew how the system worked. It was one of the reasons why she left. It was why she became a cop. And now here she was, almost two decades later, in the same town, facing the same narrow-minded views she left behind all those years ago.

'It's okay Dawn. You can't change people right away. It takes decades. But you can educate a new generation. Education is the reason I work with the Yuku Rangers.'

'You're not local, are you?'

Michael's hair colour was not often seen in the local population.

'My grandmother was of the Alawa people. She was moved to the Hope Valley Mission as a baby and then transferred to Woorabinda as a girl. My mother brought me back to our homeland when I was born, but my father wasn't from around here.'

'Where are the Alawa people from?'

Michael shook his head.

'It doesn't matter right now. Right now, I'm wondering why you came back to Cooktown. Did you know your sister was missing?'

'Not exactly.'

They sipped their drinks in silence. Michael not wanting to push. Dawn not wanting to own up to ignoring her sister's messages.

'It's a long story.'

Michael said nothing. His eyes watched her over the rim of his glass as he sipped his beer.

'That piece of fabric you found today. It brought back memories I'd rather leave behind. But my sister messages me weekly. Sometimes daily. She's never been able to let the past go.'

'I know that feeling.' Michael drained his beer and stepped over the bench seat. 'I'll grab another. You?' He pointed to her half-full wine. She shook her head.

'Didn't you want me to explain about the past?'

'Food first. I'll grab menus.'

He left the table, and Dawn to her thoughts.

Did she want to relive everything she went through back then? Did she have a choice? The fabric proved her sister's text messages weren't the usual airy-fairy nonsense.

After twenty years, Lisa might finally have snagged a clue to finding Tracey Warren's killer.

Chapter 5

Dawn reached for the glass of water on her bedside table, eyes dry and blinking. Her head pounding—her memory foggy.

How did I get to bed?

Her stomach lurched. She rolled over, heart pounding, eyes wide as she scanned the other side of the bed. Puffing out her cheeks, her tight chest eased when she found it empty.

Her phone vibrated on the dressing table. Jumping out of bed, she crossed the room and grabbed it to answer. As she yanked, the phone dropped out of her hand—reaching the end of the charging cable.

'Damn!'

Snatching it back up, she answered and pulled the cable out at the same time.

'Detective Dawn Grave.'

Her chest rose and fell as she caught her breath.

'Dawn.' Sergeant Martin's voice sounded hollow. Like he was speaking inside the bathroom.

'Sergeant?'

'We've found something. I think you had better come down to the hospital.'

'The hospital? Is it Lisa? Is she hurt?'

Dawn could hear background noise. Steel on steel, hollow and echoing. No emergency room alarms. No complaining patients. No nurses talking.

'Ask for me at Emergency Reception. I won't be far away.'

'Sergeant?'

Dawn stared at the screen, unseeing, but knowing it was blank.

Her stomach rolled again. Bile rose to her throat. The background noise wasn't new to her. She'd been to the morgue often enough to recognise the hollow, echoing sound. The stainless steel benches. The walls lined with tiles or heavy industrial vinyl.

'Oh, please. God. Not Lisa.'

She sank to the floor, pulled her knees to her chest and fought back the tears. They escaped and rolled silently down her cheeks despite her efforts.

She'd lost her brother to suicide. Or so the police claimed. Dawn and Lisa never believed it. Dawn became a cop because of it. Lisa became obsessed with staying and searching for the truth.

Did the truth cost her sister her life?

She hoped not.

Forcing herself to move, she rolled on to all fours, drew a deep breath, then another, and rose to see her reflection in the dresser mirror.

Dark circles loomed under her eyes. Her hair was matted and her skin dry and wrinkled. Even to her own eyes, she looked ten years older than she was.

'No more wine!' she promised herself as she found a wide-tooth comb and her spray-in conditioner. Everyone loved the idea of curly hair, until they had curly hair. Another reason she left Far North Queensland. The humidity made it frizz like she'd stuck her finger in a power socket.

Twenty minutes later she found herself standing at the Emergency Reception desk, lapping up the cool air floating down from the vent above her as her stomach knotted and cramped.

A nurse glanced up.

'Sergeant Martin is expecting me.'

The nurse nodded, lifted the handset on the desk phone and pressed buttons as Dawn scanned the waiting room.

The hospital was a single-storey rambling building with long verandas connecting various buildings. The reception was lined with plastic chairs, all full. Outside, tropical foliage framed more chairs, offering additional waiting space. Most were full.

'The sergeant is on his way. You can meet him outside.'

'Thanks.'

Dawn crossed the foyer and opened the front door to a fresh wave of humid air. Sweat broke out on her forehead and under her arms.

A little girl dressed in a worn tulle tutu and glittered Barbie T-shirt grinned up at her. The girl's mother, or grandmother, it was hard to tell, kept her eyes focussed on a spot on the concrete.

'Dawn. Sorry to keep you.'

Sergeant Martin strode towards her.

'Follow me.'

He turned before he reached her and headed back the way he came.

'Is it Lisa?'

She jogged to catch him.

He glanced sideways a moment, then focussed his eyes on the walkway in front of them.

'Not out here. I'll explain everything at the morgue.'

Dawn's insides tumbled.

He thinks it's Lisa.

The morgue was exactly how she imagined it, but on a smaller scale than the one she often visited in the basement of the coroner's office in Adelaide.

No long hallways of white. No dedicated receptionist. Just a coldroom like you might find in a slaughterhouse, but tidy, stark, clean.

'This is Doctor Nicholls.'

A tall, thin woman with thick grey hair and clear blue eyes peered over her glasses and gave a curt nod, followed by a royal wave.

'Excuse me if I don't shake hands. I'm gloved up.'

'All good.'

Dawn focussed on the white sheet lying over a body on the stainless-steel gurney.

'Hope you can excuse the cold. We don't have an autopsy suite here. Suspicious deaths get transferred to Cairns pretty quickly.'

'But you want to identify them first.'

Dawn's words were monotone as her eyes fixed on the sheet.

'I'm sorry to ask you to do this, but the body …'

'It's not easily recognisable.' Dawn finished for the doctor.

'It could be confronting,' she offered, without confirming Dawn's comment.

'I'm an Adelaide police detective. I've seen worse. Believe me.'

She sensed, more than saw the doctor open her mouth to say more, but she stopped. Instead, she gently, almost reverently began rolling the sheet down from the top.

'Where was the body found?'

'On the back of the Island.'

Sergeant Martin's tone said he understood the significance.

'After the tide dropped then?'

'Yes.'

The sheet continued to fold down. Dawn's heart pounded in her chest.

'I know it's going to be hard to be sure. But do you think this could be Lisa Grave?'

The doctor's voice was soft, gentle, calm.

The sheet reached the bottom of the leg.

'No.'

'Ah …'

She cut the doctor off.

'No. It's not Lisa.'

The ache in her chest eased. She turned to the sergeant.

'Lisa has a tattoo on the outside of her left ankle. The Yin and Yang one. You know, black, white.'

She waved her hand at the sergeant's blank expression.

'She got it when we were teenagers. Dad flipped.'

She nearly laughed, then recalled where she was.

'You're sure?' The sergeant scanned her face, then peered at the doctor.

'Yes. I'm sure. She also has another tattoo on her left wrist. Since the skin is gone from there, I had to wait to be sure.'

'Any other distinguishing marks, birthmarks?'

The doctor rolled the sheet up as she spoke.

'No. She has three ear piercings in her left, one up the top here.' Dawn indicated the top of the lobe. 'But the ears are gone.'

She continued, rambling she knew. In her mind, she was sure it wasn't her sister lying dead, half decomposed and torn to pieces by hungry marine animals, but still, she needed to voice all the reasons behind her belief.

'Okay. So, who is she?' Sergeant Martin interrupted her ramble.

Dawn puffed out her cheeks.

'I don't know. Have forensics been over Lisa's house yet?

'Yes. I should get the report today.'

'I have no doubt she left in a hurry. Maybe she went with someone. Maybe the someone is our dead body?'

'Our?'

'You aren't getting rid of me so easily Sergeant. Besides, I'm a detective, with over ten years on the job. You can get a detective from Brisbane, or you can use me, or both.'

'I've already called Cairns Major Crimes. Someone is on the way. I guarantee, they aren't going to let you get involved in a case which is outside your jurisdiction and involves one of your own family.'

'Two.'

'Two what?'

'Two of my family.'

Sergeant Martin frowned, opened his mouth to speak, but Dawn cut him off.

'This is connected to Tracey Warren's death. I guarantee it. And if it is connected to Tracey, it is connected to my brother's death.'

Sergeant Martin drew a deep breath. Dawn knew what he was going to say. She raised her hand.

'I'm not going to argue with you about this Sergeant. My sister sent me a text. Well, a lot of text messages, but one in particular makes a lot of sense now.'

'Dawn, Lisa has been harping on about this for two decades. And a Cooktown school uniform shirt doesn't prove a connection to Tracey's death.'

'I'm sure Lisa discovered something important about Tracey's death, or maybe Fraser's. Neither of us ever believed Fraser killed himself, and I am absolutely positive he didn't hurt Tracey.'

'I know you two have been adamant Fraser didn't commit suicide, but there was never any evidence to support your theory. In fact, there was plenty to support that his death *was* suicide.'

'The admission of guilt in the letter, supposedly explaining why he committed suicide, must have been written under duress.'

Sergeant Martin studied Dawn, until he finally broke eye contact. Had she hit a nerve? Did Martin agree with her?

The doctor cleared her throat. Dawn turned to see the body now covered, and the doctor's hands hovering on the sheet, but her eyes were focussed, with a furrowed brow.

'Sorry. Didn't mean to bring this up in front of you,' Dawn apologised.

'Actually, no, I'm sorry for eavesdropping. But I might be able to help. I know a handwriting specialist I studied with at university. He consults for the Federal Police, along with other government organisations and the private sector.

'Handwriting?' Sergeant Martin frowned.

'Yes. They can tell if someone was under duress. Shaking. If you have other handwriting samples of course.'

'I'll pay him to run the test. Maybe then I can get Fraser's case reopened. Thanks doctor. I'll be in touch.' Dawn turned to leave. 'I'm heading back to my sister's.'

Sergeant Martin followed her. 'Dawn. Wait.'

For once the warm, moist air felt good as she strode from the chilled morgue, down the covered walkway.

'I'll come with you.'

'I'm fine.' Dawn didn't slow her pace. 'I'd like a copy of the forensic report from my sister's house as soon as it's done. Has her phone been found yet? Was it in the car?'

'I can't give you that information. I keep telling you—you have no authority on this case. Or even in this state.'

'Leave that to me.'

Sergeant Martin stopped walking. Dawn kept going.

No one was going to bury this case again. No one. Not Sergeant Martin. Not the Queensland Police. Not whoever killed Tracey and probably the woman lying in the morgue now.

Dawn hoped she could find them, before something happened to her sister.

Where are you Lisa? What did you find?

She opened the door on the rusted van and adjusted her position behind the wheel. Whatever Lisa found, it was likely well-hidden and there was only one place outside the home she knew Dawn would search.

The only problem was, she'd have to face the ghosts of her past to get it.

Chapter 6

A waft of chlorine caused her nose to itch as she opened the chain-link gate. The sign hung askew, telling her the pool wasn't due to open until later in the afternoon. But she knew there was a good chance he'd be here.

A shiver ran down her spine as she watched the tall gumtrees sway in the light breeze. Gazing up, she noticed storm clouds brewing. The breeze picked up, a precursor to the downpour looming overhead.

Sweat dried on her cheeks as she faced the cool air, which she knew wouldn't last much longer. Her shirt clung to her back is if agreeing with her weather observation.

A bank of grey painted lockers lined the hallway to the changing rooms. Dawn ran her hand along the line as she studied the chipped edges, worn numbers and rusted keyholes.

Stopping, she rested her hand on the last one in the top row on the left. Smiling, she thought about Lisa's obsession with everything left. As a left-hander, she made a point of pulling her long ponytail over her left shoulder. Getting tattoos on her left side. Picking the left bed in the room they shared.

The locker on the left of the entry was no exception.

'Can I help …'

Dawn turned.

'Dawn. Is that you?'

'It is Larry. How are you?'

'My God, girl, you've grown, hey.'

'I've gotten older Larry. I don't think I've added a centimetre since I left.'

'You know what I mean.'

The man shuffled over, back more hunched and eyes duller than she remembered. Grabbing her in his arms, he squeezed without asking permission.

Dawn scanned over his shoulder and tried to block out the scent, and the visions it evoked.

'You missed your dad's funeral.'

'Is this still Lisa's locker?'

Larry frowned, then his smiled returned.

'Of course.'

'Do you have a spare key?'

Larry stepped back, eyed her from top to toe and squinted.

'I do, but I can't open someone's locker without their permission Dawn.'

'She's missing, Larry.'

'Missing?'

'Gone from the house in a hurry. I came as quick as I could.'

'She's likely gone off on one of those detox thingies. You know what Lisa is like. Goes off grid from time to time.'

'No, Larry. She texted me. She was trying to get me to come, and I didn't come quickly enough. Now she's disappeared.'

A tear forced its way from her eye. Larry stepped up and patted her shoulder.

'Now there's another body, out at Archer.'

Larry gasped.

'It's not her.'

'Thank God, or in Lisa's case, the Goddess.' Larry smiled at his own joke, but Dawn wasn't laughing.

'Why the locker?'

'She was tracking down Tracey's killer. She might have left something in there for me.'

'Neither of you could ever put that horrible business behind you. You should move on.'

'I did. I left, remember?'

Larry patted her arm. 'Yes, luv, but you haven't moved on, hey?'

Dawn gazed up into his runny, sunken eyes.

'Do you have a key or not?'

'I'll get it. But I'm warning you, Lisa is going to skin me alive when she finds out I opened it for you.'

'I'll live with that.'

Larry scurried off. Dawn gazed out at the crystal blue pool with racing lanes clearly marked out and flags hanging over the top at the halfway point like a makeshift net.

She heard a voice behind her, but it wasn't Larry's. It was the voice she hoped to never hear again. Not when she was about to open Lisa's locker. Not when she was back investigating the death of a young woman, which could be related to Tracey's death.

Her gut told her the body would be a missing girl, under the age of sixteen.

'Dawn Grave. Well, I'll be.'

The man was in his mid-forties now, still moving like the athlete he once was.

'David.'

He opened his arms. She put up her hand.

'Come on, Dawnie. Don't you have a hug for an old pal of your dad's?'

'Don't, David. Just don't.' Her hand stabbed forward palm first with the last two words. 'You can't still be coaching swimming, after all these years.'

'And why not?'

'You know why not!'

David stepped closer. His hot breath lifted Dawn's fringe as he whispered into her ear.

'I'm a bloody good coach Dawnie. No one's moving me on anytime soon.'

'David,' Larry called, as he rounded the corner of the changing rooms. 'You're early.'

David stepped back. Dawn crossed her arms over her chest, suddenly fighting the urge to go back to her room and shower.

'I've got Samantha and Melody coming in early for training. States are coming up soon.'

'Okay. Get on with it then.'

David smirked. Dawn gripped her arms firmly with her fingers, aware her fingernails were digging into the skin.

'Got the key.' Larry held it aloft.

Dawn reached for it as David stopped walking.

'Hey. You can't go into Lisa's locker without her here.'

'I'll get a warrant if I have to David.'

'Warrant? What the hell are you talking about?' The man stalked back towards her, chest out, eyes drilling into hers.

'Lisa is missing and I'm helping with the investigation.'

'You? How? Why?'

'Didn't Lisa ever tell you?'

The man's forehead creased.

'I'm a police detective.'

She conveniently didn't mention it was with the South Australian Police, not the Queensland Police.

His face paled. Her heart leapt for joy.

'What the f… I'll see about that.'

He pulled his mobile phone from his pocket and dialled.

Dawn was now sure Lisa must have hidden what she needed inside the locker. Her heart raced as she snatched the key from Larry and forced it into the lock.

Chapter 7

Dawn sat in a worn vinyl chair, old enough to make the material stiff and uncomfortable. Tension filled the room. Across the desk, Sergeant Martin chewed his lip, his eyes following the pacing man in his office.

'What were you thinking?'

The figure sat down hard on Sergeant Martin's desk and drilled her with his stare.

She shrugged without making eye contact.

'I looked you up, Grave. You've been fast-tracked, but I can see you've earned your stripes. Commendations. A senior sergeant promotion in the pipeline.'

Dawn couldn't think of an answer that would have satisfied her, if she were in his position. Only a few days ago, in the remote opal mining town of Coober Pedy, she had the exact same discussion with a local police officer who'd nearly stuffed up her own career.

She now understood why. This was family. This was her sister who was missing, not a name on a manila folder tab.

Dawn lifted her eyes, seeing the detective from Cairns for the first time. His clear, soft grey-blue eyes didn't match his stern expression.

'I'd like in on the investigation, Detective Ryan.'

He scoffed, pressed up from the desk and paced once more. Loosening his tie, he removed his jacket and hung it over the chair Dawn sat on. Sweat saturated his long-sleeved shirt, but as he drew close, she could smell his spicy aftershave and deodorant doing their job.

'You'll be lucky if you keep your job the way you're going. Searching a victim's locker without a warrant.'

Just when I was beginning to wonder what was under that shirt—he had to go and ruin it.

'Come on now, Ryan. That's bullshit and you know it. I'm her sister. I'm off duty. I asked for the key. It was given freely.'

'Not according to the guy in the next room.'

The mention of the swimming coach made Dawn leap from the chair before she could stop herself. Chest heaving, her mind raced as she tried to stay rational but failed.

She pointed towards the wall. 'That guy is a pervert. A predator of young women.'

Her hand stabbed thin air again.

'*He's* the one you should be grilling right now, not me.'

She pressed her lips shut as realisation sunk in. She never intended to tell anyone about the swimming coach. It was a secret she was willing to take to her grave, but not now. Not with *two* dead women and her sister missing.

Sergeant Martin, who'd remained silent—likely hoping none of the fallout would land on him—rose slowly from his chair, eyes fixed on her, brow creased.

'What the hell are you talking about, Grave?'

'I shouldn't have said anything.'

She waved her hand and sank back down into her chair.

'But you did. And you better be bloody sure of what you said, because David Fairweather is adored in this town. He's coached two national swimming greats, one of whom went on to win Gold in the Commonwealth and Silver at the Olympics.'

'Really! And you wonder why I'm only saying something now? Are his career achievements all you care about?'

Dawn glared at Sergeant Martin. The same man who was the local constable when she was a kid and knew all her family secrets. The same guy who coached football and gave her dad a free pass when he drove the few minutes home from the pub too drunk to even stand.

'That's not what I meant Dawn.'

'Am I under arrest?'

Dawn turned her eyes to Detective Ryan, who shook his head.

'Will you share the investigation with me, as a consultant?'

Another shake of the head. This time, with an exaggerated sigh for good measure.

She jumped to her feet.

'Then I'm leaving.'

She stormed from the room—their protests muffled in her mind as she told herself it didn't matter what they thought. Accuse one guy of something inappropriate and they all banded together in male solidarity.

Damn them. I'll do it my own way.

She regretted letting the past surface. What David Fairweather was capable of back then wasn't the issue. What worried her now, was how far he was willing to go to keep the truth hidden. And was Sergeant Martin a Fairweather worshipper? If he was, would he tell Fairweather she was ready to talk?

Did he kill Tracey? Did he hurt Lisa to keep his secret?

The contents of her sister's locker were now in police custody. It was a stupid move to push Larry to open the locker while Fairweather was there.

The guy was a golden boy. Her father said so himself. Everyone loved him. He won every swimming carnival in the state growing up. Girls fell at his feet. Guys worshipped the ground he walked on.

But not Dawn. And not Tracey, from what she could remember.

She flung the station door open, nearly knocking Michael in the face.

'Whoa. What's up?'

'Nothing!' Dawn stormed past him, towards her deliberately graffitied campervan. The random thought whether she could change vehicles jumped into her mind.

'Hey. Hang on. I only wanted to make sure you pulled up okay after last night.'

Dawn stopped.

God, I hope I didn't do anything stupid.

There was a reason she rarely drank, especially around men. Her father's history was still raw, even now, nearly twenty years after she left. She'd found out the hard way that she shared his weakness for too much drink.

'You plugged my phone in?'

She didn't mention the bit about putting her to bed. At least he hadn't undressed her. Had he?

'It was the least I could do.'

Dawn carried on down the stairs and jumped from the foot-tall curb to the road. Torrential rain in Far North Queensland meant big, deep gutters to run the water away fast. A spot of rain touched her shoulder. Large, hard and damp.

'It's about to open up, you know.' She pointed to the sky. 'I've got somewhere to be.'

'Do you need company?'

It was a double-edged question. Michael was good-looking, a nice guy by all appearances. Maybe too nice. Dawn liked her men rugged, dangerous and usually only for one night. But something in his eyes drew her in, with promises she wasn't sure he could deliver.

‘I probably don’t need company, but you’re welcome to tag along.’

She opened the door as more large drops of rain pinged the van roof.

He jumped in the passenger’s side as soon as Dawn unlocked it. ‘Where are we going?’

‘My sister’s place.’

‘You still following up, even now, after the detective from Cairns has arrived?’

‘Absolutely. No one knows Lisa like I know Lisa.’

‘You talk often then?’

The thought made Dawn stop and think, her hand hovering ready to put the key in the ignition.

They didn’t talk much at all. Lisa left messages. Dawn failed to return her calls. There was no point. They were always the same. Always about their brother Fraser’s suicide, or their dad’s drinking before he died or Tracey Warren’s murder and what they witnessed all those years ago.

All things she’d left town to avoid. All the things she never wanted to talk about or deal with.

Until now.

‘It’s a long story.’

She started the van and reversed from the curb.

‘So you keep saying. I’m not going anywhere.’

It was two minutes to her sister’s house. Not long enough she told herself.

‘I’ve been excluded from the investigation. I won’t get access to the forensic report, at least not directly, so I need to go over my sister’s place thoroughly and see what they found and what they might have missed.’

‘You think someone took her?’

‘Honestly, I don’t know. You probably know Lisa better than me.’

And there it was. The truth. Out of the bag and into the open.

Chapter 8

The campervan motor backfired as she turned the ignition off and pulled the handbrake on.

Glancing up, she studied the house closely. It was even more run-down than she'd thought the day before. It wasn't only the chipped paint and worn stairs, or the obvious lifting varnish on the polished floors.

Now, as she scrutinised the stained-glass casement windows, she could see they weren't left open to allow airflow, they were stuck open, bowed and twisted with broken hardware and rusted hinges.

'You looked pretty upset when you left the police station.'

Michael's voice made her jump.

'Sorry. Didn't mean to startle you.'

'It's okay. It's just been a long time since I saw this place and it is *so* run-down.'

'You didn't answer my question before.'

Dawn glanced at Michael, nodded she agreed, but turned back to the door and opened it to get out.

'You don't have to tell me.'

'I know.'

Dawn slammed the door and strode to the stairs. She was going to go over the place with a fine-tooth comb if she had to. Lisa wouldn't have taken off without leaving a message or calling to say where she was. Besides, her car was abandoned. And where was her phone?

She pulled her mobile from her pocket and dialled the police station, ascending the stairs as she waited for the call to connect. Michael followed quietly.

'Cooktown Police Station. How can I direct your call?'

The polite female voice wasn't what Dawn had been expecting, but then she realised the station had a few more officers and staff since she left town.

'I'd like to speak with Sergeant Martin please.'

She pushed the screen door open and wandered down the hall to her sister's bedroom.

'I'm sorry, but he is out at the moment. Can I take a message?'

'Detective Ryan then?'

'He's out too. Are you sure I can't take a message?'

'I'd like the detective's phone number. This is Detective Dawn Grave.'

'Oh.'

There was a long silence. Dawn didn't choose to fill it.

'I'm sorry, Detective, I'm not at liberty to share the detective's number with you. But I can ask him to call you back.'

'Don't bother.'

She hung up, shoved her phone into her pants pocket and entered her sister's room.

'You're not the sharing type then?'

Dawn turned to see Michael leaning against the doorframe.

'Don't get me wrong Michael, but you don't exactly seem like the sharing type either. Why so interested in this case?

He shrugged.

'Maybe it's not the case I'm interested in.' He pushed off the doorframe and entered the bedroom.

Dawn opened her mouth, but he didn't give her a chance to reply.

'What are we looking for?'

She was happy he let the subject drop. The comment wasn't what she was expecting and the last thing she wanted right now.

'Notes, a diary, receipts from places she might have visited. Bank statements. Credit card statements?'

'Okay.'

Michael crossed the room to the dressing table while Dawn checked the bedside table.

The top surface was cluttered with a half-empty glass of water, a bottle of lavender and geranium oil, alongside an empty ring stand. An old-style, wind-up alarm clock caught her eye.

The time was wrong. Lifting it, she put it to her ear.

'This clock hasn't been wound.'

Michael turned, a piece of paper in his hand.

'What's that?'

Dawn put the clock down and joined him.

'A letter.'

He handed it to her.

'To you.'

Dawn frowned as she unfolded the printed stationery featuring a little bear with coloured balloons, to reveal a handwritten letter.

She was surprised the forensic team hadn't taken it with them.

Dawn

I'm sorry to resort to a letter, but you won't take my calls, not that I like using a damn mobile. Radiation and all that. I hope you get this.

I think I've found what we need. What we've been looking for all these years. Please, don't bury this any longer. Call me. Or better still, come see me. It's been too long.

Luv Lisa
XOXO

'You read it?'

Michael nodded.

'Why didn't forensics take it?'

'It's not exactly a smoking gun, is it?'

She read it again. It was too vague for anyone but her to confidently link it to her disappearance. It could have been about a family feud, or their dad's will or where their mum was, or almost anything.

The thought of her mum made her stomach knot. She'd not thought about her since her dad died.

Now wasn't the time. She shook her head.

'I'll take it with me, since the police don't consider it evidence.'

'You really think someone would hurt your sister?'

'I don't know, Michael.'

'What was it she found?'

'It's a long story.'

'I've got plenty of time.'

'Aren't you supposed to be out at Archer?'

'Not on duty today.'

She'd totally failed to notice he wasn't in uniform.

'Sorry. I'm mucking up your day off.'

'Not at all.'

He left the bedroom and called over his shoulder.

'Which room next?'

'Down the hall to the right.'

Dawn had been so intent on looking for her sister on her first visit, she cleared the rooms like a police officer. No threat. No victim. Nothing disturbed. Move on.

Now, as she followed Michael into the room she used to share with her sister, she stopped to take it in.

The two single beds still occupied either side of the room, but on closer inspection, she realised one was covered in an old, frayed duvet, while the other boasted a new quilt with bright yellow flowers on a blue and pink background.

Her heart rate quickened as butterflies rolled around her stomach. Rushing across the room, she pulled open the top drawer of the dressing table.

Inside, were pink and white knickers, purple and orange socks balled together and a neatly folded pile of pretty coloured tops.

She turned and crossed the room to the white freestanding wardrobe. Memories rushed through her mind. Lisa's My Little Pony stickers were plastered down the outside wall, while the front door bore Kellogg's Nutri-Grain Ironman stickers.

They were always like chalk and cheese. Nothing had changed. Dawn loved sport. Lisa tolerated the swimming training.

Dawn hated cooking. Lisa loved it. Dawn never shied away from pain medication, while Lisa used aromatherapy and ate mostly vegetarian from the age of twelve.

Dawn sucked in a breath as she opened the wardrobe door. Inside, a row of diamante-studded tops and brightly coloured dresses greeted her. Reaching out, she touched the tulle fabric of a ballet tutu and knew her hunch was confirmed.

Why hadn't she told her?

'I've got to get to the police station.'

Dawn was jogging for the front door.

'What's up?'

Michael chased after her.

'It's not only Lisa they are looking for. She's got a daughter. Why the hell didn't Sergeant Martin tell me she had a daughter?'

Chapter 9

Dawn thrust the police station door open. A young female officer with a tight bun pulling her hair back so harshly her eyes appeared oriental, made eye contact before Dawn reached the counter.

'I want to speak with Sergeant Martin or Detective Ryan, now! And don't tell me they aren't here. I saw Ross's car out the front.'

The officer on duty opened her mouth but didn't get a chance to try and talk Dawn down. She must have yelled at the top of her voice, because the side door to the main office area opened to reveal Sergeant Martin scowling from the doorway.

'Get in here!'

He stepped aside and waved his hand. Dawn was vaguely aware of Michael right behind her, but they hadn't spoken a word since she leapt down the staircase like a woman with her hair on fire and jumped into her rental camper.

Dawn's chest thudded. All she could hear, as she followed Sergeant Martin through the hallway into his office, was the blood rushing in her ears. Her entire body began to shake.

Michael slipped in a second before the sergeant slammed the door closed and pointed to a seat in front of his desk.

Dawn scanned the room, but the detective wasn't present.

'What the hell is wrong with you?'

Dawn refused to sit. Instead, she paced back and forth, her back stiff, her neck stiffer.

'Lisa has a daughter. She's missing too.'

Martin frowned. It wasn't the earlier scowl—more a confused expression forcing Dawn to stop before saying the next thing on her tongue.

'You didn't know about Abby?'

'Abby.' Dawn shook her head. 'No.'

She slid into the seat before her legs gave out.

'I assumed you knew you had a niece. Abby isn't a secret. She goes to the local school. Don't you talk with your sister?'

'How old?'

'Six. Precocious little kid. Reminds me a lot of you, actually.'

'Six.'

Dawn's stomach knotted and flipped as acid rose in her throat. Six years, nearly seven if you count the pregnancy. Lisa had said nothing.

'We talk … well, Lisa talks, I listen—when I answer her calls.'

Dawn saw the sergeant's expression change and drew a long, slow breath.

'Lisa has been obsessed with Fraser's death and … you know, what we saw when we were kids. But I left town to get away, start again fresh.'

Dawn sat back in the chair. Her heart rate slowing, but the tension wasn't gone.

'I don't take her calls often. Her subject matter depresses me. And I'm busy with work.'

Sergeant Martin nodded like he understood, then shook his head sideways like he didn't get it at all.

Dawn remembered Michael and turned.

He leant against the back wall of the sergeant's office, listening, his expression hard to read. She'd worked for twenty years to keep her history buried and here she was spilling it out in front of a complete stranger.

Rising, she pulled herself together, a decision made in her own mind. One that no one, least of all Sergeant Martin, was going to like.

'I'm calling work and prolonging my break. I'm not going anywhere while Lisa and Abby are missing. Have you found Lisa's phone yet? Got her call log?'

Sergeant Martin chewed his lip, leant back in his chair, steepled his fingers under his chin and studied her face in silence—for a long time. Too long.

'You know I'm not going to give up.'

'You did twenty years ago.'

The words hit her in the gut like a sucker punch, but it was nothing compared to the day she left town.

The funeral wasn't a celebration of life. It was a dark, rainy day, not unlike today. The clouds thundered overhead. Trees swayed and bent over in the pre-cyclonic winds. The rain started as the coffin was pulled from the hearse and didn't let up.

The local minister asked their dad if he wanted to delay the funeral for the weather, but he shook his head.

The words he said that dark, stormy day stuck in Dawn's mind like a bad movie rerun now.

'Just get on with it Jamie.'

The minister nodded, pulled out his Bible and began the service, while everyone popped umbrellas.

She scanned the faces in her mind now. *Everyone* consisted of Constable Martin, in uniform. Lisa, her dad, Fraser's best mate Lachie and his parents, and a few faces she couldn't recall now, after so many years.

In any small rural Australian town, the death of a local youth, even one who committed suicide, would have brought out hundreds of mourners, even in foul weather. But on that day, they were nowhere in sight.

And the reason everyone stayed away was a lie. A complete and utter fabricated lie. Dawn had spent the weeks leading up to the funeral trying to prove it, but no one, not even Sergeant Martin believed her back then.

After watching the coffin disappear into the ground and listening to the kind words of Reverend Jamie Norris, Dawn had turned and gone home to pack.

She hadn't been back to town since, not even for her own father's funeral.

Chapter 10

Michael shadowed her as she stalked from the sergeant's office, out the side office door and through to the foyer.

'Lunchtime?'

The word from his lips made her start. Turning back, she noted his calm features.

'You have to eat, and this weather isn't letting up anytime soon. We're on a storm watch. They're predicting a category three cyclone.'

Dawn opened the front door and peered out at the sheeting rain coming down and spilling over the gutters to make ponds on the ground.

Nodding, she lifted her rain jacket and pulled it up and over her head before darting for her van.

Her feet slapped the water on the concrete as she ran down the pathway to the road. A gangplank-like ramp spanned the curb, now running a foot deep with water being shed from the heavily contoured road.

By the time she shuffled into the driver's seat, her jacket was saturated, and her shoes wet through.

'God, I hate this rain.' She spoke as Michael fought the wind to slam his door closed. The windscreen fogged instantly. Starting the motor, she fiddled with the air-conditioning and defog settings until it slowly began to clear.

'At least the sergeant agreed to send you a copy of Lisa's phone records when they come through.'

Dawn nodded. Her chest tightened as she thought about how many of Lisa's calls went unanswered.

'I should have taken her calls.'

'From what you said in there, you did, for a long time.'

'Yes, but I should have taken her call last week. I was busy, on a case.'

'Are you sure work is the reason you didn't take her call?'

Ignoring him, she struggled out of her wet rain jacket and threw it in the back, before putting on her seatbelt. Wiping the driver's side window so she could see out, she put the van in reverse with a crunch of gears and backed out slowly, hoping like hell no one was stupid enough to be speeding up the road in this heavy downpour.

'Michael, no offence, but I don't know you well enough to unburden my soul.'

She pressed the brake and slipped the car into first gear.

'There's only one way to rectify that.'

Dawn glanced over as the vehicle lurched forward, to see Michael smiling, but he smoothed his features as soon as she frowned.

'Or not.' His words were barely a whisper.

Focussing on the road, Dawn let the clutch out and tried not to skid on the soaked road as she thumped the accelerator to the floor.

A few minutes later she angle-parked on the side road outside the Top Pub. Thankfully the parking spaces weren't full. It was a short dash to the wrap-around veranda, but she was saturated by the time she reached the covered area.

'You should head up and change. I'll order drinks. What do you want?'

Dawn thought about last night. About how she didn't recall anything much of the evening and how it wasn't the first time.

'Just mineral water.'

'You sure?'

She nodded as they entered the main entrance. Simply being in the pub was a reminder of her father's antics.

'I'm sure.'

She jogged up the stairs as Michael carried on into the dining area.

Stopping at the middle landing, she watched him disappear. She knew this pub like the back of her hand. As soon as she got her licence, it was she who came to pick up her drunken dad after he'd started a fight or passed out on the bar.

Alcohol was a double-edged sword for her. It could stab her from every angle no matter what she did with it. Sheath it and she had to deal with everything in the stark light of day. Draw it, and, like last night, she was wasted beyond recollection.

She carried on up the stairs, opened her room and threw her keys on the dresser. Placing her hands down, flat on the top, she studied her reflection. At least her hair wasn't frizzy. Instead, it was stuck to her head like a wet mop.

Letting out a sigh, she gazed into her own eyes. They stared back, accusingly. She came to town to make sure her sister was okay. But Lisa wasn't alright, and neither was her daughter. As she stared at her reflection, she realised what was hurting most right now. Why did Lisa keep Abby secret?

Maybe she thought Dawn wouldn't care?

Hot tears stung her eyes, begging to be set free. Dawn blinked, forcing them away.

Who is the father? Is it someone I know?

Dawn left when she was seventeen. Lisa was barely fifteen. Was all this her fault? Should she have stayed to protect her little sister?

Of course I should have.

Turning, she opened the bathroom door, grabbed a towel, dried her hair, and considered some foundation, but decided it was a waste of time in this weather.

Returning to the bedroom, she opened her suitcase, pulled out a pair of lightweight suit pants, studied them a moment, then decided she wasn't working, and it was impractical to dress like she was.

Choosing a peasant dress thrown into her luggage at the last minute, she pulled it on and tried to smooth the wrinkles out.

Finally giving up, she collected her keys and slipped on a pair of flip-flops as she pulled the door closed.

As she jogged down the stairs, she reminded herself why she was single. Detective Ryan was her usual type. A hot, drunken sex romp was more her style. Michael was a local ranger. Dedicated to his people. Focussed on his work. And based in Cooktown.

She didn't want to take advantage of his kindness and there was no way a long-term relationship was even on her radar, let alone a long-distance one.

She made up her mind not to drink around him. She knew what happened whenever she drank with a good-looking guy within easy reach. She was thankful he was chivalrous enough not to take advantage of her stupidity last night.

A wide smile appeared on Michael's lips as she strolled past the bar and crossed the room to where he sat with a tall coke.

'Here's a menu. What do you feel like?'

She studied his dark brown eyes and ridiculously long eyelashes and pushed away the first thought that popped into her mind.

'At least the menu seems to have changed.'

She pulled it towards her as she sat.

'Thanks for tagging along with me today. I'm sorry you're probably getting to see me at my worst.'

He patted the back of her hand on the menu. It took all her composure not to snatch her hand away.

'I just want to help you find your sister and her daughter.'

'I appreciate that, but you've got a job. Why are you helping me out?'

'I thought it was obvious.'

She realised his hand was still on hers. Gently, she eased it out from under his.

'I'm only here until my sister is found.'

'And that girl's murder is solved. I'm guessing you're the type to not like puzzles.'

'On the contrary. I love them. But not a fan of unsolved ones.'

'Me too.'

He held her gaze. Dawn dropped her eyes to the menu and scanned it without comprehending the words.

'Why didn't you come back for so long?'

Dawn glanced up.

'I know it's probably none of my business, but if it has something to do with your sister, it might help if I know.'

'I doubt it. I'll grab the food today. What are you having?'

She rose to leave the table, but stopped as her phone rang in her bag. Rummaging around, she retrieved it and answered.

'Detective Grave.'

'Dawn. I've got those phone records. I'm sending them through, but you might want to know. We are bringing David Fairweather in for questioning.'

Dawn's throat clamped shut. Words stuck in the vice-like grip.

'You there?'

'I'm here,' she croaked.

'Ryan hasn't agreed you can join the investigation, but he has agreed for you to watch the interview and after what you said earlier, he'd like some more background before the interview.'

She cleared her throat. Was she ready to tell them everything she knew about David Fairweather? Golden boy. Apple of his mother's eye.

'When are you bringing him in?'

'We *are* on a cyclone warning. There's a category three hovering off the coast.'

'Michael said.'

'It would be irresponsible to try and get him in this weather, but as soon as the worst of it passes over, we'll bring him in. I'll call you.'

'Bit early in the year for a cyclone though. It will die out before it makes land.'

'Possibly, but my officers are busy preparing in case.'

'Thanks Ross.'

'Don't thank me yet Dawn. It's only a phone call on Lisa's phone records. It could be nothing.'

'I know.'

She hung up and smiled as she put her phone back into her bag.

'Good news?'

'Progress. What are you eating?'

'Chicken salad.'

Dawn's eyebrows rose.

'What? I like my greens.'

'Chicken salad it is.'

Chapter 11

The scent of rotting vegetation wafted on the warm, damp air. The wind died down an hour before, the rain with it. Knowing the rain would return any minute, Dawn had made the mad dash for her family home as dark, threatening clouds formed up over the hills.

Now, she listened as large raindrops began hitting the iron roof, the noise slowly going from a tap to a drum as the dark clouds turned day to night.

Michael had offered to come with her, but she sent him home to his own family. A cyclone warning was nothing to scoff at. Scanning the twisted hinges and loose balustrading, Dawn wondered how the old Queenslander had survived this long.

Pushing away from the front balcony railing, she rushed through the house, desperate to secure it as the rain intensity picked up and overtook the earlier onslaught.

Pulling on a casement window handle, she quickly realised it was jammed and moved on to the next, only to find no locking mechanism to keep it shut.

Steam rose in the air but stopped once the heavy droplets picked up pace.

A bang made her jump. Scanning the hallway, she listened to the thumping sound of water on the roof and waited. The noise sounded again. Every nerve in her body tingled as she crept towards the sound.

'Who's there?' she called as she crept towards the last bang she'd heard. It sounded again. She forced herself not to jump, to stay the course as she tentatively stepped to the kitchen doorway, body hard against the wall.

Peering around the corner, she scanned the kitchen, ready to bolt, but smiled as a drenched cat made a frantic dash to enter through the swinging screen door before it slammed one more time.

The striped ginger tabby's back was arched, tail flicking, eyes wide and fur drenched.

'You picked the wrong day to go hunting, my friend.'

She dropped to her haunches. The cat shook then turned and pranced by her with a haughty expression, like she was the intruder.

'Pleased to meet you, too.'

Dawn watched the cat retreat down the hallway and turn into her sister's room. Following, she kept her distance. Staying quiet wasn't an issue as the roof sheets rattled and the entire structure creaked with the rising wind speed.

Maybe I should have stayed at the pub?

She glanced at the ceiling, but there was no point. She couldn't see if the iron roofing was being ripped off or the rotted weatherboards flung from the siding.

It was time to buckle down for the full force of the storm and upstairs wasn't the right spot to do it. But she couldn't leave the cat.

Approaching the bed, she stopped to study the animal as it lay purring and licking to dry itself.

It was why she liked cats, not dogs. Cats enjoyed their solitude. They relied on no one. This animal didn't need her to towel it dry or feed it. Lisa was gone, missing, and her cat had gone hunting.

'You and I are more alike than you think.'

She sat on the edge of the bed. The cat stopped licking—paw held mid-air with an expression clearly asking Dawn if she had a good reason to intrude on its personal space.

'It's pissing down out there and you're not going to like it, but we need to get under the house, into the garage, in case this cyclone hits and rips the house off its stilts.'

The cat ignored her, returning to lick its paw and clean its ear.

The sound of smashing glass made Dawn jump. The cat leapt into the air and darted out of the room.

'Damn!'

She followed, but the cat was gone.

'Sorry kitty, but I've locked everything up as best I can. I need to get downstairs, with or without you.'

Dawn grabbed her rain jacket, struggled into it and pulled up the hood. Zipping up the front, she stepped out the front screen door, right into the chest of a darkly clad figure.

Hands grabbed her by the shoulders. Her instincts took over. Thrusting both arms up between those holding her, she turned her palms out and pushed outwards. The grip on her shoulders was broken, but the element of surprise was gone.

Rational thought disappeared as Dawn rushed to the stairs. Finding herself on the ground in seconds, she fumbled in her jacket for her keys.

An image of them on the kitchen table flashed in her mind. Frantically she scanned her surroundings. The door to the understorey flew open and slammed shut in the rain. Dismissing it as a hiding place, she desperately tried to orientate herself.

Darkness closed in with the looming clouds, as sheeting rain obscured her view. Lightning flashed across the sky, illuminating the balcony. Dawn caught a glimpse of the figure, standing at the top of the stairs. Unthinking, unplanning, she ran.

Reaching the tree line, she stopped to catch her breath as driving rain pelted down, stinging her skin beneath the thin waterproof jacket.

She needed shelter. Somewhere safe to wait out the storm. There was only one place she knew of. It was the last place she wanted to go right now, but the only option left.

Catching her breath, she carried on, being careful to watch her footing. One slip in this tropical forest and she could be injured, stranded in the cyclone, likely dead before morning.

To Dawn's dismay, the abandoned sawmill was still standing. Rusted iron, worn timber beams and debris littered the small clearing. Ducking inside, Dawn found a corner where the building was still intact. Water gushed like a river from the iron creating a cascading waterfall on one end.

Dawn sank into the driest spot she could find, drawing her legs under her raincoat. Her heart raced as she tried to slow her breathing.

It was David Fairweather. She was sure of it. The height. The build. The gall of him turning up to the house unannounced. It had to be him. He must have found out the police were bringing him in for questioning. But how?

And why come after her?

She wrapped her arms around her shoulders as the wind intensified. The loose iron roofing overhead clanged, the sound echoing through the hollow building. Swirling wind threw ancient sawdust into the air. Dawn ducked to avoid it.

The scent of eucalyptus hung in the air, despite the mill being disused for decades. This was once their cubby house. The place they came to smoke and drink and kiss boys and …

It was all a lifetime ago now. They'd come to hide out here the day they found Tracey Warren floating in ankle-deep water at Archer. Fraser drove home, past the police station despite Dawn's protests. She begged him to stop and tell them what happened.

As soon as the car stopped, he'd flung the driver's side door open and stomped his way to the sawmill before Dawn or Lisa could protest.

They followed, yelling at him to stop, but he didn't. They jogged to keep up with their big brother. Nearly nineteen, working, with a licence, he was the man of the house their dad should have been.

Their lives had changed after their mother disappeared without a trace. They'd grown up so fast. Dawn was fifteen, Lisa twelve, Fraser sixteen. Her big brother juggled school and part-time work back then, so they wouldn't lose the property.

Dawn jumped back to reality as thunder rumbled across the darkened sky, covering her ears. She wasn't trying to block out the weather, or even the rattling and smashing of the building. She needed to bury the memory of *that* day.

Fraser, pacing back and forth. Dust rising under his feet as he wore a path in the sawdust and clay floor.

We need to tell the police!
We can't. I've ...
What, Fraser? What is going on?
They'll think I did it.
Don't be stupid. You were with us. We found her.
But I was with her, out there, last night.

He'd been right. They did think he did it. Now, as a police officer, she understood why they'd suspected him, but there had been no evidence. Nothing. All they had was an eyewitness account, placing his car out there the afternoon before.

Fraser said he took her home, but there were all sorts of rumours flying around town within days. The police were under pressure to find the killer. Fraser was their only suspect.

But Dawn knew he wasn't. She should have said something. But she remained silent. Then her brother was dead. Everyone was saying it was suicide—that her brother was guilty and killed himself from remorse.

It wasn't true. Dawn knew it back then. Lisa did too. But they couldn't prove it. Lisa kept trying. Dawn left town.

Tears ran down her face as she wrapped her arms around her knees and huddled like a beaten child. Burying her face in her arms, she sobbed like one. Regret eating into her soul.

Chapter 12

The sound of lorikeet chatter broke into Dawn's dream. Her eyes opened to a stream of light filtering through the side opening. Blinking, she tried to focus past the grit and mucus in her eyes.

As she unfurled herself from the foetal position, her right leg cramped. Stretching it and pulling the foot back, she breathed through the pain. She was dehydrated. The irony of being in a downpour of more than a metre of rain and being thirsty made her laugh out loud.

Pushing herself to her feet, she scanned the dilapidated building. The ghost of years past seemed to dim in the light of day, but Fraser's last words to her echoed in her mind now.

We all know who did this. We just need to prove it.

Drawing herself up, she stretched and made a promise, more to herself than anyone else. This time she wasn't leaving Cooktown until Tracey's killer was caught. But now it wasn't only Tracey dead. There was another woman. And Lisa and her daughter Abby were missing. She had to find them.

She stumbled back to the house, thirsty, hungry and lost in her own world.

Climbing the stairs, she lost her balance as one rung dislodged under her foot. The old house needed a demolition order. When she found Lisa, she was going to do something about it.

The power was out. Not unusual after a storm. It could be a few hours, or a week before it was restored, depending on the damage.

The clothes she wore were muddy and wrinkled. She needed something to wear other than suit pants.

Lisa's taste was a long way from hers, but it would have to do. As she opened the antique wooden wardrobe, the smell of camphor filled the air. Smiling, Dawn recalled her mother insisting all the cupboards and drawers be made of camphor laurel wood because it kept the silverfish and cockroaches out of the clothing.

She found a loose-fitting shirt with a floral pattern and drawstring at the neck. The scent of washing liquid and camphor laurel reminded her of every piece of clothing she'd ever worn as a child.

When her mother disappeared, they'd been heartbroken, but her unannounced departure broke their father. Peggy Grave was a model mum. Chair of the school's parents and citizens committee, volunteer coach at the swimming club, full-time mum, part-time journalist. She was the perfect mum.

There had been a note. Dawn never saw it. Apparently, her father burned it when he read it, but no one searched for her mum. One day she was there. The next, she was gone. Forever.

Shaking herself free of memories, she realised again why she left Cooktown. So much baggage. So many unanswered questions. Even now those memories kept her awake at night.

Grabbing her keys, phone and bag, she hurried down the stairs and into the campervan. She would have loved to switch the vehicle out, but the depot was in Cairns, over four hours' drive away.

For now, the green graffiti-covered, politically incorrect slogan–sprayed vehicle was all she had.

She drove into town, scanning the aftermath of the storm. Battered buildings, trees down, water sitting in large ponds on vacant blocks of land.

Pulling up outside the police station, she parked and stepped out of the car to find the roadside gutter full of debris, the pavement covered in broken tree limbs and twigs, the lawn so saturated it couldn't absorb any more water.

Sticking to the paved walkway, she picked her way to the police station entrance.

The female duty officer glanced up, smiled and waved her through. That was a good sign.

Opening the door, she wandered down the hallway to the main office and stopped a moment to watch as officers scurried back and forth between phone calls, desks, and filing cabinets.

'Where the hell have you been?'

Dawn turned at the sound of Sergeant Martin's voice. The man's entire body was rigid, hands firmly planted on hips, face a mix of relief and anger.

'I went home.'

'You weren't there when I sent Ryan out to get you before this storm went crazy. What were you thinking, being out there in that pile of sticks in a cyclone?'

Dawn shrugged.

'Out of practice, I guess.'

Then a thought struck her.

'Ryan. When did you send him out and why him?'

'All my officers were flat out, and he wanted to speak to you anyway, so he was the obvious choice.'

'What time did he come out?'

'How the hell would I know? Ask him.'

Dawn's mind raced. Could the hooded figure have been Ryan? He was the right build. Then why didn't he identify himself? Maybe it wasn't him. Maybe he came later.

'He's in my office.'

Dawn was stuck to the worn lino floor like a statue. For a moment, scenarios ran through her mind, but nothing made any sense. If it was Ryan, he would have called out to identify himself when she ran off.

'I'll go see what he wanted.'

Dawn hurried past the sergeant as he continued wrangling his staff like a seasoned campaign general. Orders were given and followed without question.

The scene made Dawn homesick for her own station.

Ryan rose from the spare chair in the sergeant's office as she entered. 'There you are.'

'The sergeant said you've been looking for me. What time did you come to the house?'

'A little after three. Why?'

Dawn tried to read his expression. He seemed calm, relaxed, genuine.

'I was gone by then.'

'That bomb of a van was there.'

He took a step closer. Dawn took a step back. Ryan frowned.

'Are you okay?'

'I'm fine. What did you want to speak to me about?'

'I've been comparing the notes on the Tracey Warren case with our new case and Martin updated me on your history.'

He waited. Dawn offered nothing.

'You knew the victim.'

'Everyone knew the victim. It's a small town. Everyone knows everyone's business here.'

'You say that like it's a bad thing.'

Dawn shrugged. There were times when knowing the local kids kept them out of trouble. Like when Sergeant Martin was a constable and used to tell any local youth who stepped out of line that he'd tell their parents. It was a good strategy.

The police didn't want to prosecute, and most parents cared enough about their kids to set them straight.

But there were times when local knowledge was a minefield to be navigated carefully. Like when her mum ran off. The rumour mill went mad. Then her brother's arrest.

Dawn shook her head. 'It's a fact. Nothing more. What do you want to know?'

The next question wasn't what she was expecting. Everyone thought her brother killed Tracey, even Sergeant Martin.

'Cause of death on our latest victim is a very close match to the Warren case. Close enough to raise questions about Warren's suspected killer.'

'You mean my brother.'

Ryan's nostrils flared as he sucked in a quick breath.

'So you have signs of sexual assault, drowning, self-harm?'

'All of those things.'

'Detective, my sister is missing. The last text she sent to me said she had proof Fraser had nothing to do with Tracey's death. To me, that means she had proof who the real killer was.'

'The doubt about your brother's guilt is why we are putting every available officer on the case to find her, and her daughter.'

Dawn sat on the corner of the sergeant's desk. Ryan lowered himself back into the chair.

'Why are you suddenly telling me all this?'

'I kept you out, at arm's length, because of your connection to our missing victim, and …'

'My brother being the only suspect in Tracey's death.'

Ryan nodded.

'And now?'

'And now, I could use some local knowledge, and your training makes you the right choice. You don't only have knowledge of the old case—you know police procedure. You know what I need to know.'

Dawn sighed. Her entire body ached from her night on the ground in the sawmill. Her heart ached with the loss of her brother all over again. Her mind was screaming with the need to find her sister and niece. She shook her head. She wasn't giving up on Lisa and Abby.

Never.

'Where do you want to start?'

'Let's start with David Fairweather. You made some serious accusations yesterday and now we know he was in contact with your sister before she disappeared. I need the whole story.'

'I've got no proof, only my own experience.'

'It's a start.'

Chapter 13

The Top Pub was quiet. Most of the town was out mopping up after the storm, which as Dawn suspected was downgraded to a tropical low by the time it hit Cooktown. She suppressed a twinge of guilt. As much as she wanted to help clean up, finding Lisa and Abby was her *only* priority right now.

'Dawn. My golly gosh! Ben said you were in town, and I told him he must have been seeing things.'

The short woman, with thick jet-black hair and smiling oriental eyes scurried out from behind the bar, arms outstretched. The publican's features were a complete contrast to her accent.

Mari was born and bred in Cooktown, a descendent of the early Chinese settlers who came to run businesses during the gold-mining years.

'Mari, you haven't changed a bit.'

The woman grabbed Dawn into a bear hug, holding her so tight she thought she was in a prize-wrestling match.

'You can still charm the balls off a brass monkey, luv. I'm greyer, flabbier and I think I've shrunk an inch, but I'll take a compliment when I can get one.'

She turned back to her husband at the bar. 'They don't come often enough these days.'

The barman shrugged, but the grin on his face said he knew his wife was baiting him.

'Who's the man then?'

Dawn almost forgot Detective Ryan was behind her. Glancing over her shoulder, she noticed his smirk and scowled.

'This is Detective Ryan, from Cairns.'

'Oh. My mistake. I thought ….'

Mari looped her arm through Dawn's and guided her to a table, leaning in close so no one else could overhear.

'I hear you became a cop and all. And now poor Lisa. Any luck tracking her down?'

'We have a few lines of inquiry.'

Dawn slid into the booth seat offered.

'That's very official.'

Back in the day, Mari was the gossip queen of Cooktown. Publicans hear everything going on in town, and it was Mari who did her fair share of scaremongering when Tracey Warren's body was discovered.

Mari waited for further explanation, but realised none was coming. Pursing her lips, as though words were trying to escape, she remained silent. Finally, she gave a curt nod of understanding.

'What can I get you? Bit early for beer or wine. How about a coffee?'

'Cappuccino is good for me, thanks Mari. Ryan?'

'Same for me, thanks.'

'I'll grab you a menu. You're as scrawny as a day-old calf.'

The publican scurried away.

'Do you know everyone in town?'

Dawn sighed at the detective's question.

'I did. But I'm sure I don't anymore. The town hasn't changed much. There's the new hotel up the road. A few more fancy houses along the top of the cliff, overlooking the water. Most of the locals are still here. But there are lots of new faces too.'

Ryan rolled up the sleeves of his long-sleeved shirt. Sweat pooled under his arms.

'It's too sticky up here for long sleeves.'

'A legacy of my schoolboy days.'

‘Private then?’

He nodded, opened his mouth to speak, but stopped as Mari slid two cups onto the wooden table, along with two single sheets of laminated paper.

‘I don’t think we’ll be too busy today, so take your time. Luckily the power is back on, so we have a full menu on offer.’

‘Thanks Mari.’

The publican stepped away, then stopped. Turning back, she placed her hand on the tabletop and waited for Dawn to make eye contact again.

‘Luv. You had a shit go of things back then. I hope the town can redeem itself now. Your sister has stuck it out. Made new friends. Won a few old ones over. We aren’t bad people. Everyone was scared. You understand?’

Mari waited. Dawn studied her a moment, then broke eye contact. What could she say? *Sure, all is forgiven. You all watched my dad implode and did nothing, then either drove my brother to suicide or made him a scapegoat and let the real killer go free?*

‘I’m here if you want to chat luv. That’s all.’

Dawn nodded. She didn’t trust herself to speak. How on earth had Lisa put up with it?

She already knew the answer to that. Meditation, new-age thinking, Buddhism, too much weed. You name it, Lisa adopted it.

Mari shuffled away, head down.

‘Sounds like a tough childhood.’

Dawn lifted her shoulders and sighed.

‘A lot of it was good. We had freedom here. It was safe, or so we all thought.’

‘David Fairweather.’

‘David Fairweather.’

Dawn sipped her coffee while she tried to formulate exactly where to start.

As though reading her thoughts, Ryan gave her direction.

'Tell me how you met him. Then what happened to make you dislike him so much.'

'My mum and dad were fixated on swimming.'

'Wondered about that. Your names—Dawn and Fraser. Australian swimming legend right there.'

'Yep. And Lisa, named after Lisa Curry.'

'Your dad a qualified coach?'

'He was, until his protégée, Fairweather, won a few national events and then everyone wanted him to coach their kids.'

'But it was your dad who coached Fairweather?'

'What can I say. We love our sporting heroes.'

'So, what went wrong? Where does Tracey Warren fit in?'

'I was too young to see it. I should have said something.'

Ryan waited as tension rose. Dawn scanned the menu but couldn't focus. She did say something to her dad, and he'd told her to keep her mouth shut and not rock the boat.

'Fairweather was a creep. He's the reason I quit swimming.'

'Sergeant Martin said you were bound for greatness.'

'Everyone hoped I was, but it wasn't likely. I never had the killer instinct needed to reach the heady heights. I loved swimming. I enjoyed the community. Friendly competition was fun. I didn't even mind the early morning training, every day.'

'What happened?'

'Fairweather had me at a private early morning session.'

'Your dad wasn't there?'

'No. Fairweather said he was too emotional. Always pushing, always yelling, putting me off my game.'

'Was he?'

Dawn thought about it a moment. Her dad certainly got annoyed if she wasn't standing on the veranda ready when it was time to get to practice.

'He competed when he was younger. Then an injury retired him. It was back before shoulder surgeons could do what they can do now. I think he was living vicariously through me.'

'So, what happened?'

Dawn had only mentioned the incident to her dad once. Then to her sister and brother when they found Tracey's body. But she'd glossed over and downplayed the details at the time. Since then, she'd never told anyone about the day she quit swimming.

She glanced up into Ryan's grey-blue eyes. Once again, she was distracted by his broad shoulders and athletic build. Like Fairweather, he was confident, assured. He was the type of guy Dawn had a habit of jumping into bed with, only to leave in the dim morning light before they could ask anything more of her.

Pulling back her shoulders, she focussed on the task at hand. Spilling her guts to Ryan wasn't ideal—she rarely let her guard down—but this was a police matter. This wasn't personal. She wasn't unburdening herself in his arms. That was something she'd never do.

Take a breath and toughen up Princess!

'Training was done. I was in the girls' locker room, changing out of my wet swimmers. I wrapped the towel around me after drying off, then I felt his eyes on me.'

Dawn reached for her coffee and gulped down a mouthful. Her empty stomach gurgled in protest as her hand began to shake. She assured herself it was the caffeine overload.

'The sun was barely up yet, so the visibility wasn't brilliant, but I could tell it was him. He gawked for a minute. I grabbed my bag and clutched it to my chest, over my towel, and headed for the cubicle. He stepped into my path. He was close enough I could smell the cigarettes on his breath.'

Ryan didn't take notes. He waited, patiently, appearing to be removed emotionally, but the twitch of his jaw told her he was seething on the inside.

'I was fifteen at the time. I stepped out to go past him, he intercepted me again.'

Dawn took another sip, then licked her lips. She wasn't going to give him too much detail. Not here. Not now.

'He touched me. I shrugged him off. I don't know why, but he stepped aside and let me pass to the cubicle. I didn't understand it back then, but I do now.'

'You were his first.'

'Yes. I was his first attempt. I think he realised he'd picked the wrong personality. Not sure if it was the look in my eyes. My body language. When I think about it, probably both. Tracey was different. She was eager to please. Desperate to win.'

'You think he groomed her?'

'I am certain of it.'

'You tell anyone?'

'My dad.'

'And he didn't believe you?'

'Oh, he believed me. He told me to keep my mouth shut or he'd lose his spot as assistant coach.'

Ryan was silent a moment. Dawn gazed at her hands, heart pounding, chest aching.

'I can see why you didn't go to his funeral.'

Dawn's eyes flicked up, Focussing hard on the detective.

'I do my homework. Did anyone else know? Martin? Did you make a formal complaint when you got older?'

'No. I left here when I was seventeen, after my brother's funeral, and swore I'd never return.'

'Yet here you are. Did your sister know?'

'Yes, and my brother. I told them when Tracey was murdered. Although, I think Fraser already knew about Fairweather.'

'What makes you say that?'

'He was dating Tracey. It made him the prime suspect.'

'And you think Fairweather had something to do with Tracey's murder.'

'Yes, and I think he forced my brother to write the suicide note.'

'That's a huge leap Dawn.'

Dawn lifted an eyebrow at the use of her first name.

'Sorry. Detective.'

'Except now my sister is missing and his number is in her call log.'

'But there's nothing to connect him to your brother's suicide or Tracey. Why would he be stupid enough to have links to your sister if he planned to do anything sinister to her?'

'I don't think he did. Plan to that is. Maybe Lisa found a link. She told me as much in her text.'

'What did she say, exactly?'

'Here. I'll show you.'

Dawn reached into her shoulder bag for her phone, being careful not to reveal her weapon.

Why hadn't she kept her bag on her last night when she headed downstairs for cover against the cyclone? Then maybe she'd have been able to shoot Fairweather instead of running from him.

'Here.'

She opened the call record for her sister as a stab of guilt made her stomach ache. There were so many unanswered calls and messages.

Passing it to Ryan she avoided eye contact a moment. He was going to think she was a bitch for not returning the calls, but he didn't know Lisa. He didn't have to listen to her hypotheses and warped ideas for all these years.

She always claimed karma was going to get whoever killed Fraser, but she was going to give it a hand.

'This is pretty cryptic.'

'Yes, but it says she has proof.'

'It doesn't exactly say proof.'

Dawn reached for the phone and read the message again. Ryan was right.

I think I've found what we need. What we've been looking for all these years.

'Found what we need could be about anyone. Anything.'

'But it has to be him. He came to the house yesterday.'

Ryan's body stiffened. 'When?'

'Before you came by. I took off into the bush when he was there. He didn't follow. You said you came around three.'

'I didn't pass anyone on the driveway.'

'Well, we can ask him when we bring him in for questioning then.'

'There's no *we* here Detective. You're on the bench. I agreed to include you in the investigation, from behind the scenes, because of your local knowledge, but you will be watching the interview from afar. There is no way you are getting into that interview room.'

Chapter 14

Dawn watched as Ryan ordered their meals at the bar. The drunk from the previous night eyed her from his perch on the last stool at the bar.

She smiled and waved with as much sarcasm as she could muster. He averted his gaze, but then slipped from the stool and staggered towards her.

How could he be drunk? It's only ten in the morning.

'Your dad was a good bloke, you know.'

Dawn remained silent. Struggling to place him from her childhood memories, she tried to picture him twenty years younger, maybe a tad more tanned and less jaundiced.

'You don't remember me, do you?'

'Should I?'

The smell of stale whisky wafted her way. Dawn held her breath.

'Excuse me.'

Ryan stepped between the man and their table with his back to the guy, eyes questioning her, as though she might need rescuing.

She shook her head. The old-timer was no threat, but her interest was piqued. What did he know about her family? Her father?

'I'm sorry, but I don't remember you. What's your name?'

The old man wobbled on unsteady legs, then shuffled away without a backward glance.

Mari reached their table with napkins and cutlery.

'Who is that guy?'

Mari glanced over her shoulder.

'Ned Clements. He's harmless.'

'He seems to know me. Keeps talking about my dad, but I don't remember ever meeting him.'

'He's one of your dad's old drinking buddies. Not sure they had much to do with each other outside these four walls, but they certainly did enough chinwagging back in the day to put a mothers' meeting to shame.'

'What time does he start drinking?'

She thought maybe it was worth catching him sober one day to talk. If her dad confided in him, there was a chance he might know more about where her mum disappeared to.

Mari bent close so no one could overhear.

'He never stops, luv.'

'Oh.'

Her hopes were dashed, but as she glanced his way, she could see there was some semblance of coherence about the way he gazed back towards her.

'Sounds like my dad.'

'Sorry, luv. You understand, we always tried to keep it to a minimum.'

'I don't blame you, Mari. Or Ben. You were always good to him—to us.'

She noticed Ryan listening intently. Mari must have too.

'Can I get you another coffee?'

'No thanks, Mari.' She turned to Ryan.

'What about you Ryan?'

'I'm fine.'

He waved his hand. Mari stepped away from the table.

'You really did have it tough growing up here.'

'I don't need your sympathy Ryan.'

'It was only an observation. It could be pertinent to my investigation.'

'Our.'

'*My*.'

He grinned. She let herself smile back.

Out the corner of her eye, Dawn noticed movement. Turning, she waved as Michael stepped up from the courtyard into the main bar area.

His eyes drifted from her to Ryan and back, as though he were making some sort of decision. Dawn saw him draw himself up, shoulders back.

She rolled her lips to stop from smiling. It had been a long time since anyone fought over her. Not that she was entertaining any romantic interests. Cooktown was the last place on earth she wanted to meet anyone or pursue a relationship.

She'd be gone as soon as she found her sister and niece.

'Michael. Come join us.'

She shuffled over to make room on the bench. A grin split his lips, showing his snowy white teeth.

'This is Detective Ryan. Ryan, this is Michael, the ranger who found my sister's car and the fabric with the Cooktown school emblem.'

Ryan stood and held out his hand, which Michael shook. They sat in unison, eyes focussed on one another as silence ensued. Until Michael finally turned his glance to Dawn.

'I've been looking everywhere for you. I thought you might need help cleaning up at the house.'

'Did you come out to the house yesterday?'

Michael shook his head.

'So it *must* have been Fairweather.'

She tried to wipe the smug expression from her face, but obviously failed. Ryan rolled his eyes. 'Eat, then we'll find out.'

Michael scanned Ryan's face, then hers. 'Can I help with anything?'

'I don't think so. For now, we have a suspect to interview.'

'I think you mean *I* have an interview.' Ryan didn't wait for Dawn to react. 'He could just as easily be a witness.'

Dawn didn't bother arguing. Her gut told her Fairweather was involved. She didn't know how yet, but she intended to find out.

Michael wasn't ready to give up.

'I'm keen to keep looking for Lisa. I don't mind helping out. I've searched a few spots in the Archer Point Park I thought she might have gone for help, but since her car was abandoned, I'm not sure how far she could have gone.'

Dawn shoved her fears aside, and focussed on being a cop. It was all she could do right now. Procedure would keep her mind active, with no room for anxiety or guilt.

'We need to ID the victim. Then we can probably work out if she went with Lisa to Archer Point or drove her own vehicle. Maybe Lisa took the dead girl's car. Do you have any forensic evidence from Lisa's car to support someone else being in it?'

Ryan shook his head.

'Nothing out of the ordinary in the car and the victim was gnawed at pretty badly by fish. No obvious ID yet. Still waiting on DNA, and the post-mortem report.'

'Did you find anything of interest in Lisa's locker at the pool? Fairweather seemed very keen to make sure I didn't get my eyes on it.'

'Nothing popped out at me, but you can take a look after our interview.'

Ryan was about to go on, but Michael interrupted.

'This could be nothing, but I heard your victim might be one of ours.'

Ryan frowned. 'What makes you think that?'

Michael shrugged. 'The doctor who prepared her for transfer to Cairns is a friend of mine. She said, on closer inspection, she noticed the victim's hair was dyed lighter, but coarse, like our mob. She wanted to let me know to check for any missing girls in the community.'

'Hopevale?'

'No, my rangers. I work with at-risk youth. They come and volunteer, learn a bit about their heritage. Hopefully we can instil some pride and focus, and they can finish school and go on to higher learning or at least bypass the glue sniffing and alcohol treadmill.'

'Very admirable.'

Ryan's tone was weird. Dawn scowled. He ignored her.

She knew what it was like to go off the rails as a teen. Shortly after she dropped swimming, her mum and dad started arguing, a lot. Then her mum disappeared, and her dad picked up his drinking.

She often thought they were arguing over her quitting swimming. After her mum disappeared, her dad and she argued constantly. In the end, she started skipping school. Picking up a long list of drop-kick boyfriends. One who was a vandal, another a local petty thief. It had only been a matter of time before she got into serious trouble.

Constable Martin could have shoved her into juvenile detention, but he didn't. He could have dobbed on her to her father, but he knew it would be useless. Instead, he gave her an ultimatum. Arrest record or join the local football team.

When she complained she'd be the only girl, his answer surprised her.

'Not for long!'

He turned out to be right.

She found a new appreciation for Michael in that memory. But she needed to focus on now, on finding a murderer. In her gut, she was sure Lisa wasn't dead and there was no doubt in her mind her sister's text, the death of Tracey Warren and maybe this new victim, were all related.

She turned to Michael.

'Have you checked in with all the female rangers?'

'Yes, and one is unaccounted for.'

'Let's check her out then.'

Mari bustled up to the table to place two plates down.

'Michael. What can I get you?'

'He can share mine.'

Dawn suddenly wasn't hungry anymore and the faster her food was gone, the quicker Fairweather could be interviewed and she could run a search on this missing girl.

Chapter 15

The interview room was like most Dawn had seen. Coming from Major Crimes in Adelaide, and previously, a smaller regional station, she saw more than her fair share.

Small, drab, grey or greenish. A table, chairs, recording equipment. No windows, only harsh fluorescent lighting overhead, casting ghostly, bluish light that made everyone appear anaemic.

Even Fairweather, with his tan and sun-bleached hair appeared gaunt under the lighting.

Sergeant Martin pressed *record* and introduced all present.

'Why am I here?'

No one answered Fairweather. Instead, Ryan scanned details on a piece of paper inside a manila folder. Eyes down, finger running along the page and not a word leaving his lips.

Dawn grinned at the technique. Give him time, and enough silence, he might incriminate himself.

'Am I under arrest?'

Fairweather sat, hands clasped together on the table, clenching and unclenching to an unheard beat.

His eyes darted from Sergeant Martin to Ryan. One in uniform, the other in the same grey pants and long-sleeved shirt, now rolled back down and cuffed.

'What the hell is going on?'

More silence. Until Ryan finally glanced up and made eye contact.

'You are simply helping us with our enquiries Mr Fairweather.'

'Enquiries about what?'

He sat back, hands in his lap, eyes still darting around, unable to find a resting spot. Dawn knew Constable Jamison had said nothing definite when he picked Fairweather up in the police LandCruiser.

She knew she shouldn't, but she was enjoying watching him squirm. Maybe now Fairweather would understand how she felt, half-naked in the pool changing rooms while he loomed over her.

She hadn't told Fraser for a reason. She knew if she'd told her brother, Fraser would have been down there in a flash to take a punch. But Fairweather was bigger, stronger and more experienced. And even when she did tell Fraser, after Tracey was murdered, it was only once she was sure her brother wouldn't try to retaliate.

Ryan sucked his teeth and ran his tongue over them before opening the file and turning it to face Fairweather. Inside, a photo of Lisa's abandoned car at Archer Point sat on the top.

'Do you recognise this car?'

Fairweather leant forward, glanced at the photo, then searched the sergeant's face. Martin's eyes were on the picture, not Fairweather.

'Yes.'

'And you know the vehicle how?'

'What is this? Everyone knows what car Lisa Grave drives.'

'And what is your relationship with Ms Grave?'

A smile crept across Fairweather's face. Dawn shivered. He leant back, placed his hands behind his head and turned towards the two-way mirror.

'Which Ms Grave?'

'Lisa Grave.'

Ryan slapped the tabletop, drawing Fairweather's attention. She could tell Ryan was fighting his instincts to look at the two-way mirror—to look at her.

'None of your bloody business.'

'Just tell him David. This isn't a game.'

Fairweather glared at the sergeant, who appeared calm, even a little bored.

'Your phone number is in her mobile call log. There aren't many. From all accounts, Ms Grave doesn't use her phone much, but on the day she went missing, and the few days before, your number appears seven times in her call list.'

Fairweather nodded, a sneer causing his top lip to lift.

'What can I say. It's my magnetic personality.'

'Let's stick with the facts, shall we?' Ryan mocked. 'I'll ask you again. What is your relationship with Lisa Grave?'

'We have no relationship.'

Fairweather crossed his arms and plunged back in the chair with a huff.

'Then why so many phone calls and why did you go out to her place yesterday, during the storm?'

Fairweather's gaze snapped to meet Ryan's.

'How the hell …'

'You came unannounced, when you knew Lisa Grave was missing. You were aware the house would be unlocked. What were you hoping to find?'

'Not her bloody sister staying there, that's for sure. She's been gone twenty bloody years because she hated the place and then she goes and stays there.'

'So you admit to being at Lisa Grave's home yesterday between the hours of two and three?'

'It's not a crime.'

'Why were you there?'

Fairweather drew a long breath and blew it out in frustration.

'I knew she was missing. Everyone knows. I went out there to batten down the hatches. The storm was upgraded to category three. I know she leaves the place open like a bloody breezeway.'

'So you were simply being neighbourly?'

'Yes.'

'Then why all the calls?'

Fairweather's shoulders slumped. Dawn had never seen him resigned to defeat so easily. He was an arrogant arse. Always the ladies' man. Always full of his own self-importance. Maybe the last twenty years had seen his notoriety wane.

'I kept calling because she wasn't answering my texts.'

'What were the texts about?'

Fairweather glanced at the two-way glass, then locked his gaze on Sergeant Martin.

'Is she in there?'

The sergeant said nothing.

'She's not going to like this.'

Martin glanced at the glass. Ryan remained focussed on Fairweather. Dawn's blood ran cold. Her skin broke out in a clammy sweat.

'I was trying to get access to Abby.'

Dawn used every bit of her self-control not to rush into the adjacent room and rip Fairweather's throat out. This time, Ryan's gaze shifted to the glass. Inside, her stomach rolled as their eyes locked, unknowingly, through the two-way mirror.

'Why would Lisa Grave give you any type of access to Abby, after knowing your history?'

'What history?'

'Why did you need access to Abby?'

'Because my wife left me two years ago and since then, I've been trying to get unsupervised visits with my daughter.'

Chapter 16

Dawn sat rigid behind the wheel of her campervan, staring out the windscreen at the police station, struggling to breathe. She thumped the steering wheel as her vision narrowed, her pulse raced, and every pore of her body leaked sweat.

It was a lie. It had to be a lie. How could Lisa possibly sleep with David Fairweather? After all the history. After everything he'd done. How?

A hand touched her arm.

'Just breathe slowly.'

She knew how to overcome a panic attack. She'd dealt with them most of her adult life, but they were rare these days. Becoming a cop, then a detective, had empowered her. Given her a sense of control—which was slipping away into the abyss with every hour she spent back in her home town.

Michael wasn't allowed to watch the interview. He had no idea why she'd stormed out the front door, down the steps and jumped into her rental van. But he'd followed, a few steps behind, ready to catch her if she passed out.

'I'm okay.'

He waited another few seconds before speaking. 'Do you want to talk about it?'

She shook her head. 'No. I want to find my sister. I want to follow up on your missing ranger.'

'The mobile phone reception is still out and so is the power in a few areas. I think texts are still getting through.'

'I've already asked Ryan to run your girl for a vehicle registration. It might give us a lead. In the meantime, we should visit the school. What year is she in?'

'Year 11.'

'Let's talk to her teachers, or the principal. Maybe they know something.'

'Are we allowed to do that? We don't know if your victim is her or not yet?'

'We won't say she is. You're a concerned friend. Trying to track her down.'

He nodded. 'I'm good with that, but how about we take my car? It's humid as hell and I reckon my air-conditioning is way better.'

Dawn glanced around the sparse interior of the older model HiAce and had to agree.

'Deal.'

A few minutes later, she was angling the vents at her chest, lifting her shirt and trying desperately to dry the sweat soaking her bra.

Michael chuckled from the driver's seat.

'What's so funny?'

'Nothing.' His voice was an octave too high.

'I'm sorry, but if I don't cool off soon, I think I might pass out.'

'Don't be sorry. It's not every day I get someone in my vehicle flashing her bra at the air vents.'

'No, really! I thought with those puppy dog brown eyes you'd have the local girls swooning.'

He glanced at her sideways. She turned to gaze out the window.

'Who's the principal these days?'

'Same one as when I was here.'

Dawn turned back. Her perplexed expression was met by another chuckle.

'I dropped out of school in Year 10. When I decided I wanted to be a ranger, and lead the local youth, I thought I better set an example.'

'You went back to school?'

He nodded.

'A mature-age student. The senior girls in my year would have been all over you. I bet you got plenty of attention.'

'I did.'

He parked his vehicle in the angle parking outside the school oval and applied the handbrake. The corners of his mouth turned up slightly as he tried to keep a straight face.

'I hope you disappointed them.'

Visions of Fairweather flooded Dawn's mind. She shook them away. Not every guy was a pervert.

'Of course. And before you ask, we have very strict fraternisation policies in the work I do. Open door policy, absolutely no *one on one* time with those in our care without supervision. I've even had to refuse to give students a lift home. Luckily, we've got some good funding, and the local taxi service picks up from pretty much anywhere.'

He opened the driver's side door without another word. Dawn sat a moment before opening her door, ready to join him.

Fairweather hadn't raped her, but their encounter was enough to scare her. In some ways, she was quite paranoid, but then her dating choices in men was abysmal. She had divorce papers to prove it.

Her phone pinged in her pocket as she slammed the door closed. Retrieving it, she opened the screen as she joined Michael on the pavement.

'It's Ryan. Says your girl's full name is Jessica Mills, no middle name and no registered vehicles in her name or her mum's.'

'No surprise there. Cars aren't exactly owned by locals. I've seen her drive out to Archer in a few different vehicles. I'm guessing they are shared around the community.'

'Maybe make a list of the make and models you recall.'

'But I won't have registration details.'

'The models might be enough.'

Dawn placed her phone back into her shorts pocket and wondered if she should have dressed in more professional attire, then dismissed the thought. She wasn't working. She was helping Michael find a missing girl.

They had no confirmation it was Jessica's body undergoing an autopsy today and she had no jurisdiction to work without Ryan's supervision on this case.

Dawn was personally familiar with the principal's office and could likely find it blindfolded. But today she was a visitor. A stranger in her own home town.

Michael led the way up the concrete path to the main office building. Three flagpoles held limp, wet flags. The Australian flag, the Indigenous flag, with the red, black and yellow sun emblem and another Dawn couldn't quite recognise without seeing it flying.

The grass squelched underfoot as they cut the corner of the pathway to avoid a fallen branch.

A group of adults with high-vis shirts scurried about picking up debris and trimming back battered bushes.

'I'm surprised the school is open today.'

Dawn surveyed the damage as they passed.

'They'll have town kids in, skeleton staff I'm guessing. Most of the outlying areas will be flooded in for a few days.'

'Dawn. How are you?'

The voice caught her off guard. Turning, she recognised Larry waving from the centre of the group.

'Larry. Is there anywhere you don't volunteer?'

'I'm still on the P & C.'

It always amazed Dawn how much Larry did for the community. He was a family guy, with a lovely wife and two sons.

'You have kids here?'

He shook his head.

'No. Grandkids. But I like helping. You know how it is.'

A thought struck her. Stopping, she turned to the man who always had a charming smile for everyone.

'How long have you been with the P & C?'

He frowned, like the question was unnecessary because everyone knew the answer, then grinned as he no doubt remembered she'd been away a long time.

'Twenty-five very fun-filled, fulfilling years.'

'Really. I might want to catch up with you someday and ask you about my mum.'

His frown returned, this time, it didn't disappear.

'Dark times for you Dawn. Maybe you should let the memory rest.'

'Michael. Come in. I got your call.'

A short, balding man with broad shoulders and slim hips waved from the entrance. Dawn glanced over, then back at Larry who had returned to his gardening undeterred.

'Dawn, this is Tom Fletcher. Tom, this is Dawn Grave.'

Michael seemed to be struggling for the right word to describe her presence.

'A friend of mine, helping me find where Jessica has wandered off to.'

'Come in. Lovely to meet you Ms Grave.'

'Call me Dawn.'

She shimmied past as he held the door, then stepped aside and waited for him to draw up alongside Michael.

'How long has Jessica been missing from school?'

Michael jumped straight to the question Dawn would have asked.

'She missed roll call Friday last week and again yesterday, but lots of kids did with the cyclone looming.'

Dawn let Michael do the talking.

'Is she still living out at Hopevale?'

The principal opened a door and ushered them through into a reception area. They passed the main desk, turned left down the hall and strolled to the end where two doors were labelled with name plates.

'As far as I know. I haven't tried to contact her family yet.'

He opened the door facing the front of the building and entered.

'I tried earlier today. The mobiles and power are still out in Hopevale.'

Michael sat in the seat the principal offered. Dawn joined him in the one alongside. The principal rounded the desk and pulled a file from the top drawer, then rolled out his chair and sat.

They huddled around the wide timber desk as he turned the file around so they could see.

'You asked about her grades. I don't usually share this type of thing beyond direct family, but I know you're doing a great job with these kids Michael. They are lucky to have you.'

'I've been where they are, Tom. Everyone deserves a break.'

Dawn understood more than most how true that statement was.

'Did anything pop out at you?'

'Jessica is bright. When she first joined your program, her grades picked up, but she's been struggling through Year 11 this year.'

'Year 10 was good though?'

'It was in the first half. Her grades were excellent, then they dropped to average in the second semester.'

'Did her teachers say anything? Was she being disruptive?'

Dawn joined the conversation, unable to keep her thoughts to herself.

'On the contrary. The only comments were how Jessica was withdrawn, less attentive, often distracted in class.'

'Any counselling offered?'

The principal chuckled.

'Our funding only goes so far Ms Grave. We have guidance counsellors, but they are snowed under. Jessica isn't a priority, because she is still passing, not at a high level, but she's sneaking over the line.'

'I don't suppose we can get a list of her friends, so we can see where she might be?'

Dawn could see Michael knew the answer to his question before he asked it.

'I'm afraid not. Showing you her grades was a courtesy. I'm sorry I can't be of more help, but our student's personal information comes under the privacy act.'

Michael rose. Dawn joined him.

'The police are searching for Jessica now. I've lodged a missing person's report. If you think of anything else, call the station and let them know.' Michael held his hand out to the principal.

'I will.'

They shook hands. The principal held his hand out to Dawn. She shook it. He held on, eyes focussed on her face.

'You don't happen to be related to Lisa Grave?'

'Yes. She's my sister.'

Dawn pried her hand free. 'Why?'

'You both look so much like your mother. Lisa is a member of the P & C these days. Lovely soul. Always happy. Always got a kind word to say to everyone.'

'Have you seen Lisa lately?'

Dawn's heart rate kicked up a notch.

'Not since last Monday's meeting. I make it a habit to attend as many as I can.'

He studied Dawn's expression. 'Why? Is something wrong?'

'My sister is missing.'

'Heavens. There's a spate of it going around then.'

He was smiling at his own joke, until he wasn't.

Michael frowned as he clarified the situation. 'No, Tom. She is genuinely missing.'

'I'll be sure to check with the rest of the committee then. I'll get back to you as soon as I can.'

'Thanks.'

Michael turned to leave. Dawn studied the principal's face. He was too smiley, too charming, too something she couldn't quite put her finger on.

'Dawn. You good to go?'

She watched the principal's eyes track from Michael to her, then back to Michael as he buried his hands in his pockets and waited for her to leave.

'I'm good.'

She strode out the office door, leaving Michael jogging to catch up.

Chapter 17

They drove back to the main street in silence. Dawn gazed out the window, lost in thought. Michael focussed on the road, his body tense, his hands gripping the wheel.

'Are you going to tell me what got your hackles up before we left? Tom is a great guy. Gives so much time to those in his care.'

'I'm just tired. I didn't exactly sleep well last night.'

Fairweather's hooded figure flashed into her mind. Was he telling the truth? Did he go out to secure Lisa's house? Why would Lisa have slept with him?

'Dawn. I don't know you very well yet, but I can tell when you're pissed off.'

As she thought about his use of words, she smiled, despite her mood. His use of the word *yet* needed clarification before there was any misunderstanding.

She wasn't staying in Cooktown. She was going back to her very fulfilling job in Adelaide and the last thing she wanted was to be in a relationship, with anyone.

'It was something he said. I honestly don't know exactly what it was. He was talking about Lisa, then joking, then not. I bristled. That's all.'

'I don't think he realised how serious this is. You said so yourself. Lisa is a free spirit. Maybe he knows her better than he's letting on?'

'Are you implying my sister sleeps with everyone in town?'

'What? No! That's not what I meant.'

Dawn shook her head and put her hand in the air to stop him talking. The gesture didn't stop him.

'Is there something you're not telling me?'

'Nothing that is any of your business.'

The fact her sister might have slept with the man she hated most in this world—other than maybe her father—was painful enough. The idea of Lisa throwing herself into the arms of every man in town was unbearable. She forced the idea from her mind.

She'd seen the principal's wedding ring. She knew Fairweather was married when Abby was conceived.

Shaking her head, she forced the thought away. She was in no position to pass judgement. Two married men, a drug addict, a stockbroker who banged anything with legs and a long list of one-night stands she'd never remember the names of.

She was a walking, talking encyclopaedia of ruined, corrosive, manipulative relationships.

Hot tears stung the back of her eyes. She closed them and dropped her head back onto the headrest.

'I'm sorry. You're right. I just found a car, met someone who I thought was different and wanted to help her out.' When she didn't respond, he went on. 'When I get you back to town, I'll head back to where I came from.'

She kept her eyes closed. He wanted her to stop him. He needed her to say it was alright, she was wrong. He was only being nice. But she kept quiet. She wasn't going to be manipulated again.

More importantly, she was not going to lead him on.

As they drove down the main street, Dawn gazed out the window. Groups of people picked up debris, mended fences and swept the pavement. Two council trucks were piled high with rubbish.

She was so absorbed in finding her sister—in trying to get Fairweather arrested—that she missed the destruction left behind by the storm.

The RSL hall roof was missing a few sheets of iron. No doubt there would be water damage. A group of old men huddled around looking like they wanted to help, as a dozen high-school aged boys swept the water out, boarded up the roof and did their best to secure the building until major repairs could be done.

Her body shuddered, and tears rolled down her face before she could stop them. This return to town embodied everything she loved and hated about this place growing up. The sense of community, pride and care was enormous. Yet everyone had secrets and her family's were spilling over for everyone to see.

Or maybe everybody already knew some of them and it was she who was the mushroom. Hiding away, not knowing, not wanting to find out, hoping the bullshit she told herself would feed her and keep her safe.

'Look. I'm sorry. I was being a jerk.'

Michael parked the four-wheel drive outside the station and turned the engine off.

She shook her head. She didn't want to make him feel bad. This wasn't his fault.

'It's not you. It's this place. I can't explain it. I've missed it, but I haven't. Does that even make any sense?'

She opened her eyes. Michael held out a tissue. She took it and wiped her face. When she glanced his way, she could see him gazing out the window at all the work going on.

'How about we get changed and give everyone a hand?'

Dawn drew a breath. Part of her wanted to do just that, but the other part desperately needed resolution. Who killed Tracey, and now probably Jessica, and where was her sister? Where was the niece she never knew existed?

'I shouldn't. I need to find Lisa.'

'Ryan is on the job. It's getting late. There isn't much more you can follow up today. Is there?'

Michael was right. They were at a dead end. Until the post-mortem came in, they had no official ID or cause of death, even the place she was found yielded nothing. As for Lisa, she'd been through the house. She'd checked the reports on what was found in the car. She knew where Lisa had last been seen. It wasn't much to go on.

All she could do now was hope the P & C members could shed some light on things. Even Lisa's phone records weren't of any help, except to lead to Fairweather, who so far proved to be a dead end.

'Okay. Let's do it.'

Chapter 18

Steam rose and hovered above the road and pavement. Every pore on Dawn's body oozed sweat as she shoved rubbish into a disused fertiliser bag with gloved hands.

'Yowie, is that you?'

A hand touched her shoulder lightly. Only one person called her Yowie and Dawn hadn't heard it for over twenty years.

'Ronnie?'

Dawn turned to face the woman whose features were only vaguely familiar. The hair colour was different, body shape more rounded, even the height seemed wrong, but the voice was unmistakable.

'It is you. What the hell? I thought nothing on earth would ever bring you back to town.'

Dawn resisted the urge to settle her frizzy hair and wipe her clothing with filthy gloved hands. When they were teenagers, Ronnie was the gorgeous girl they all aspired to be. While Dawn was broad-shouldered, boobless and ungainly anywhere but the swimming pool.

'I'm here for Lisa.'

'Oh. Of course. I heard about her going missing. No news yet?'

'Not yet. But we are getting there.'

'We?'

'I'm working with the detective on the case.'

Dawn didn't mention Michael was helping, or that she was a police officer. News travelled like wildfire in country towns and Cooktown was no different.

'Lisa talks about you all the time. But aren't you Adelaide based? You can't work here, can you?'

Lisa talks about me.

Did Ronnie know she was a cop? If Lisa told people, then everyone would know already. There was no point trying to hide it.

'I'm off duty, but I'm still in the loop with what's going on. Professional privilege.'

'Have you met Abby? She's such a cutie. Goes to school with my Liam. I think they'll make the perfect couple when they get older.'

Dawn laughed out loud. When she was younger, everyone thought she'd marry Bradley Summerset, but *that* was never going to happen.

'Abby is missing too.'

'Oh no. That's terrible. Lisa can be a bit flaky at times. When you left, she was a bit lost really. Got into reiki and yoga and started hanging crystals everywhere. I think she missed you terribly.'

'We were close.'

'Were?'

'I've seen Lisa a few times. She's come to visit me in Adelaide, we talk on the phone occasionally.' Dawn considered how many calls she'd sent to voicemail over the years and cringed. 'But we've drifted apart since …'

'Veronica, get your arse over here.'

Ronnie jumped and spun around as Dawn peered over her shoulder to see who was yelling at her old friend like she was a barmaid taking too long with his beer.

'Brad?'

Dawn questioned the man as he stormed towards them.

'Veronica. I said get over *here*.'

He grabbed Ronnie's arm and tried to haul her towards him.

'Brad, is that you? It's Dawn.'

Dawn never expected a parade at her return to town, but Brad's expression made her feel like a terrorist on the top of his *most wanted* list.

'I know who you are. I know what your brother did too. I assume you're not staying long.'

He dragged Ronnie away without another word. One of the few girls Dawn could call a friend when they were in school, glanced back over her shoulder and mouthed the word *sorry*, but didn't pull away from Brad's grasp.

Dawn watched them cross the road and continue cleaning up a hundred metres away.

'What was that about?'

Michael was as stunned as Dawn.

'Brad was one of my brother's mates. I wondered why he never came to the funeral, but then I shouldn't have. Hardly anyone turned up to bury Fraser.'

'Why?'

Dawn realised Michael hadn't heard the story, which surprised her. But then again it probably shouldn't. Twenty years was a long time, and the town wanted to forget. Now they wouldn't be able to, because another young woman was dead, and Fraser couldn't be the scapegoat this time.

'It's a long story, but when my brother committed suicide, he was found with a note confessing to the murder of Tracey Warren.'

'You mean the girl whose school uniform you thought we found?'

'The very same.'

Remembering the suicide note reminded Dawn about the handwriting professor. She needed to follow up with Dr Nicholls and see if she could call in a favour with a friend from the Adelaide forensic lab.

‘I think I’m done for now. I need a shower and I’ve got a few calls to make.’

‘You do look a bit grubby.’

Michael used the back of his sleeve to wipe a mark from Dawn’s cheek.

‘It’s alright for you. Your dark skin covers a multitude of sins.’

‘Good to know it’s good for something.’

Dawn put a gloved hand on his arm.

‘I’m sorry.’

‘It’s okay. Growing up this colour wasn’t a bed of roses, but I’m proud of my heritage.’

‘You should be. I get it must have been hard for you though. But you’ve done so much for yourself, for your people.’

‘I was lucky. Plenty aren’t.’

‘That’s not only an Indigenous thing. In my line of work, I see a lot of disadvantaged people, teens, adults. Poverty, domestic violence. These are social issues, and they don’t discriminate.’

Dawn thought about her missing mother, her drunk father, how close she came to being an assault victim. If it wasn’t for Ross Martin, she could have easily been another statistic.

‘You’re right, but I’m only equipped to do what I can, and working with my community, doing what I can for Indigenous culture is all I can manage.’

Dawn’s stomach tightened as she glanced around her. Standing at the end of the main street, gazing out at the ocean past the river entrance, reliving the memories of her childhood, she realised something she’d never considered before.

Shaking the feeling aside she focussed, forcing the guilt away.

She left because this town held memories that nearly tore her apart as a teenager. She left for a good reason. Not even guilt was going to make her stay, once she found her sister.

'Let's go. I need to make those calls.'

Chapter 19

The fogged-up mirror in the bathroom was a blessing. The last person Dawn wanted to see was herself right now. Ronnie's words rolled around her head.

When you left, she was a bit lost really.

'I was seventeen.' She reassured herself aloud.

Grabbing a towel, she dried her body roughly, in no hurry to remove all the moisture. Instead, she left the bathroom naked and damp and stood directly below the buzzing ceiling fan, arms held out, breathing slowly, trying to cool off and compose herself.

She remained still until the last drop of moisture evaporated, then reached for clean underwear and her mobile.

Dialling, she hoped the phone lines were back up. As the ringtone sounded loudly in her ear, she sighed in relief and waited.

'Forensics, Penny speaking.'

'Penny. It's Dawn. How did the wrap-up of the case go?'

'Brilliantly. Between you and Jenny we got everything tied up neatly, like a bow on a Christmas pressie. He's going down for setting the teacher's wife on fire, too.'

'Good news. I'm sure Jenny's happy to put the whole thing behind her. Did she take up my offer to become a detective?'

'Not yet but give her a few years.'

'Years. We could do with her on staff now, not in a few years.'

'Well, I think Nick and she are pretty settled. Unless you can get the farmer to leave the cattle station, I think you'll have to wait it out.'

'Damn. Relationships can kill a woman's career.'

'Tell me about it.'

There was a moment of silence and Penny filled it.

'Now you can't tell me you rang to get a wrap-up of the Coober Pedy case. What do you need?'

'You know me too well. I've got a handwriting specialist looking at something for me. I was hoping I could give him your number so you can link in with him on the case. It's a cold one.'

'Love cold cases. Send it my way.'

'You sure? It's not on the books. There's no overtime coming your way—this is a Queensland case.'

'Dawn. How long have we known each other? Don't answer that, we both know it's too many years. Us girls need to stick together. Give him my mobile, I'll follow it up off the clock.'

'You're a gem.'

'Diamond, of course.'

Dawn chuckled, despite the tightness in her chest. Despite the feeling her world was imploding and if she didn't find her sister soon, she might fall into a pit of despair.

'Thanks Penny. I appreciate it.'

There was a quiet second.

'Is this about your brother?'

Dawn drew a deep breath.

'It's tied to family, yes.'

'I'll get right onto it.'

'Thanks Penny.'

'Talk soon.'

The phone line went silent. Dawn tossed her mobile onto the bed and followed it with a dramatic flop, arms outstretched, still half-naked. She lay under the spinning fan, watching the blades blur mesmerisingly.

The rush of adrenalin finally abated. Rolling from the bed, Dawn dressed and forced herself to head downstairs for some food. If it wasn't for Ryan's call earlier, she'd have curled up in bed and slept the early evening away, wallowing in depression.

If she failed to find Lisa and Abby, then her whole family would be gone. She'd be alone. Scoffing at herself, she slammed the dresser drawer. Who was she kidding? She *was* alone, had been since the day she left her family—left Cooktown.

All the one-night stands, short-lived relationships, drinking, gambling, partying. She'd been alone throughout it all. How could she not have seen it before now?

****

The buzz in the front bar and dining room caught Dawn off guard as it filtered up the stairs.

'First beer is on the house and don't try for two because I've got a memory like a steel trap.' Mari's voice rang out with authority and power belying her tiny frame.

Pushing her way through the crowd, Dawn spotted Ryan fending off a tall, blonde backpacker with curvy hips and a bust to match. He didn't appear to be trying very hard, until he saw Dawn approaching.

The woman spun around, glared, then scurried away, as though Dawn had spoilt her fun.

'Don't stop on my account.'

She slid into the seat opposite.

'Stop what?'

His grin said he knew exactly what she was implying.

She leant over so he could hear her. 'You said the autopsy report was in.'

Ryan scanned the room.

'It's a bit busy in here to discuss. How about we go to my accommodation?'

Dawn considered Ryan's eyes. Was he trying to hit on her? Possibly. Did she care? Probably not.

He was an attractive guy, with muscles in all the right places, broad shoulders, stylishly cut wavy hair and a five o'clock shadow that put George Michael to shame. He was everything she looked for in a hook-up. A little arrogant, attractive, not interested in anything long term.

As much as she wanted the release of a quick romp, she wanted to find her sister more and there was no doubt in her mind the recent body and Lisa's disappearance were connected.

'Do they have a lounge or bar?'

Ryan smirked. 'It's got a balcony opening to the street, if being in the public eye makes you feel safer.'

'Safer.' Dawn scoffed.

Ryan shimmied out of the seat. Dawn followed, admiring Ryan's butt in the form-fitting cargo shorts he'd changed into.

A few minutes later, Dawn gazed out the window of Ryan's accommodation. Sitting at the top of the hill, a few streets back from the main street overlooking the Endeavour River estuary and sunset, the renovated Queenslander was geared up for holiday letting.

'This place must have cost a bomb.'

Ryan shrugged his shoulders. 'I whacked it on my Visa.'

'You paid for your own accommodation?'

'I'll put in a claim for reimbursement when I get back.'

'The Queensland police force must be a lot more generous than SA. This place is way outside the allowance I get when travelling.'

Dawn thought about the run-down motel she stayed in at Coober Pedy. The orange bedspread came out of the sixties and was worn enough to indicate it wasn't an attempt at fashionable decor.

'They won't cover it all.'

Dawn let the subject drop. Where Ryan stayed and how much it cost was the last thing on her mind right now.

'Wine?'

'No thanks.'

An eyebrow rose, but he didn't push.

She knew alcohol and Ryan were a mix she'd regret. What was going on with her? A week ago, she would have jumped at this scenario. A scene flashed before her eyes. Ryan sweaty, naked, tequila shots and lines of salt laid out on his naked chest.

She must have blushed.

'You okay?'

Drawing a calming breath, Dawn nodded. 'Yep. I'll grab a water. Can I see the autopsy report?'

Ryan pointed to a file sitting on a round coffee table between two matching couches with plush cream-coloured fabric.

The thought Ryan hadn't taken it to the pub with him made Dawn wary she was being set up. But she was a big girl and knew how to say no.

Do I?

Ryan poured her a glass of water, placed it on the bar before opening a tall, fully stocked wine and beer fridge to retrieve a beer. Flipping the top off, he shoved the bottle into a stubby holder and collected her glass of water.

She rolled her lips, considered if one wine would be okay, but quickly decided it wouldn't. Not today. Not with all the stress and a good-looking guy within easy reach.

If she slept with Ryan, she'd risk her access to this case and there was no way she was willing to do that.

Sitting, she reached for the report.

'Didn't you want to sit on the balcony?'

Ryan hoisted the glass towards a wall of windows with billowing curtains.

'Yep.' She rose, opening the file and reading as she walked.

'Like your friendly ranger friend said, the victim is likely Indigenous. Hair texture, skin colour, eye colour, are all consistent with Torres Strait Islander or Aboriginal traits. The coroner found water in her lungs, so, as suspected, she drowned.'

Ryan strolled onto the deck and pulled out a patio chair ready to sit as he explained what was in the report.

'If you already knew what was in the report, why am I here?'

'You asked to see it.'

Dawn puffed out her cheeks. *Definitely a set-up.* She pulled out the chair at the end of the table, as far away from Ryan as possible, and sat, slapping the report on the table and began reading.

'It says here it's fresh water.'

'Chlorinated to be exact.'

'So, we're back to Fairweather?'

'No. We're back to someone drowned the girl elsewhere and dumped her body out at Archer Point. How many private pools are there in Cooktown?'

'I don't know, but this is about the swimming team. I know it is.'

'We've got no evidence to support that.'

'We need DNA to confirm the girl's identity.'

'I'll go see her mother tomorrow.'

'I'll come with you, and I think Michael should be there too.'

'You got the hots for the local ranger, then?'

'No.' *Do I?*

An uncomfortable silence grew between them.

'He's local, works with the Indigenous youth. Speaks the language, understands the culture. The Aboriginal people have different views on death and can be very uncomfortable speaking the name of the dead. I don't understand it all. But we need to be culturally sensitive.'

'What a load of crap. Politically correct bullshit is what it is.'

'If you don't take Michael and this blows up in your face, don't blame me.'

Dawn pushed away from the table. 'Are you dropping me back or should I call a taxi?'

Ryan's chair squealed on the tiles as he rose and crossed the patio towards her. His eyes were hungry. Dawn's pulse quickened.

Her sister's face flickered into her mind as Ryan grabbed her around the waist and pulled her hard against his chest, planting his lips on hers.

A rush of blood left Dawn's head and she returned his frantic kisses as he lifted her by the butt cheeks onto the table.

Wordless, confusing thoughts about Abby and Lisa, and Cooktown and the old Queenslander she grew up in rolled through her mind, creating a weird sensation like a wave of cool air.

'No!' She pushed Ryan away with her palm and turned her lips from his.

'You want this.'

'Yes. But no! I want to find my sister and niece.'

'You're not going to get anywhere tonight.'

Ryan's breath was hot against her ear—his body firm against hers, as she sat on the patio table, out in the fresh air, out in the open where anyone could see. Except the balcony was higher than any other building in the area. They had privacy if she wanted it.

'I said no. Are you taking me home, or am I calling a taxi?'

She shoved him away.

'You send out all the wrong signals, you know.'

'I can send out whatever signals I want. No means no.'

Ryan scoffed. 'I'll drop you back.'

'Ryan.'

She waited until he made eye contact again.

'You're right. I sent out the signals. Normally, a quick round in the bedroom with you would relieve tension, satisfy us both. But this place ...'

She waved her hand to encompass the skyline.

'It doesn't matter. Let's go.' He didn't want to hear her excuses. He didn't want to know how coming home was hurting her. Or changing her. Or both.

'Are we good?' Dawn asked as Ryan stalked past the billowing curtains towards the front door.

'I'll never mention it if you don't.'

'Done.'

Chapter 20

Michael leant against his four-wheel drive as he waited outside the police station. Dawn led the way down the concrete pathway from the station entrance. Ryan followed, sulking despite his statement the night before.

'Hey.' Michael waved but dropped his hand to his side when he saw Dawn's face.

Ryan shook the keyring hanging from his index finger. 'I've got the keys to the police LandCruiser, Wonder Boy. Let's go.'

'I think we should take my car.'

'And why would I want to do that?'

'The locals know me. You'll get a better reception. Rocking up in a police cruiser isn't going to open doors for you.'

'He's right.' Dawn agreed.

Ryan huffed, turned, and stormed back to the station to return the car keys.

'What's up with him?' Michael asked as soon as Ryan was out of hearing.

'Needs to get laid, I reckon.' She couldn't help but grin to herself. She could hardly talk. Every fibre of her body was tense.

Michael watched Ryan disappear inside, then turned to face Dawn, studying her like he had a question to ask but didn't know how to say it.

A slight shake of his head told Dawn he'd decided not to ask at all.

'What did the autopsy say?'

'That the body is likely your missing girl, so we need DNA to confirm. She drowned.'

'Really? She was a competitive swimmer, so I'm not buying it, and I don't think Jessica was stupid enough to swim out at Archer this close to the wet season.'

'She wasn't. The coroner found fresh water in her lungs. Highly chlorinated, likely swimming pool water. We're getting a sample of the town pool sent off to the lab. As soon as the results are back, we can arrest Fairweather again and hopefully he'll confess this time.'

'This time?'

'I think he killed Tracey Warren all those years ago.'

'Think or know?'

'It's only a hunch.'

'I can't believe he's the father of your niece.'

'I shouldn't have told you. It was a slip-up. I need to speak to Lisa to confirm. I'm not taking the word of a pervert.'

'You don't believe him?'

'I don't *want* to believe him.'

Ryan strode down the pathway. Michael opened the driver's side door and slid in. Dawn jumped into the passenger's seat. Ryan huffed as he was relegated to the back seat.

The drive to Hopevale was tense. More than thirty minutes of stilted small talk was giving Dawn a chronic headache. She rubbed the back of her neck as they pulled up outside a chain-link fenced yard with an overgrown lawn.

A threadbare velour couch, in a faded pale shade of pink, occupied most of the veranda. Two locals lounged against the sagging cushions. The guy was in his early twenties, a rolled-up smoke in one hand, a bottle in the other.

Dawn glanced at her watch. It wasn't even ten in the morning.

Michael hopped out of the driver's side, smiled and casually approached the front gate. Three dogs came bounding towards him.

Dawn joined him but eyed the dogs warily.

'Michael.'

A rounded woman with almost black hair, deep brown eyes and a bright floral pink blouse smiled openly.

'Daisy. This is Dawn Grave, and …'

He stalled as he realised he didn't know Ryan's first name. Dawn couldn't fill the gap. She didn't know either. No one wanted to call him Detective Ryan before they got Daisy on side.

He answered for them. 'Clint Ryan.'

'Is Jessica in?'

The woman glanced at the man on the lounge, then back to Michael.

They'd not spoken a lot during the trip, but all of them agreed they needed to tread lightly and see if there was any indication Jessica's family knew what might have happened to her.

As Dawn observed them now, she was sure they didn't.

'Not since I told you she was missin', Mick.'

'So she hasn't called, and no one else has seen her? Is her car missing?'

'She doesn't have a car Mick. You know that.'

Daisy was frowning at Michael now.

'Can we come in?'

'What's goin' on Mick?'

'Do you have anything of Jessica's we can use for DNA, like a hairbrush or toothbrush?'

Daisy glanced over her shoulder at the man on the lounge once more. He was busy relighting his smoke, but glanced up as the conversation stopped.

Daisy waved for him to get up.

Lazily he rose, put his beer bottle down and drew on the now lit smoke.

'What you need her DNA for?'

The whites of his eyes popped against his dark skin. Dawn watched his wary expression turn into a sneer.

She joined the conversation. 'Are you sure we can't go inside?'

They shifted their gaze to her.

'Who is ya, anyway?'

Daisy pointed to Ryan. 'This one looks like a cop.'

Dawn suppressed a grin at Ryan's expression, then focussed on Daisy's face. Taking a deep breath, she considered how to broach the subject. If they didn't play this right, the family might deny them DNA access. Then they'd be left with nothing.

'Daisy, I'm Lisa Grave's sister. Do you know my sister?'

The woman's gaze ran up, then down Dawn's body, taking in her features, her stature.

'Ya look a bit like her, but not much.'

'She took after Mum.'

'Your brother offed himself, hey.' The man interrupted. Dawn shifted her gaze to him as her stomach knotted.

'You know about that?'

'Yeah. Ya sister was trying to get Jesse to talk about stuff.' The man hawked and spat, not hiding his distaste.

'Shut it, Lionel. Nothin' wrong with Lisa.'

'I'm sorry to tell you this, but we've found a body.'

'You reckon it's Jess?' Daisy wavered, reaching for the lounge as Lionel stepped forward, smoke hanging from his lip, arms outstretched, ready to support her.

Michael stepped forward reassuringly, lowering to his haunches as Daisy dropped to the lounge. 'We don't know, Daisy, but we need to check.'

'It can't be my baby. It can't.'

'We just need DNA to confirm one way or the other, Mrs Mills.'

Dawn joined Daisy and like Michael, crouched down on her haunches so the woman could meet her eyes.

'Do you know anything about the questions my sister was asking …'

'Your daughter.' Michael finished for her.

She took a second to remember the reason Michael was there. If Jessica was the body they had in the morgue, then speaking her name now might be offensive.

'Not much. But it all happened after Bub joined the school council thing.'

'The P & C?'

Daisy nodded. Dawn frowned. Children didn't join the P & C as far as she knew.

'Then the swim club.'

A light bulb flashed in Dawn's head. Ryan shifted from foot to foot behind her, no doubt reaching the same conclusion.

'Have you seen my sister, Mrs Mills?'

The woman glanced up, eyes filling with tears, hands shaking. Finally, she nodded up the road.

Lionel patted her back and sniffed before he spoke. 'She rocked up whiter than usual with her kid.'

'Her car was found abandoned. How did she get here?'

'No idea.'

'So you didn't see her arrive?' Ryan interjected.

'Nah.'

Dawn popped to her feet, DNA forgotten. 'Where is she?'

'Up at Deloris' place.'

'Number?'

'Twenty-two.'

Dawn scanned Ryan's face.

'I'll get the DNA with Michael. You go see where your sister is.'

Ryan's eyes softened for the first time that day.

Dawn's filled with tears.

Chapter 21

The humid air filled Dawn's lungs, making each step towards number twenty-two harder. Dark rain clouds loomed, as though wanting to enshroud her sister, keep her hidden.

The gate creaked when she pushed it open. Ignoring the barking dogs, she focussed on the front screen door, full of holes, sitting ajar, doing nothing to stop mosquitoes or flies entering the home.

Yet, for Dawn it was a brick wall standing between her and her sister. She faced it, frozen a moment, before knocking on the doorframe.

'Deloris.' The woman's name finally left her lips. 'Are you home?'

Sounds echoed down the hall. Voices, the noise of a door closing.

'Comin'.'

Was that come in *or* coming*?*

Dawn waited as the sound of footfalls on the wooden floor grew louder.

'What 'cha want?'

'I'm Dawn Grave. Daisy said my sister, Lisa, is here?'

'Don't know no Lisa.'

'Lisa!' Dawn called loudly, hoping her sister would recognise her voice, but why would she? Other than a few visits, they'd only spoken over a phone line, and even then, only occasionally. You couldn't recognise a person's voice over texts.

'Lisa. It's Dawn!'

The sound of movement, a door creaking, footsteps. Dawn held her breath.

'Oh my God, Oh my God. It's you. It's really you!'

Deloris stepped aside as a whirlwind screamed past and shoved the screen door wide open with a bang.

Arms wrapped around her neck like a vice. Her sister's tears soaked her blouse within seconds.

'Abby. Baby. Come see your Auntie Dawn.'

Dawn was speechless and surprised to find warm tears running down her own cheeks as a small girl with huge blue eyes and long, blonde ringlets peered around the corner.

The strangest thought struck Dawn.

How does she stop those curls from frizzing?

'Come on, baby. This is Auntie Dawn.'

The name finally sank in. Dawn turned within Lisa's grasp to face the little girl.

'Hi, Abby. Nice to meet you.'

She dropped down from Lisa's embrace to the child's level as the little girl scrutinised her with suspicion.

'I'm sorry I haven't met you before now.'

And she was. Deep in her heart, she knew she was. How could her sister have had a baby and not even tell her? Did she even give Lisa a chance?

'You ready to go, Grave?' Ryan called from outside the front fence.

Dawn glanced up into Lisa's frowning eyes. 'We've got room in the car for you two. Grab your gear.'

'I'm staying here. The locals can keep me safe.'

'I can keep you safe Lisa. And I need to know what's going on. Your texts were cryptic as hell!'

'If you'd taken my calls, you wouldn't have had to decipher them.'

Abby reached for Dawn's hand, making her glance down into the deep blue pools.

Abby glanced at her mother.

'Can we go home now, Mummy? I want to see Cherry. She's got to be hungry!'

'Who's Cherry?'

'Our cat.'

Lisa smoothed Abby's hair.

'That cat's got an attitude.'

'Like someone else I know.'

Lisa scooped up her daughter and turned to Dawn. 'You armed?'

'Of course.'

Lisa bit her lip, studied her daughter's face, glanced back at Ryan and then Michael standing in the yard. Finally, she nodded to herself.

'You need to know what I saw, anyway. He police?'

Her head nodded towards Ryan.

'Detective.'

'I guess he'll do then.'

Chapter 22

Abby hopped from Michael's car and ran full speed up the stairs before anyone could utter a word. Dawn watched as the little girl scurried around the veranda, eyes peeking into every corner. Finally, she stopped, plonked her hands onto her hips and grumbled.

'There you are Cherry. My goodness you had me *so* worried.'

Dawn closed the rear passenger door as Lisa did the same on the other side. Michael and Ryan opened the front doors and followed silently behind.

'Which one are you sleeping with?' Lisa whispered as Dawn joined her at the bottom of the double staircase.

'What?'

'Don't play coy with me. They both look like someone stole their favourite toy.'

'Well, I'm no one's toy. We've got to get your statement. Stop fooling around.'

'Sorry. I'm a bit ragged and the state of your love life was always a great distraction when we were younger.'

Dawn followed her sister up the stairs. 'What are you talking about? I hardly dated in school.'

'So many missed opportunities.'

Lisa's wistful tone had Dawn searching her memory for a connection.

'Is David really Abby's father?'

Now seemed like the best time to ask the question—while Abby was busy fussing over her cat, who seemed to be lapping up the attention.

'He told you, then?'

'So it's true!'

'We can talk tonight. Not now. Not in front of Abby.'

'She doesn't know?'

'She does, but it's a long story and complicated now.'

'Why now?'

Lisa touched the dreamcatcher at the top of the stairs and held it between her fingers like it would answer the question for her.

Closing her eyes, she was silent a moment. Dawn waited, but when Ryan and Michael caught up, she thought it best to let the question go.

'Michael. Can you keep an eye on Abby while Ryan and I get Lisa's statement?'

'Sure.'

He gave her a wink and crossed the balcony towards the little girl. The cat was now over the pampering and desperately clawing its way free of her grasp.

'Cherry!'

She ran off after the scurrying ginger tabby. Michael followed.

'Cup of herbal tea? I think I need camomile. How about you, Detective?'

Lisa flashed a smile. Ryan glanced to Dawn, then back.

'Regular tea for me thanks.'

Lisa let go of the charm, turned, pulled her shoulders back and opened the screen door. Holding it, she ushered them inside.

'How about I get the tea, you start talking.' Dawn asked as they entered the kitchen.

'You'll never find anything. I've shifted stuff around since Dad died.'

A stab of guilt hit Dawn's heart.

'I'm sorry I didn't come. I was flat out at work.'

'Of course you were.'

Lisa made a side eye at Ryan.

'Don't look at me. I work in Cairns, she's Adelaide based.'

'I bet you use work as an excuse to get away from family stuff too.'

'Hang on a minute Lisa. You might have done some soul searching and be enlightened, but that doesn't give you the right to judge anyone else.'

'You mean judge you?'

Ryan stepped between them—hands held up like he was directing traffic. 'Come on, ladies.'

Dawn deflated as she dropped into a cane chair beside the kitchen table. In all the conversations she'd had with Lisa since she left home, not once had her sister voiced any concern over her absence.

Lisa dragged a chair out and sat down next to her. 'I'm sorry. It's been a stressful few days.'

'For both of us. I thought you were dead.'

'I nearly was.' Lisa grasped her hand. 'If I'd been sitting in my car, instead of going for a walk, I likely would be.'

'Tell me what happened. How did you end up out at Hopevale?'

'By sheer luck. Or maybe it was divine intervention.' Lisa gazed skyward out the corner of her eye. 'Either way, I couldn't have planned it.'

'Start at the beginning. Before you ramped up the text messages—which I'm so sorry I didn't answer by the way. I was outback, in the middle of the desert, chasing down a killer.'

Lisa gripped her hands tighter.

'It's okay. You do important work. I get it. I wouldn't have kept texting you, but this time, this time I was sure I was on to something and if what you say is true, and if Jessica is dead, then I must have been on the right track.'

Ryan hovered, keeping his distance. Dawn watched him leaning against the kitchen sink, listening, waiting.

'So, what got you revved up? And why did you abandon your car?'

'It wasn't a choice. I was walking and saw car lights rock up. I'd been waiting for a few hours, and no one came, then they did, and it wasn't who I was expecting.'

'Lisa. You're all over the place. Why were you waiting out at Archer Point of all places? Who for?'

'Sorry to butt in, ladies, but you're both going around in circles. This is all personal. Grave, you're too close. I need to do this.'

Dawn opened her mouth to protest, then stopped. Ryan was right. Her head was a muddle of emotions and everything coming out of Lisa's mouth was even more confusing.

Nodding, she directed him to take a seat across the table from them and drew her chair closer. For once in her life, she wasn't going to sit across from a witness. Lisa needed her support, not her questions.

'Okay, we should be doing this down the station.'

'No.' Lisa and Dawn said in unison.

'I don't know exactly who is involved and I'm safe here, with Dawn.' Lisa turned back to her sister. 'You said you had a gun.'

Dawn smiled. 'I do.' She patted her handbag still slung across her chest.

Ryan took charge of the conversation. 'Okay. Start from who you were supposed to be meeting out at Archer Point.'

'Jessica.'

'Why?'

'When I met Jessica, she'd recently been elected to the Student Council as a Year 10 rep. Popular girl. Smart, kind, funny, bright, cheerful. All the things you'd expect in a rising school leader.'

'How did you meet an SRC rep? Your daughter is only six?'

Ryan was asking all the questions Dawn should have. Tension eased from her shoulders.

'The P & C have at least one member of the SRC at each meeting. Jessica was a regular.'

'So why were you meeting Jessica last Friday afternoon?'

'Jessica's personality had been changing, rapidly. I spoke to her after the meetings from time to time. We were building up a friendship. Abby and I visited Hopevale each weekend, when we could, helping out with community stuff. The locals are totally into native herbs and I've been teaching a class on the medicinal value of indigenous plants, so I was researching with Deloris.'

'So you became friends with Jessica. Why the meeting?'

Ryan was trying, not very successfully, to hide his frustration. Dawn smiled to herself. Lisa was always such a people person. Never in a hurry to get to the point. Always focussed on the journey, not the destination.

They couldn't have been more different.

'I'm getting there. You need the whole picture. Don't you detectives thrive on details?'

Ryan sighed. Dawn bit her lip to stop a chuckle escaping.

'Jessica was invited to join the swim team. Between that and the P & C, maybe it was the pressure but some of the things she did reminded me of Tracey, before she was killed.'

Dawn wiped the smile from her lips as Ryan sat forward, suddenly focussed.

'What changed? What did you notice?'

'Just stuff. It's hard to put my finger on, but it doesn't matter. I was right because one day, I found Jessica crying after a P & C meeting. Her brother was late picking her up and she was shaking like a leaf. When I tried to console her, she pulled away, like I was going to hurt her.'

Lisa turned to Dawn.

'Everyone knows I wouldn't hurt a fly. Right Dawn?'

'That's right, Lisa.'

She nodded to Ryan. He nodded back.

'So Jessica was upset. Did you find out why?'

'Not exactly, but I had my suspicions. David is on the P & C too, and the swim team. I bet he took one look at Jessica and convinced her to join so he could do to her what he did to Tracey, and you.'

'If you believe David could do that, why did you sleep with him?'

The words were out of Dawn's mouth before she could stop herself. The mere mention of Fairweather set her blood racing.

'I don't know. He's a charismatic guy. I was lonely. Dad had just died. What was I, twenty-eight, twenty-nine?'

'He was married.'

'I'm not proud of it,' Lisa snapped. 'In fact, I regretted it almost as soon as the affair started, but he was so persuasive.'

'What about Tracey? What about what he did to me?'

'You know David. Always a plausible explanation?'

Dawn struggled to breathe—darkness closed in around her. Ryan filled the silence. 'How so?'

Dawn tried to focus. There were parts of Fairweather's attack she never told anyone, especially not Lisa. David had leered at her and blocked the path to the cubicle. But there was more.

The sensation of his hands on her backside, his body pressed against hers, made her stomach roll. She blinked away the bright sparkles intruding on her vision and breathed deeply, holding it a moment before releasing the air slowly.

'He said he didn't realise you were changing, and was stunned when he walked in. He didn't want to scare you, but he was worried you might tell someone he was in the changing room, and he could have been sacked from his coaching job, which would ruin his chances of becoming a schoolteacher.'

'Fairweather is a schoolteacher?' Ryan bolted up from the table. 'Why the hell didn't anyone tell me?'

Lisa frowned as she studied her sister's face for an answer.

Bile rose in Dawn's throat. Nausea swept through her. Before she realised, she was lurching to her feet. The table scraped back with a cringing noise, as her chair flipped backward.

Dawn rushed out the back of the kitchen as Abby rushed in, Michael a few steps behind. Dawn threw her hand over her mouth until she reached the railing, then hurled vomit over the edge.

It cascaded towards the ground, across the railing and splattered back all over her blouse as Michael drew up alongside, then retreated a few steps.

'I'll get you a cloth.'

Thankfully he was inside as another wave washed over her. Sweat dripped from her brow. She tried desperately to compose herself.

She didn’t want to have to tell anyone what she’d been through. It was her secret. And some secrets were best left buried.

Chapter 23

Michael handed her a wet face cloth and a glass of water. Dawn wiped her face, then turned towards the tree line, trying to come up with an excuse. Maybe they'd believe it was food poisoning?

'Must have been something I ate?'

'Do you need to go to the doctor, the hospital?'

'I'm fine. Thanks for the water.'

She rinsed her mouth out, then drank the rest in one long gulp.

'Careful, you'll throw it all back up again.'

'You sound like my mum.'

Dawn started to walk back inside, but Michael gently stopped her with a hand on her arm.

'You sure you're alright?'

'I'm fine. Shouldn't you be at work?'

'I phoned in yesterday to book in leave.'

'Why?'

'To help you find Lisa.'

'Well, she's been found.'

'But Jessica's murderer hasn't, and Lisa might still be in danger.'

'Michael, you're not a cop.'

'Neither are you, up here.'

Dawn sighed.

Michael followed her as she returned to the kitchen.

Abby sat on the edge of the table, a peeled carrot in one hand, a cup of water in the other. Eyes bright, smile wide.

'Auntie Dawn. You look terrible.'

'Thanks sweetheart.'

Ryan rose as she rejoined them.

'Kid's right. You look shocking. We'll pick this up later. I'd like to check on a few things. Speak with the principal again.'

'I'll come with you.'

'No. You stay here and clean up.' He glanced at her blouse. She blushed. 'Keep an eye on your sister. Sounds like she's opened a can of worms.'

'What did I miss?'

'Michael, any chance you can drop me back into town?'

He nodded at Ryan, then turned back to Dawn. 'I'll be back in ten minutes. Do you need anything at the shops?'

'Milk, apples, bananas.' Lisa opened the fridge. 'That should do for now.'

'Okay.'

Michael turned to leave, then stopped, hovering over Dawn who'd sat back at the kitchen table.

'I'm fine. Get going. Ryan, keep me in the loop.'

'Will do. I think we need to find out where our friendly swim coach and teacher was Friday night.'

The men left, letting the screen door slam behind them. Thunder rolled overhead as storm clouds filled the sky.

'Oh, goody. We're going to get another lightning storm. I love lightning. How about you, Auntie Dawn?'

'I like it, too. You go out on the veranda, and I'll join you in a second. I need to change first.'

She helped Abby down from her perch on the table and watched as the little girl skipped out the door.

'I'm sorry Dawn. I shouldn't have slept with him. But he was so charming.'

'It's not your fault Lisa. I should have told you the full story. Then you wouldn't have given him the time of day.'

'But then I wouldn't have Abby.'

It was true. From a monster, came a beautiful little girl who had filled a void in her sister's heart. One left by Dawn herself.

'What happened out at Archer? How did you get to Hopevale?'

'I left Abby with a friend, so I could go to meet Jessica.'

'Why Archer of all places?'

Lisa shrugged. 'I honestly don't know. Jessica picked the place. It was supposed to be after school, around four, but I waited for an hour. It got hot in the car, so I parked under the trees and went for a walk. The sun was dropping below the hills when I got back and saw headlights coming down the road.

'I waited by my car a minute, but then I got this funny feeling. Like why was Jessica so late? My nerves were rattled. I can't explain exactly why. I think the Universe was telling me something.

'I jumped the fence and hid in the grove of trees, near the water's edge. You know, where we used to light the fires and set up our chairs, back when we were kids?'

Dawn nodded. She missed those days so much. Cool winter evenings, after a warm sunny day of fun. Sitting by the fire, drinking rum and cola and talking crap like teenagers do. The sensation of sun-baked sand between her toes and the rising tide touching her feet as the warm, tropical water rolled in at a rapid pace.

'I remember.'

'Well, I hunched down there and watched the car stop next to mine. The headlights faced me, so I couldn't make out the vehicle. I only know it was a dark colour.'

The cop in her took over. 'Any other details?'

'The light was fading fast. The headlights were elongated though, not round. Whoever it was, went to the boot of the car, opened it, dragged something out and dumped it on the ground. Dawn. The sound. It made my blood curdle … even thinking about it now.'

Lisa shivered. Dawn reached for her hand and squeezed.

'I think it was Jessica, but I couldn't see what it was for sure. I know it was heavy because it made such a loud thud as it hit the ground. The guy picked it up like it weighed nothing, threw it over his shoulder and walked straight past me. Even though he was so close, I still couldn't see his face.

'He waded out to the mangrove island. He was only gone a minute, maybe two, then I heard a splash and another minute or so later, he was back, with only a blanket in his hands.'

'You think he dumped a body out there?'

'I didn't hang around to find out. When he first arrived, I thought he might just be a bloke dumping rubbish, but when he started going through my car and called my name. I panicked.

'I scurried through the trees like a scared possum. When I reached the road, I ran up the other side and past the car park entrance, then ducked back into the tree line.

'It took me nearly two hours to get to the main road. By the time I hitched a ride into town and collected Abby, I was exhausted.'

'So how did you get out to Hopevale without your car?'

'Ronnie dropped me out.'

'Ronnie?'

'Yeah, she was babysitting.'

'Ronnie knew where you were all along?'

'Sure. Why?'

'Lisa. We've had the SES out hunting for you. We've got every available cop on the case. No one told us you were safe.'

'Well, she wouldn't, would she?'

Dawn gaped.

'Why would she? I told her what I saw. Who I thought it was.'

'You told her you thought it was David?'

'No. I told her I thought it was Jessica's body.'

'Why didn't you go to the police?'

'I already had. You. That's why I sent you the last message.'

'So why didn't you stay at Ronnie's?'

'Because she agreed with me. She thought getting out of town was best, too.'

'So why didn't she tell me where you were, when I told her why I was here?'

Lisa bit her lip. 'I don't know.'

'Maybe we should find out?'

Chapter 24

The sound of the occasional heavy raindrop pinged the iron roof as Dawn changed out of her dirty blouse, into one of Lisa's brightly coloured tops and left the kitchen to keep her promise to Abby. By the time she lowered herself onto the cane lounge, the drops had intensified—hitting the iron like rapid fire from an automatic rifle.

Abby gazed out at the thunderclouds, giggling as the darkened sky was illuminated with forks of lightning. The occasional rumble of thunder made her jump, as the entire house vibrated.

'Mummy says it's the gods grumbling at each other, not me, so I don't need to worry.'

Dawn fought the urge to roll her eyes, and opened her mouth to explain how thunder was nothing of the sort, but stopped as Lisa joined them outside.

'I've asked Ronnie to come over for a drink and watch Abby while I help with your investigation.'

'She buy it?'

'I think so.' Lisa sat down next to Dawn and Abby cuddled up close as another bolt of lightning split the sky.

They sat in silence a moment, then Lisa asked.

'Do you think Ronnie could be involved in this somehow?'

'I don't know, but she didn't give you up, so maybe she was only being extra cautious, or …' Dawn ran the scene through her head. Ronnie was happy to see her and maybe, if given the chance, she would have told her about Lisa, but Brad interrupted her.

The front screen door creaked, then slammed. Abby jumped from the lounge and bolted for the kitchen. Dawn missed the warmth of her body instantly.

'It's Auntie Ronnie.' The little girl called as she disappeared inside.

'She never misses a beat, does she?'

'Not usually.'

'What's with the gods being angry bullcrap?'

'It's what Mum used to tell us. Don't you remember?'

Dawn searched the recesses of her mind. Finally, she shrugged.

'You should tell her the scientific reason.'

'Why? She'll learn it in school. Why take all the magic and mystery out of life?'

'Because gods don't actually control the thunder and lightning.'

'How can you be so sure?'

Dawn opened her mouth to start a full-on argument over theology versus science, but Abby's deflated figure stomping out onto the veranda stopped her.

'What's up?'

'It's not Ronnie. It's only Michael.' Her bottom lip drooped.

Michael opened the back screen door wide.

'Sorry Abby.'

He held up a bottle of wine. 'I picked up a few extra things from the shops. I hope you don't mind.'

Lisa stood, swooping the bottle from his grasp before Dawn could utter a word about not drinking wine. She needed to keep her wits about her tonight.

'Hello. Anyone here?'

The female voice sounded from the left side of the house, coming around the wide veranda.

'I heard voices out here, so I thought I'd come straight out back.'

Ronnie poked her head around the corner. Dressed in an A-cut floral kaftan with tan coloured sandals and swept back hair in a loose bun, she seemed relaxed.

'Come around. Michael was just opening the wine. Would you like a glass?'

'Michael?'

Ronnie scanned the faces before her but didn't get the chance to ask questions.

'Auntie Ronnie!'

Abby's ringlets bounced as she ran and leapt at Ronnie, who caught her without hesitation.

'Abby. Will you hop down and help Michael find the glasses?'

Dawn needed Abby kept busy while she asked Ronnie questions. Questions she thought might upset the woman, and it seemed Abby thought a lot of her Aunt Ronnie, who wasn't an aunt at all.

The last thing Dawn wanted to do was upset Abby. Was she seriously vying for her niece's attention? Probably.

Abby hardly knew who she was. It seemed Aunt Ronnie had been around Abby all her life.

I haven't been there for her. Why should she favour me over a fake aunt who has at least acted like one?

'Okay, Auntie Dawn, but only because *you* asked.'

'Thanks, Abby. You're such a good girl.'

Win for Auntie Dawn!

Abby disappeared into the kitchen, Michael a few steps behind her. He stopped in the doorway and glanced back at Dawn, a question on his face she couldn't interpret.

'You want me to find some snacks too?'

'That would be perfect. Take your time.'

He nodded he understood what she needed him to do.

'Ronnie. So good you could duck around.'

'I thought I was keeping Abby busy so you could go over your investigation. What are you investigating anyway?'

Like she doesn't know!

'Take a seat, Ronnie. I need to ask you something.'

Dawn ushered Ronnie to the lounge she'd been sitting on earlier and pulled up a single cane stool for herself.

'Do I need a lawyer?' The question had a hint of sarcasm, and Ronnie was smiling, but her eyes were pinched.

'I'm not a cop here Ronnie. I'm only trying to keep my sister safe. She told you what she thought she saw. I'm wondering why you didn't go to the police when you heard we were looking for her?'

Ronnie sat at the edge of the lounge—her eyes darted from Lisa to Dawn without resting on either long.

'It was none of my business.'

'But what about after you knew a body was found out at Archer Point?'

'Still none of my business.'

'But why not tell me when you saw me on the street?'

Ronnie shrugged.

'So it had nothing to do with Brad?'

'Brad. What's he got to do with anything?'

Too quick. Too defensive.

'I'm trying to work out why you let me, and half the Cooktown police force, run around in circles when you knew where my sister was and had a good idea of the identity of the body recovered from the water at Archer.'

'The same reason your sister didn't, I guess. I don't want to upset anyone in town. I don't want to be hiding out in one of those hovels in Hopevale.'

'Hovels?'

'They barely have running water out there.'

'That's an exaggeration, Ronnie.' Lisa jumped in to defend her Indigenous friends.

Michael stepped out with two wine glasses, handing one to Ronnie and one to Lisa. 'We tend to enjoy the simple life.'

Ronnie waved the wine away and rose. 'I don't think I'm staying. I thought I was coming to look after Abby. I'm done. You want any information about what Lisa told me, my family, or anything else, you call my lawyer. Lisa knows who he is.'

The haughty tone set Dawn's hackles into overdrive.

Ronnie stalked from the veranda without a backward glance and Dawn let her get almost out of sight, but couldn't help herself.

'Your family. An interesting topic considering we were talking about Lisa and the possible murder of Jessica Mills.'

Ronnie jerked to a stop, but didn't turn.

'I'll definitely call your lawyer, after I work out what it is about your family you don't want to talk about.'

Ronnie turned back, her eyes wild with fear, or anger. Dawn couldn't be sure which.

'Brad said you were trouble. He said you'd be back on the bandwagon trying to clear Fraser's name and he was right.'

Ronnie stalked back towards Dawn, her finger stabbing the air, her back rigid.

'You're the one who racked off, left your family behind. You leave *my* family alone. You hear me!'

'Fraser. What has Jessica Mills' death got to do with Fraser?'

Ronnie's face lost all colour. 'Nothing. Nothing at all.' She spun on her heel, visibly shook herself like she needed to wake herself up, then stormed away. This time she didn't stop. This time, Dawn said nothing.

Everyone was quiet until they heard Ronnie's car engine firing up and rev loudly as she backed around and floored it.

Thunder rumbled across the sky. The house vibrated.

Abby tugged Lisa's hand. 'Why is Auntie Ronnie angry like the gods, Mummy?'

Dawn was wondering the same thing.

Chapter 25

Abby sat on the central, worn wooden kitchen table, her legs dangling and swinging back and forth as she chatted about the weather, her cat, the fun she had playing with the kids at Hopevale.

Dawn's tension eased with every word, and the familiar smell of fried onions and garlic wafting throughout the kitchen brought back fond memories.

Lisa buzzed around like a bumble bee, cutting, stirring, frying, all with a huge smile on her face. Despite the last few days, Dawn was relaxed, at peace in a way she'd not experienced since her childhood, living within these walls—building forts in the trees and riding her bike to get milk for Mum or the paper for Dad.

Lisa's voice broke into Dawn's daydream. Her sister turned with a wooden spoon in hand.

'I know it's not the greatest of circumstances, but I'm glad you're here, Dawn.'

'It's been too long. I should have come back earlier.'

Dawn studied the worn-out wallpaper, the flaking floors, the old cooktop their mother had used. Nothing about this place had changed, except it was all worn out. There were so many memories here. She'd run away from them all, not realising she was turning her back on many happy ones, too.

Why hadn't she returned earlier? Not even once.

'Who is Ronnie's lawyer anyway?'

'Her brother-in-law, Trevor.'

'So, what does Brad do?'

'He's an accountant. The boys went to university in Brisbane after you left.'

'Of course. I forgot they were twins. Never had much to do with Trevor. Brad was one of Fraser's best friends, but he never turned up to the funeral.'

'Nobody turned up for the funeral, Dawn.'

Michael returned from packing bags into the car. 'Can I help with anything?'

'Help yourself to a glass of red and take a seat.' Lisa pointed to the open bottle on the table. 'And grab one for Dawn while you're at it.'

'Not for me, thanks.'

Lisa's eyebrows rose.

'I need a detox.'

Lisa nodded unconvinced, and returned her focus to the bolognaise sauce and spaghetti simmering on the cooktop.

'Are you sure we need to stay at the pub?'

'Sorry. But yes. I need to help Ryan with the investigation, and I know Ben and Mari can keep you safe when I'm not around.'

Abby frowned. Her bottom lip pouted.

'Why Auntie Dawn? I don't want to leave Cherry again.'

'Maybe Ben will let you take her to the pub? You'll need a kitty litter tray, though. Why don't you go find it?'

Abby's face lit up as she shuffled from the table to the closest chair and then down to the creaking wooden floor. Dawn watched her hair fly behind her like a cape as she raced down the hallway.

'She's a cute kid, despite her father.'

'Have you heard back from the detective yet?'

Lisa ignored the jibe and Dawn scolded herself for saying it. Her niece was gorgeous—nothing like her father except for the blonde hair.

She should have apologised but didn't.

'Not yet. He shouldn't be long.'

'He better not be. The spaghetti is nearly cooked.'

'I've got it Auntie Dawn.'

'Well done.'

A knock on the front screen door was followed by a familiar voice.

'Can I come in?'

Abby dropped the kitty litter tray and sprinted down the hall, flung the door open with a bang and greeted Ryan.

'Hello Detective.'

Dawn heard Ryan chuckle.

'Hello Abby.'

When they appeared in the kitchen, Abby had Ryan's hand in hers and was literally dragging him into the kitchen.

'How did you go?'

Lisa interrupted, her eyes darting to Abby and back to Dawn. 'Let's talk about all that after dinner.'

'Good idea.' Dawn crossed the room, opened an overhead cupboard and pulled out plates, ready for her sister to dish up.

Lisa waved tongs in the air. 'You good to stay for something to eat Detective?'

'Fine by me. As long as Michael is good with it.'

Dawn frowned and Lisa stifled a giggle as Michael shrugged like he didn't care, and Ryan nodded to Lisa he would stay.

Dawn pulled out another plate and placed it on the bench as Lisa began dishing out a rich bolognaise sauce, minus the meat.

Dinner was friendly, full of small talk and listening to Abby's endless chatter. Once they were finished, Lisa began clearing the dishes.

'Let me help with those.'

Dawn stacked her plate with Michael's, crossed to the sink and started running water.

'I'll wash, you dry.'

They giggled like schoolgirls. They'd fought over dish duty all through their teenage years.

'Fine by me, but I've got no gloves, so you'll have to deal with the dry hands.'

'I'm good with that. I'm not exactly model material.'

She held up her jagged fingernails for inspection.

'You got that right.'

Michael rose from the kitchen table. 'I'll take the litter tray down to the car. Do you have a cat cage to transport Cherry in?'

'In the laundry, over there.' Lisa pointed. Michael left the kitchen.

'Abby. Why don't you go and get your pyjamas on? We'll go to the pub soon.'

The little girl's eyes grew wide with horror.

'I can't go out in pyjamas Mummy.'

'But you'll be going straight to bed when we get there. Go get changed now.'

'Okay Mummy.'

Abby slunk off down the hallway, stomping her feet as hard as she could.

Dawn handed the first plate to her sister. 'She's going to be a handful.'

'What do you mean going to be?'

They giggled again.

Dawn turned to face Ryan sitting quietly at the table, eyes watching them intently.

'Did you get anything out of Fairweather?'

'Yes, but it isn't good.'

'Why?'

'He's got an airtight alibi for Friday afternoon, from four until midnight.'

Dawn stopped, freshly scrubbed dish in hand. 'What?'

'He was with Bradley Summerset.'

'You've corroborated that?'

'Not yet, but we'll do it first thing tomorrow.'

'Good to hear you're not fighting me joining you.'

'I didn't say you were included in the *we*. Constable Jamison might like to join me.'

Dawn scoffed as she handed another plate to Lisa. 'Where does Brad live?'

'He lives up on the hill, on Webber Esplanade. The next best view in town after the Grassy Hill lookout.'

'No wonder Ronnie didn't want to rock the boat. That's a sweet location. How on earth does an accountant in little old Cooktown afford a place up there?'

'His dad purchased the land up on the hill back when we were in high school. Got it for a song, from all accounts. Then subdivided it and made a bomb.'

Ryan handed his empty wine glass to Lisa. 'I'm out of here, ladies.'

'I'll see you at the station at seven a.m., then?'

Dawn didn't leave any room for argument. Ryan opened his mouth to argue anyway.

She cut him off.

'Seven a.m., or I'll camp outside Brad's place until you get there.'

'You're impossible, you know.'

'So I've been told.'

Ryan's shoulders sagged in mock defeat.

'Just remember, you have no jurisdiction here.'

'That's the only reason you're coming.'

'All packed and sorted. I'll hang around until you're settled,' Michael announced, eyes scanning Ryan and Dawn with suspicion.

'I'm out of here.'

'I'll walk you out,' Michael offered.

Dawn watched them leave. Lisa waited patiently for the next dish.

'You know they're going to fight over you.'

'Michael and Ryan? Don't be silly.'

Dawn busied herself vigorously washing cutlery.

'They both like you.'

'I'm leaving once this case is over.'

'Michael said you were leaving once you found me.'

'Did he?'

'Leaving! You can't leave, Auntie Dawn. You only just got here.'

Dawn and Lisa swung around at the sound of Abby's high-pitched voice. If it weren't for the little tear rolling down her cheek, Dawn would have burst out laughing.

There she stood, not in pyjamas as instructed by her mother, but a pink tutu, a Wiggles T-shirt covered in glitter, tucked into the waist band. Her hair was messily pulled back into a half ponytail, half bun with red and purple ribbons tied at odd lengths.

'I'm not going anywhere yet, Abby.'

Lisa rolled her lips together to hide her smile. 'That's not your pyjamas.'

'But I can't go out in public in my pyjamas, Mummy, and now you made me cry, I'll need to freshen up. Auntie Ronnie says you must keep up appearances. *Can't let people see you crying Abby*. She always says it when I'm sad.'

'Does she?'

The hair on the back of Dawn's neck rose to attention.

What was Ronnie hiding? Why was she crying? What didn't she want anyone else to see?

Chapter 26

The rain thudded on the tin roof of the pub, but from the lower storey it was quiet enough to talk over.

Dawn eased the tension from her shoulders as she jogged down the wide staircase into the front bar. Ben waved from the counter. Mari glanced up, then focussed her dark brown eyes back on serving a couple of guys in work shorts, with button-up shirts, scruffily tucked inside.

She stopped at the bar and waited for Ben to serve Ned what should have been his last drink for the night, but Dawn knew Ben wouldn't stop passing out the grog. Responsible service of alcohol didn't extend to guys like Ned.

It should, but small country pubs like this one relied on regulars like Ned to keep the doors open.

'Thanks for looking out for them, Ben. I'll be staying back at the house tonight. You sure they'll be safe here?'

Ben reached under the counter. The barrel of a shotgun peaked over the top for a split second before it disappeared.

'Always in easy reach.'

'Luckily for you I have no jurisdiction here, or I'd have to charge you with failing to secure your firearm, Ben.'

The barman's thick beard parted with a wide grin.

'You've been in the city too long.'

She returned his smile. 'You've been running a pub too long.'

'Grab a drink before you leave. Michael over there has been nursing his beer since you got here.'

'I'll grab a water, thanks, Ben. Last time I drank here, I forgot half the night.'

Ben chuckled. 'Your dad never knew when to stop either.'

Dawn lifted her chin but suppressed the urge to shoot back a smart-arse remark. There was no point. She couldn't defend the comment, because she knew she was so much like her dad when it came to alcohol.

'You're gonna get yourself in trouble, missy.'

Ned's slurred words were accompanied by his raised beer and wavering arm.

'Shut it, Ned, or I'll cut you off for the night.'

Ben wiped the bar top down and glared at Ned.

'Your dad said you was too much like her.' His words slurred. 'Never could let sleeping dogs lie.'

'Stop your jabbering, Ned. You're full of crap mate.'

Ben glanced up and caught Mari's attention with the wave of his hand. 'Time to get Ned a taxi, luv.'

'I'll call them now.'

Mari rushed through the rear doors with an arm load of dishes.

Dawn turned to Ned. The old man pulled back so he could focus better.

'What are you talking about?'

'What?'

'You said my dad talked about my mum to you. Said I was too much like her. What *sleeping dogs* can't we let lie?'

'Did I say that?'

'He's got alcohol-induced dementia, Dawn. You can't trust a word he says.'

Mari scurried out from the kitchen, pulling her apron off and throwing it on the bar as she reached Ned.

'Time to go Ned. Taxi is here.'

'Oh, thanks, luv.'

She helped him slide from his stool. Staggering, he stayed upright with Mari's help and disappeared out onto the veranda to meet his ride.

'What was he talking about?'

Dawn turned to Ben.

'Your dad talked a lot of bullcrap when he was here with Ned. Drink can make a man say all sorts of rubbish.'

'Ben. My mum disappeared without a trace. I requested information on her missing persons' report when I first made detective. Nothing. None was ever filed.'

'Your dad always said she ran off with another guy. He thought she was having an affair with someone from the P & C, but couldn't prove it.'

'Did someone from the P & C disappear at the same time?'

'Not that I know of.'

Ben handed her an iced water and nodded towards the back of the room. Dawn turned to see Michael sulking over his beer.

'Damn!'

'Looks like your date isn't too impressed with the wait.'

'He's not my date.'

'Maybe you should tell him.'

Dawn watched Michael glance up. He smiled. She returned the gesture. He was an attractive guy, but he was the last thing she needed right now. The quicker she found out who killed Jessica, the quicker she'd be able to tie the young woman's death to Tracey's.

Maybe, after two decades, she'd be able to clear Fraser's name—her family name—for good.

Michael rose as she joined him.

'All settled in?'

'They are. Thanks for all your help.'

'The least I could do. When I found Lisa's car out at Archer Point, abandoned, I couldn't help but see it through.'

'Now you can get back to work.'

'I guess.' Michael sipped his beer. 'Or I could help with your investigation.'

Dawn bit her lip.

'Michael. Whoever killed Jessica, could have also killed Tracey Warren. This isn't an episode of *Scooby Doo*. We could be dealing with a sexual predator, a killer.'

'Is there evidence of sexual abuse?'

Dawn wasn't comfortable sharing intimate details with family or friends about sexual-based crimes. They never took it well. She considered her answer carefully.

'The bodies were found in water, so DNA evidence wasn't present. Unfortunately, sea creatures had attacked the …' *genitalia,* she thought, but didn't say, 'bodies enough to make it impossible to confirm, but there were signs of trauma.'

'If you're right, and Fairweather was sleeping with both girls, why the twenty-year gap?'

'What do you mean?'

'I'm not a cop, but when you work with disadvantaged kids you get training. Mandatory reporting—how to be on the lookout for signs of abuse. If Jessica was his latest victim, and Tracey was maybe his first …'

Dawn finished Michael's train of thought.

'Who were the victims in-between? It's a good point. He won't have waited twenty years to abuse another girl.'

'And if he had more victims, why didn't he kill them?'

'Maybe you can be of some help, after all.'

Dawn raised her glass of water and clinked Michael's raised beer glass.

Chapter 27

The same young female officer sat behind the front desk. She waved her through to the office area with a bored expression. Dawn stopped to lean over the front counter before entering.

'Reynolds?'

'Yes, Detective?'

'Do you get front desk duty often?'

The young constable rolled her eyes.

'Pretty much every time I'm on shift.'

'Who does the roster? Sergeant Martin?'

'No. Senior Constable Constable.'

Dawn laughed. Then cleared her throat when Reynolds didn't join her.

'Constable Constable is his real name?'

Reynolds nodded.

'Oh, I bet he can't wait to make sergeant.'

Reynolds pressed her lips together. Her brown eyes sparkled.

Michael chuckled under his breath behind her.

'Maybe I'll have a word with him.'

'Good luck with that, ma'am.'

'Call me Dawn or Detective.'

'Will do.'

Reynolds hit the security button to unlock the door. It buzzed, and Dawn gave a casual wave before stepping through. Holding it, she waited for Michael to join her.

Directly inside the hallway, Sergeant Martin's office door was on the right. Two interview rooms occupied the left. Further down the hall, they turned right, heading towards the main office area. Voices filtered down the passageway as they drew closer.

Two groups of tables either side of the room created a corridor down the centre. At the end were two glass office doors, with a wall of windows either side.

To the left of the corridor, a mobile whiteboard was set up with pictures of Jessica Mills at the centre.

She sensed Michael tense behind her. She understood why. One image of the young woman was a school photo. The rest were graphic images of Jessica's lifeless body. Turning, she scanned his face.

'Are you okay? This is pretty confronting for the uninitiated.'

'I'm fine. We don't usually share images of the dead. The same as we don't use their name.'

'Oh. I'm sorry. This is going to be hard for you then.'

Ryan cleared his throat. Dawn turned to see him standing beside the whiteboard, marker in hand. Two uniformed constables sat at the left-hand bank of desks, with Sergeant Martin perched on the edge, facing the whiteboard.

Ryan caught her gaze. 'What's he doing here?'

'We were talking last night.'

Ryan's eyebrows lifted.

'At the pub.'

Why did I need to clarify that?

'He raised an interesting question: Why only two victims?'

'Two not enough for you Grave?'

Ryan's smart-arse retort wasn't entirely unexpected, but his motive was hard to deduce. Was he annoyed she'd talked about the case with Michael?

'I'd like to know why the hell we're allowing two civilians in on this case anyway?'

A stocky constable of medium height rose from his low-backed wheeled chair. His features were sharp, despite his build, and everything about him seemed out of proportion.

'Senior Constable Constable, I presume.'

She held out her hand to offer a handshake and noticed Ryan tongue his cheek from the corner of her eye. Constable Jamison failed to hide a grin.

'Your reputation precedes you.'

The senior constable eyed her suspiciously.

'No one answered my question.'

He turned to Sergeant Martin for an answer, but it was Ryan who did the talking.

'That's because it's a stupid question. Grave is a detective. She's handled enough murder cases to understand the process and she's previously from around here. We've asked her to consult on this case.'

Ryan drew a breath before plunging on.

'Ranger Michael, on the other hand …'

'Has extensive knowledge of the location where my sister's vehicle was found and where Tracey and Jessica's bodies were dumped. He's also come up with an interesting point. If we still think Fairweather sexually molested these girls and killed them, why aren't there more victims?'

'You beginning to doubt Fairweather is our guy? I thought you were deadset on him.'

Ryan crossed his arms and waited.

'He's involved. I'm only saying, have we been through old missing persons cases involving young girls, aged thirteen to seventeen, to see if there are more possible dead bodies we should be looking for?'

'Serial paedophile *and* murderer. Big leap.'

'Exactly. So I'm thinking maybe he's the paedophile, but what else do the girls have in common? What other motive could have gotten them killed?'

'You're assuming the two murders are linked.'

'MO is spot on. Finding a link needs to be our top priority.'

Dawn glanced around. This was a small town. She wanted to talk about Ronnie, about Brad's family, but out in the open office area wasn't the right place.

'Can we find somewhere a little more private? I've got a line of enquiry that might go nowhere, and I don't want to rock the boat if it's a dead end.'

The senior constable puffed out his chest and stepped into Dawn's personal space. 'You don't trust the local police?'

'Let's just say this could be above your pay grade, *Constable*. I'll brief the sergeant and Detective Ryan, but you're *need to know* for now.'

'What the …'

'Shut it, Rick.'

Martin waved his hand towards his office.

'Make yourself useful and chase up Jessica's mobile phone records and canvas the school, her friends, anyone you can think of. Someone must have seen her Friday, before she was killed.'

He waved Dawn towards his office but turned as Michael followed.

'If it's so sensitive, Michael can wait out here too, for now.'

Michael opened his mouth to protest, but Dawn shook her head. She could fill him in if it went anywhere, but for now, she didn't want everyone knowing Ronnie could be involved in two murders.

For now, she didn't want to admit it to herself either. But her old friend's behaviour yesterday sparked her interest. Ronnie rarely got upset, at least she never used to. It had been a long time though, and anything was possible.

Could Ronnie have killed those women? Was it Brad having an affair with them and not Fairweather?

She shook the thought away as Martin closed his office door and flicked the blinds shut. She reminded herself to stick with the facts. It was what the lead detective in Adelaide would be telling her right now. She shifted back into work mode, removing herself from her past, from her friendships, from anything capable of impairing her judgement.

Chapter 28

Ryan and Martin listened as she went over Ronnie's outburst from the night before and filled them in on Lisa's unofficial statement.

'You're saying Ronnie babysat Abby the night Jessica died? That fits with Brad Summerset being Fairweather's alibi. He said they caught up for drinks.'

'It's what Lisa said last night.'

'We need to get an official statement from Lisa. I'll send a constable to the pub.'

Martin crossed the door ready to give the order.

'Send Reynolds.'

'Reynolds? She's on the counter.'

'She's always on the counter.'

Martin's face scrunched as he considered Dawn's comment.

'Apparently your senior likes to keep her there. You haven't noticed?'

'I hadn't, but you're right. Okay. I'll let her do it. Probably best to send a female, anyway, considering the situation.'

Dawn wanted to protest that it wasn't a girl thing, but decided now wasn't the time.

Gently. Gently.

Martin was never a chauvinist. He'd encouraged her to join the police force twenty years ago. This wasn't the sergeant's doing. Old habits were hard to break, and change took time. It happened faster in the city, but things were getting there in the bush.

'We'll interview Summerset, then I think we need to get some CCTV footage from the school. See where Jessica went after she left on Friday.'

Ryan opened the door ready to leave.

'You coming?'

'Of course.'

Dawn strolled through the open door.

'Do you have Summerset's address?'

'I do, but like I said last night, it's the biggest house on the highest hill so we can't miss it.'

As she stepped out, she spotted Michael leaning against the desk closest to Sergeant Martin's office door.

He rose. Ryan waved him back down with an open palm.

'Sorry, junior. We have official police business to attend to.'

Michael hovered, backside a few inches from the table. His gaze fell on Dawn.

She tried to smooth things over. 'Can you check on Lisa and Abby for me?'

'Sure. Anything else you need done?'

'Would you be able to ask the other rangers about Jessica? Casually. Did she have a boyfriend? Had they noticed anything strange with her behaviour lately? Maybe they know something about her home life we should be aware of.

'Questioning friends, associates, is something *we* should be doing.' The senior constable's voice was sharp. As Dawn turned, she noticed him staring at Sergeant Martin to back him up.

'He's the best person for the job. Michael is far more likely than us to get anything out of the rangers.'

Dawn focussed on the sergeant.

The senior constable jumped to his feet, nostrils flaring like a bull ready to charge. 'We have Indigenous officers based in Hopevale who can do it.'

Dawn frowned and met Sergeant Martin's gaze.

A silent question passed between them.

Why was this such a big deal?

Dawn was ready to make an argument about it, but Martin interceded.

'Let it go, Rick. Michael knew Jessica well. He works with the kids all the time. They'll open up to him rather than a police officer, even one of their own mob.'

Dawn tapped her foot, waiting for the senior constable to agree. She shouldn't have cared. The sergeant had already told him to back off, but she wondered why Ryan stood by the hallway, saying nothing. He was lead detective. Maybe because it involved Michael?

'You good Michael?'

Dawn studied his dark brown eyes and waited for him to nod.

'Maybe I'll see you at the pub for lunch?' he called after her, as she hurried to join Ryan already striding out. The senior constable glared at her when she passed his desk. The hairs on her arms stood to attention as a wave of unease flowed over her.

She was still trying to shake the feeling when they pulled up outside the Summerset home.

Lisa was right. It was a mansion, and the view was breathtaking.

Ryan whistled.

'Maybe I should have been an accountant.'

They slammed the car doors in unison. The sound travelled. A curtain flickered in the front window.

'They probably think you're a Jehovah's Witness or something, in that suit.'

'I'm not on a cycle.'

'That's Mormons.'

Dawn waved her hand at the now sunny sky.

'How on earth do you wear a suit in this climate anyway?'

The rain-soaked vegetation and soil visibly released steam. The humidity was as close to one hundred per cent as Dawn ever remembered it being.

'It's only September. Wait until December.'

Ryan knocked on the front door.

It opened a crack on the security chain almost instantly.

An uneasy sensation ran along Dawn's spine.

Who used a security lock in Cooktown?

Ryan glanced her way. He was thinking the same thing.

'Ronnie. Can we come in? Detective Ryan has a few questions for Brad.'

The door closed, the lock rattled, then the door swung open.

'Mrs Summerset, sorry to bother you. Is your husband home?'

Ryan stepped forward as Ronnie stepped back.

The foyer was larger than Dawn's apartment back in Adelaide. A planter lined the right-hand side, full of tropical indoor greenery. Two, full-width steps led up into the open-plan lounge area. To the left was a closed door.

Ronnie nodded towards the ornately carved teak door, twice as wide as a regular one. Dawn glanced up at the swirls and filigree inset above, topped with a panel of frosted glass. Light filtered from the skylights in the foyer ceiling, no doubt adding even more light to the office within.

Ryan tapped on the door. The knock echoed through the tiled foyer.

'I told you not to disturb me, Veronica.'

'Mr Summerset. It's Detective Ryan with Cairns Major Crimes. I'd like to ask you a few questions. Can you please open the door?'

Ryan stepped back and waited.

Dawn could hear drawers opening and closing. A filing cabinet clunked shut seconds before the lock on the door clicked.

'Detective. What can I do for you?'

Brad's smile vanished as his eyes fell on Dawn.

'What's she doing here?'

'Detective Grave is assisting us with this investigation.'

'She's a cop?'

'Detective.' Dawn corrected him.

He hesitated, then stepped back and opened the office door. Dawn glanced back at Ronnie. It was bright in the foyer, with the skylights and wide entrance windows, but still, the woman was wearing sunglasses indoors.

Dawn hesitated joining Ryan a moment, but followed inside. The door clicked shut behind them.

'Last Friday night, where were you, Mr Summerset?'

'Straight to business. Don't you want to take a seat?'

Brad indicated two tan leather and black metal chairs opposite a beige leather sofa, a glass-topped coffee table between them.

'We won't keep you long. If you can confirm where you were last Friday night.'

'What's this about?'

'We are just following up on something mentioned to us during a police interview.'

'What things?'

Brad's eyebrows furrowed.

'Just tell him where you were Brad, and we'll be out of your hair.'

Brad sucked in a breath as his shoulders rose and his mouth opened.

'How on earth does the sister of a killer become a cop anyway?'

'Detective.'

Dawn struggled to stay calm.

'Mr Summerset,' Ryan's chest rose, his shoulders pulled back, 'you can answer our questions here, in the comfort of your *very* swanky office, or you can come down the station, but the only past tense I'd like you to focus on right now is *last Friday night!*'

Brad's eyes blazed. Did he honestly think Fraser killed Tracey? And why mention it now, when there was a fresh body found at the same location? It didn't make any sense.

'I had a few drinks, played a round of billiards with a mate.'

'Here?'

'Yes, here.'

'Which mate?'

'David Fairweather.'

Dawn listened as Ryan continued with another question, but something was niggling in the back of her brain, and she couldn't quite figure it out.

'How long have you and Mr Fairweather been friends?' she interrupted Ryan.

'Decades.'

'Decades? What is the age difference between you and David. Ten years?'

'I don't know. I've never asked.'

'When you were eighteen, he was twenty-eight, or thereabouts. What does an eighteen-year-old have to do with a twenty-eight-year-old?'

The sound of someone clearing their throat made Dawn spin around. She hadn't even heard the office door open. Larry danced into the office, a broad smile across his face, eyes sparkling. 'I'm sorry Detectives, but Brad won't be answering any more questions without a lawyer present.'

Dawn caught a glimpse of Ronnie peering in from the hallway, a toddler in her arms and a boy around Abby's age holding her hand.

'I hope you understand. I'm only looking out for my son's best interests.'

Dawn glanced at Larry, then back to the hallway to find it empty.

'Of course.' Ryan answered Larry, who spotted her frowning at the empty foyer and turned to see what she was looking at.

'Sorry Dawn. I'm only doing the dad thing.'

Dawn returned her focus to Larry, who was still smiling. She'd known the man since she was a child, but what did she really know about Larry Summerset?

She forced a smile and hoped it came over sincere.

'No problem Larry. If we have any further questions, we'll be sure to contact Trevor.'

Larry led the way from the office. Dawn risked a quick look over her shoulder as she left the room.

Brad sat behind his desk, head in hands, shoulders sagging.

Chapter 29

Dawn slammed the car door and yanked her seatbelt out, only to have it lock halfway.

'He's hiding something.'

'Who? Brad or Larry?'

'Larry's a sweetheart. Volunteers at the swimming club, the school and who knows where else.'

Ryan clipped his seatbelt on and started the car.

'Where did the money come from for that house?'

'Lisa said Larry purchased the land on the cheap and subdivided. Could be good timing, but I think we need to do a double-check. Where to next?'

Dawn finally got her belt to stop jamming.

'The school. Let's get the CCTV footage and see if anyone saw Jessica at school Friday. She might have missed roll call, but she could have arrived late. Or skipped out for a while.'

Dawn's phone buzzed in her pocket. She pulled it out and answered.

'Detective Grave speaking.'

'Dawn. It's Ross. We've managed to get a quick DNA turn around. The body at Archer was Jessica Mills.'

'Thanks Ross. I'll tell Ryan. We're on our way to the school to get camera footage, but I've got a question. Maybe you can run the background, or maybe you know. Where did Brad get his money from? Being an accountant in Cooktown can't be this lucrative. Has he got organised crime connections or something?'

'I thought you knew. When Larry was a council worker, he got wind of some land up there being rezoned for housing. Snapped it up for a song from all accounts. Kept a block for himself and his two boys, then sold the rest for a bomb.'

'Lisa said, but have you seen inside Brad's house? I can't see how they made so much from one subdivision.'

'If you think Brad's place is impressive, check out Larry's. He lives across the road from Brad, on the other side of the cul-de-sac.'

'Thanks Ross.'

Ryan's eyebrows rose at Dawn's tone as he backed the vehicle from the driveway. Dawn held her finger up for Ryan to wait a second before driving away.

'Can you confirm how much the land sold for? Even back twenty years ago, it would have fetched a lot of money, and I'm struggling to see how a council worker like Larry found the money to buy the land in the first place. And even if he made good money, I can't see it being enough to build *these* homes, drive luxury cars.'

'True. Maybe he put a syndicate together. A few local investors? Maybe they went on to invest elsewhere.'

'Maybe. I'd like to know for sure.'

'I'll get Reynolds onto it. She just got back from taking your sister's statement.'

'Everything all good there?'

'Ben's keeping an eye on them.'

'Thanks.'

'You're welcome. We go way back. I'm glad I can help.'

Dawn hung up and pointed to the Mediterranean-style villa opposite Brad's. The terracotta tiles and whitewashed walls weren't opulent on their own, but the two-storey high, ocean-facing windows and sparkling blue suspended pool would have cost a mint, even twenty years ago.

'*That's* Larry's place.'

Ryan whistled.

'I've got the sergeant doing a little digging.'

'You're pretty good at this, you know.'

'You said you read my record.'

'I was just blowing smoke up your arse. I figured you were another token female fast-track.'

Dawn didn't take offence. She knew a few women in positions who shouldn't be there. Women certainly deserved a fair go and should be treated equally, but that didn't mean they should be promoted when they weren't ready. If they did, officers' lives could be at risk.

It was the same when politics influenced who got what job. Money and privilege saw plenty of men in positions they didn't deserve.

'And now?'

'I'd ride with you any day Detective.'

Dawn suppressed a grin. She wasn't sure if she should take the piss or take the compliment. She decided on the latter.

'Let's get to the school and check out this CCTV footage. We've got a positive ID. Jessica Mills is our victim and my gut is telling me this is linked to Tracey Warren. If Fairweather isn't our connection, then we need to find out what is.'

'The school? The swim team?'

'Both, or something else. Let's ask the principal a few questions about Tracey Warren while we're there?'

'Like what?'

'Like any other activities they shared. Friends or family in common. Guidance councillors, teachers?'

'Fairweather teaches at the school, he's on the P & C and he's the swimming coach.'

'True, but if Brad's statement is correct, his alibi is legit, Fairweather is in the clear for Jessica's murder.'

'That's *if* it's legit and they aren't in it together.'

Dawn thought about Brad pulling Ronnie away from her. Making snide comments about her brother. Was he protesting too much?

'Let's see what Principal Fletcher has to say.'

Ryan pulled away from the curb and steered the vehicle down the steep hill. Dawn couldn't help but take in the view of the Endeavour River, winding its way inland like a serpent. She didn't miss the fresh batch of dark storm clouds heading their way either.

Chapter 30

Ryan parked in the official police and ambulance parking zone. Dawn didn't protest as raindrops the size of five cent coins started to fall from the sky.

Ryan pointed to the looming grey clouds rolling over the hills, closing in, surrounding the school and flung his door open. 'Let's make a dash for it before that opens up on us.'

'I forgot how bloody wet it gets up here.'

Dawn hopped out, slammed the door and ran for the veranda covering the school office entrance, reaching it as thunder rolled overhead and sheets of rain cascaded over the guttering.

'And how damn quick it comes in from a clear sky.'

Shaking off, she opened the front doors and shivered as cool air hit wet skin.

A short brunette receptionist with huge eyes and eyelashes to match, glanced up.

'Can I help you?'

Ryan pulled out his badge. Dawn didn't bother. Her SAPOL credentials would only confuse matters.

'I'm Detective Ryan, this is Detective Grave. Can we see Principal Fletcher, please?'

'He's at lunch right now. Can I help you at all?'

She fluttered her eyelashes.

'I'm sure you can.'

Ryan flashed a wide grin. Dawn forced herself not to roll her eyes.

'We've had unfortunate news about one of your pupils.'

He leant forward, over the high countertop and whispered.

‘We can confirm the body found recently was one of your missing students and we need access to her school file, along with an old file you might need to dig up for us.’

‘I don’t know if I’m allowed to do that Detective. Student records are highly confidential.’

‘Of course they are, but you’d like the killer caught before another student is harmed, wouldn’t you?’

Dawn admired the detective’s tact. When she first met Ryan, she expected him to be arrogant, pompous even, but he was capable of handling a delicate situation and putting on the charm when needed.

‘Well, the current student I can help you with, but the old one would be archived, and I don’t have access.’

‘Who does?’

‘No one. We are only required to keep student records for a short time after they graduate or move to another school.’

‘That’s unfortunate.’

‘Why? What old records were you chasing?’

‘Ones from before you were born,’ Dawn interjected.

‘Oh.’ Her eyelashes fluttered again.

‘Is there anyone around the school who would recall students from over twenty years ago?’

Ryan continued with his charming smile.

‘The principal might. Then there are the P & C members. A few of them have been on the committee for that long.’

‘A few, like who?’

‘Mrs Baxter.’

The woman tapped her finger to her lip.

‘And of course, Larry. I think Larry’s been on the P & C *forever*.’

‘Larry Summerset?’

Ryan clarified what Dawn already knew.

'Yes, that's him.'

'Any teachers?'

'Mr Fairweather, Ms Prentice. That's probably it. We get a lot of teachers straight out of university, doing their regional service so they can move on to pick a school closer to home.'

'Thanks for your help.'

Ryan glanced at the girl's chest and Dawn was about to kick him in the shin, when she realised he was scanning the name tag.

'Rhianna. Thanks. You've been so helpful.'

He glanced at his watch.

'Do you think you might be able to disturb the principal now and grab the file for us.'

'Of course.' She rose from her chair. 'He'll be in the staffroom. I'll give them a bell.'

She picked up the phone and dialled.

'Which student file did you need?'

'Jessica Mills.'

The blood drained from Rhianna's face as she slipped back down to her chair. A voice on the other end of the phone echoed out. The receptionist gazed off into space a moment but composed herself.

'Ah. Can you ask the principal to come to reception. There are two detectives here to see him.'

She hung up.

'You knew Jessica?'

Dawn considered coming around the counter to make sure the receptionist didn't faint and hit the lino floor.

'Everyone knew Jessica. Does her mum know?'

'The Hopevale police are delivering the news.'

Ryan spotted the principal striding down the hall from the opposite end to his office and nudged Dawn.

'Can you tell us a little more about Jessica?' Dawn coaxed as the principal drew up alongside the counter.

'Detectives, what can I do for you?'

His smarmy smile was back.

'We've formally identified our victim.'

'Tom, it's Jessica.' Rhianna choked out.

Fletcher cleared his throat. Was it at the mention of Jessica's name or being called Tom by his receptionist?

Either way, his expression was impossible to read as he flattened his features and straightened.

'Come into my office.'

He lifted his hand to point the way.

'We'll need all the files you have on Jessica's Mills *now*.'

Ryan's tone said it wasn't up for debate.

'Of course. Rhianna. Get yourself a cup of tea and bring the file into my office as soon as you can.'

'Yes, sir.'

Formality was restored. Yet, something about the way the receptionist looked at the principal set Dawn's gut into gymnastics mode.

Chapter 31

Dawn opened the file to read while she led the way back to Ryan's vehicle.

'What's your take on the receptionist and the principal? Sleeping together?' The grin on Ryan's face made his opinion blatantly obvious. Dawn didn't buy into the innuendo.

'Not sure it's relevant. Rhianna's reaction to our victim's ID on the other hand, way more interesting.'

Dawn opened the car door and flopped into the front seat.

'I hope the principal doesn't take too long with the CCTV footage. Maybe we'll get a clearer picture once we've seen it.'

'Maybe, but one thing is for sure. This case is linked with Tracey Warren—I'd bet my firstborn on it, if I thought I'd ever have one.'

'Not planning on kids then?'

Ryan started the car, and turned the air-conditioning fan up to full speed, before pulling on his seatbelt.

'No, not planning on them. You need to have a partner to have kids, or at least a sperm donor—unless immaculate conception suddenly became a real thing.'

'That's pretty easily fixed.'

Ryan didn't bat an eye.

Was he offering?

Dawn cleared her throat.

'There's a link between Jessica and Tracey. How are we going to find it?'

Dawn held her breath hoping her change of subject clearly redirected the conversation.

Ryan was silent as he backed the vehicle out of the angle park.

'Old newspaper articles.'

'What?'

'You've been away from a small town too long Grave. Everything, every school captain or SRC election, P & C fundraiser, or local council announcement. Every bloody piece of local news goes in the town paper.'

'Why didn't I think of that?'

'Because you've been in the big smoke too long.'

Dawn scoffed.

'Adelaide has a population of a million, with a further hundred thousand or so out bush. It's not exactly a metropolis you know.'

'True. But I get a lot of regional cases.'

'Why? Did you piss someone off?'

'Not exactly.'

Ryan parked outside the library, turned off the engine and pointed.

'Ready for a microfiching expedition?'

He laughed at his own joke.

Dawn kept her face deadpan.

'See what I did there?'

She rolled her eyes and opened the passenger's side door.

'Oh, come on. Don't you ever laugh?'

He opened his door and jumped out, slamming it closed in his hurry to catch up to her.

'Not when I'm tracking down a murderer, and one who might decide my sister is his next victim.'

'Not young enough.'

He seemed convinced with his own argument.

‘I don’t think these girls died because of sex or sexual assault. Michael’s right. If Fairweather messed with young women before, then killed them, why don’t we have more victims?’

‘Let’s go fishing and find out.’

Ryan lunged forward and opened the glass door.

Dawn passed through, he followed.

A grey-haired woman in her mid-sixties tapped her toe to an unheard beat, her head bobbing, her body grooving, as she searched the shelves, book in hand. Sliding it back in its place, she turned to collect another from the trolley of returns and stopped, hand hovering mid-air.

‘Morning. Can I help you at all?’

She pulled a set of earbuds from her ears and left them dangling around her neck.

‘Yes. Thanks. I’m Detective Grave, this is Detective Ryan. I’m wondering if you have microfiche for the local paper editions? If so, how far back?’

‘You’re new then?’

The woman’s tanned brow furrowed.

‘Detective Ryan is from Cairns, and I’m a consulting detective from Adelaide.’

The woman studied Dawn’s face closely.

‘You look familiar.’

Her eyes sparkled.

‘Did you say Grave?’

‘Yes.’

‘You Lisa’s sister? Peggy’s daughter?’

‘Yes, I am.’

The woman lunged forward, grabbed Dawn by the shoulders and pulled her into a bear hug, nearly knocking her over. The sweet scent of hairspray made Dawn’s eyes water.

Out the corner of her eye she saw Ryan stifle a chuckle, his lip turned up on one side in a crooked grin.

'You look so much like your mum.'

Dawn struggled to remember exactly what her mum looked like now. Peggy Grave disappeared without a trace over twenty years ago. Dawn was only fifteen when her world turned upside down.

Dawn wiggled free of the woman's grip. 'I'm sorry. I don't recall your name.'

'Sharon Quinlan. Most people call me Shaz. I was on the P & C with your mum, back in the day and my son is the same age as …'

She bit her lip to stop from saying the name Dawn would never forget.

Dawn filled the gap. 'Fraser.'

'Yes, luv. They were the best of friends.'

'Lachie? You're Lachie's mum?'

'Yes, luv.'

'I'm sorry. I should have recognised you. You came with Lachie to Fraser's funeral.'

'He was a sweet boy. A bit of a larrikin at times, but always watched out for our Lachie.'

Ryan cleared his throat.

'Oh, sorry. What papers were you chasing?'

'The local rag, community service pages.'

'How far back?'

Sharon pushed the trolley back to the main counter, parked it carefully, applying the brake, then crossed the room towards a large metal filing cabinet with wide, shallow drawers.

'To Tracey Warren's last year.'

Dawn followed Sharon, nearly slamming into her back as the librarian stopped abruptly and turned.

'Are you reopening the case?'

'Possibly.'

'Is this about the body found out at Archer Point on Sunday?'

'Possibly.'

'Oh dear!'

'The microfiche would be very helpful. If it goes back far enough.'

Ryan made another attempt to pull Sharon back on task.

The librarian sucked in a deep breath, drew herself up and slowly let the breath out in what appeared to be a well-practised meditative technique.

'It certainly goes back that far. But maybe I can save you some time. What are you looking for?'

'We are trying to figure out what other community groups and activities Tracey took part in. Her parents have moved away. So while we try and track them down, we thought we'd start with the papers.'

Dawn felt bad about the white lie. They weren't tracking Tracey's family down at all. Not until they knew for sure they were dealing with the same murderer.

'Tracey was a bright girl. She joined the swimming team, was sports captain and, as if she wasn't busy enough, she took on a student leadership role.'

Dawn's skin tingled with goosebumps.

'What kind of student leadership role?'

'SRC council chair.'

Dawn glanced at Ryan. He was on the same wavelength as her.

'You said you were on the Parents and Citizens Committee with my mum. Were you still there when Tracey was killed?'

'I was.'

'Did Tracey attend the meetings often?'

Shaz nodded emphatically.

'Every month, without fail. She was there taking notes, sharing the SRC news, pushing for funding options for the Indigenous students. My goodness, they were really struggling back then. Still are, I guess, but I understand there are a lot more grants available to help the Aboriginal kids get an education now.'

'Do you know where we might get a copy of the P & C meeting minutes from back then, or even from recently?'

'Well,' Shaz pursed her silver-pink lipstick–clad lips, 'the secretary usually records them, then they get audited with the end of year financials, then they go into storage at the school. Not sure how long they keep them, but since they are an arm of the Queensland Education Department, my guess is a while.'

'You've been extremely helpful, Sharon. Thanks.'

Ryan plastered his flirty cop smile on.

Was Shaz blushing?

'My pleasure Detective.'

A thought popped into Dawn's head.

'Can we ask you to do something that is almost impossible in a small town like Cooktown?'

'Of course.'

'Can you please keep this visit to yourself for now?'

Shaz tapped her nose.

'No one will hear it from me, luv.'

Dawn smiled, said her goodbyes and rushed from the building. Ryan was only one step behind.

'What are you thinking?' he asked before the library door closed behind them.

'I'm thinking we've found our connection, and we need to get a warrant for those minutes before someone decides to lose them.'

Chapter 32

Sergeant Martin peered over a stack of folders as Dawn entered the sparsely decorated office. Two filing cabinets occupied the left wall. A large, worn desk with a flaking vinyl inlay and high-back office chair took up a lot of space in the centre. In front, two guest chairs were placed at odd angles a few feet apart. There were no personal touches, nothing homely. Not even a photo of Martin's wife, kids, grandkids.

Dawn pulled one of the chairs out. Ryan reached for the other. Her chair squeaked as air evacuated on impact.

'You two have been busy.'

Sergeant Martin slid the files aside. Dawn glanced at the tabs, wondering if they were old, new or ongoing.

'I've just gotten off the phone with the Summersets' attorney.'

'Really?'

Dawn directed her question to the sergeant, but glanced Ryan's way.

'We must be on to something then.'

His grin likely mirrored hers.

'On to what? Remember you're only a consultant Grave. And, Ryan, what the hell did you do at the Summersets to get them so pissed?'

'My job.'

Ryan's tone was flat, but Dawn could see a twitch of tension in his jawline.

Martin scratched his head and sighed.

'You were supposed to be confirming Fairweather's alibi. That's it. The Summersets are a big deal in this town these days.'

'Exactly what we were investigating.' Dawn interjected.

'What do you mean?'

'When I left town, Larry was a council worker. Brad was a veritable pain in the arse. If he wasn't driving like an idiot, he was out on his motorbike tearing up our backyard.'

'He was one of Fraser's friends, wasn't he?'

'They weren't besties, but yes.'

A memory popped into Dawn's head, stopping her in her tracks. How could she have forgotten it?

Ryan turned in his chair to face her. 'What is it?'

'Brad. He dated Tracey Warren before Fraser.'

The sergeant leant forward, his hands flat on the desk, eyes wide and focussed. 'You're trying to draw lines when you've barely got dots, Grave. I admit, when we found the school emblem out at Archer, I was ready to join those dots, but now we know Jessica's body was dumped out there, it makes sense it was hers.'

'The MO is the same. *That* links the cases, but we're pretty sure they weren't killed by a sexual predator.'

'And probably not Fairweather,' Ryan added.

Dawn picked up the details. 'And we found another link between the two dead girls.'

'Will you two stop finishing each other's sentences and tell me what the hell is going on.'

Ryan waved towards Dawn to carry on, a smirk tugging at the corner of his mouth.

'Both girls were on the swimming team.'

'So Fairweather could still be in the picture.' The vein no longer pulsed at the sergeant's temple.

'Except Brad is his alibi and we found out the girls were both student reps on the SRC council and attended P & C meetings regularly.'

Sergeant Martin sat back, pressed his fingertips together like a church steeple and brought them to his chin. Silence hung as they let him digest the information.

'They all link to Fairweather still. How solid is his alibi?'

'We only have Brad's word for it. But Fairweather isn't the only one on the P & C with links to the swimming team.'

'You're talking about Larry Summerset. I don't think I'm going to like where this is heading,' Sergeant Martin sighed.

'Did you get anywhere on the land purchase?'

'Still waiting.'

'I'd like to get a warrant for the P & C minutes. Going right back to when Tracey was still alive.'

'We don't have grounds for a warrant.'

'But they are public domain. They were probably published on the school website and circulated to all the parents back then.'

'Look, Dawn. This is a shitshow waiting to happen. You're not officially allowed to be investigating this. Ryan is here to follow up on *Jessica's* murder, not a cold case.'

'Jessica's death is linked to Tracey's, and the P & C minutes are linked to Jessica in any case.'

'You don't know that. It's all circumstantial. I don't want to create a media circus. If we get a judge to sign off on a warrant for the P & C minutes, the local paper will get word of it and all hell will break loose.'

'Can we at least follow up on the money? I have a colleague in Adelaide who says it's always about the money.'

'Sex, love, money or power.' Ryan recited them like rules in a playbook, ticking his fingers as he went.

'In this case, maybe all of the above.'

Dawn rose from her chair, slid it neatly back towards the desk so it wasn't at a cockamamie angle and indicated with her head for Ryan to do the same.

'I've got an idea.'

Sergeant Martin rolled his chair back and rose. 'Am I going to like your idea?'

'No warrant, okay? I think I might be able to get the minutes another way. But can we hurry up the financials behind the land deal on the hill? Something doesn't feel right about it.'

'Tread very lightly. No press. No searches without my say-so. And no more interviews without running it by me first.'

'None?' Ryan turned back, his hand on the office doorknob. 'You'll be hamstringing my investigation, Sergeant. I've got a job to do.'

'And I'll be here after you've both gone home. You turn over a rock and something crawls out that isn't case related, but stinks, I'm left cleaning up the mess.'

'If it stinks, it shouldn't stay buried,' Dawn huffed.

'People are okay with buried, Grave.'

'I'm not. My brother is buried and labelled with a crime he didn't commit. Now we have another body. Similar circumstances. Now we can prove who actually did it.'

'Be careful Dawn. Townspeople don't like old news much and opening old wounds is never a good idea.'

'I can't promise anything.'

Dawn nodded for Ryan to open the door. When he did, she walked out and he followed. Once the door was closed, she waited for him to draw up alongside.

'Did you see the files on his desk?'

'Yeah. What's up?'

'The one on top. The one he closed when we came in.'

'There were heaps of them, all closed.'

In her mind's eyes, she could see the corner of a photo sticking out. It was all she needed to know what was in the file. It was a scene she'd never forget. Not as long as she lived.

'The top one was my brother's.'

'How could you tell?'

The memory flooded back. Bright teal painted concrete floor and walls.

'Fraser. We'll be late for dinner. Come on!'

Silence.

'Come on Fraser. Dad said you'd give me a lift home after you finished swimming practice.'

Dawn hated the odour drifting from the boys' toilets. Going in to find her brother was the last thing she wanted to do, but he was her lift home.

The vapour from the urinal made her eyes water as she entered. Fraser would be really pissed off if he was having a pee and she interrupted him.

'Fraser!'

She called out, took another step and waited.

Still nothing.

Two more steps in.

Silence.

Dreary darkness closed in as she turned the corner. Ahead, two cubicles and a stainless-steel urinal took up the end wall. A basin to her left, a small high-set window to her right.

A shiver ran down her spine.

He'd gone home from swimming practice and forgotten her.

Damn! She hated this place.

It gave her the creeps, not just for the eerie silence and smell. Her own memories rose to create panic. She pushed them down as her heartbeat quickened and she turned to leave, but something caught her eye.

Behind the left-hand cubicle door, was a piece of fabric on the floor. Denim jeans. How?

She stepped closer, despite her fear and anxiety, one foot in front of the other, tentatively placed tiptoe first.

'Fraser?'

The door was closed but the 'engaged' symbol wasn't turned. The door wasn't locked.

'Are you okay?'

Silence.

Dawn's heart thudded in her chest. Rushing sounded in her ears. She pushed on the door. It wouldn't open. Someone was leaning against it.

'Fraser. Stop stuffing around.'

Silence.

A crow cawed outside. Dawn shivered.

She peered under the bottom of the door. A waft of crap and urine hit her nose. Her eyes watered instantly, she gagged. Her instincts screamed at her to run away. To get help. But she was drawn in like a mosquito to a blue light.

Opening the other cubicle, she climbed on top of the toilet and put her hands over the edge of the cubicle partition. With a quick push off, she pulled herself up and glanced over.

It was only a quick glance, but it was a sight she'd never forget. Eyes bulging. Tongue lolling.

'I saw a photo poking out of the folder. Only the corner. But it was enough.'

'Why has the sergeant got your brother's old case file out?'

'I'd like to know the answer to that question too. But for now, we need to get the P & C minutes.'

'You heard the sergeant.'

'Yes. But I've got an idea.'

'So you said.'

Ryan sounded as dubious as the sergeant earlier.

Chapter 33

The short drive from the police station to the Top Pub didn't give the air-conditioner time to kick in. The windscreen was fogged up by the time Ryan parked the car outside the pub, and steam rose from the road as sweat ran to the small of Dawn's back.

'This weather is worse than I remember. Was it always so humid in late September?'

'La Nino, or is it El Nina or whatever it is they call it. The weather is changing. The ice caps are melting and all that stuff.'

'So that's a no. I'm not going nuts and it isn't usually this wet in September?'

Dawn opened the door. Ryan did the same.

'We've had years like this before, but not for a while.'

'I'll grab Lisa and Abby. You get a table, I'm starving.'

Ryan gaped a moment, ready to argue he wasn't taking orders from her, but Dawn was gone before he could protest.

Taking the stairs from the main entrance, up to the second floor, Dawn used her key to open the door to her room. She expected to find Lisa and Abby hiding out like she'd told them to, but the room was empty.

Adrenalin kicked in. Dawn relocked the door and ran down the stairs, her mind filling with horrible images of Lisa's hair floating in the water, her eyes cold and dead.

As she reached the bottom rung, she nearly collided with Michael's chest. His hands gripped her arms firmly, preventing her from losing balance.

'Sorry. I was coming to get you. Ryan said you were upstairs.'

'Where is Lisa?'

'She and Abby are in the bar, grabbing lunch.'

'Why are you here?'

Michael frowned.

'I was keeping an eye on them for you.'

'Why on earth is Lisa out of the room. We still don't know if she's in danger.'

Michael shrugged.

Dawn huffed and pushed past, striding into the bar, ready to blast her sister. The scene that greeted her made her stop in her tracks. She sensed Michael standing behind her, politely waiting.

She shouldn't have gone off at him, but Lisa, and now Abby was all she had left of her family.

'She's a cute kid.'

Michael's whisper, over her shoulder, tickled her ear and sent a tingle down her spine. Goosebumps exploded on her skin, despite the moist, warm weather. She tried to ignore them.

Focussing on Abby, she smiled at her niece, whose legs dangled over the edge of the bar and swung back and forth, heels hitting the timber. Her hair was tied up in two pigtails, hanging to her shoulders and curling into perfect ringlets.

Ben nodded and smiled diligently as Abby's finger waggled in his face. Lisa bit her lip, trying not to laugh, and old Ned watched them both, eyes trying to focus as they flicked from Abby to Lisa and back again.

Dawn approached the bar. Ryan met her with a glass of wine in hand.

'I'm not drinking, and neither should you. You're still on duty.'

'Have it your way.'

Ryan turned and handed the glass to Lisa who accepted it without a second thought. Then he turned back to Dawn, made sure she was paying attention and sculled half his beer in one long gulp.

'What can I get you Dawn? A water, soft drink?' Michael offered. Ryan grunted.

'Water is good. Thanks for asking Michael.'

Lisa lifted Abby from the bar top.

'Grab us a seat, Abby, over there.'

She pointed. Abby glanced over, then back up at her mum.

'Can I have pasghetti?'

'You had spaghetti for dinner last night.'

Abby pouted.

'But I love pasghetti. But can I have the proper one?'

'You get the table. I'll order your *proper* spaghetti.'

Abby smiled and skipped towards the long table in the courtyard Lisa had pointed to. Dawn nodded for Ryan to follow Abby.

He rolled his eyes, but followed.

Michael, a stack of glasses in one hand and a bottle of water in the other, glanced at Dawn and read something in her eyes.

'I'll see you at the table.'

'Thanks Michael.'

She turned to Lisa, about to ask a question, but stopped when she noticed the expression on her face.

'What?'

'You need to decide which one you want to date.'

'What the hell are you on about?'

Lisa laughed aloud.

'Have you had a boyfriend in the last twenty years?'

'I ...'

Dawn didn't want to discuss her one and only serious relationship. It was a disaster in more ways than one.

'I didn't think so. If you could read men as well as you can a suspect, you'd have noticed those guys fighting to impress you.'

'Ryan, Michael? No way!'

'Yes way.'

Dawn glanced at the table where Abby helped Michael pour glasses of water for everyone, only spilling a few drops, as Ryan supervised. It didn't take long before they both glanced her way.

'See.'

Lisa waited for Ben to take her order, then turned to head over and join her daughter.

Dawn stopped her with a gentle hand on her arm.

'Can I ask you a favour?'

'Sure. What do you need?'

'You said you were on the P & C, right.'

Lisa nodded.

'We need the minutes. Recent ones, since Jessica joined the meetings, and some old ones from the archives, but Sergeant Martin doesn't want to raise any suspicions and won't request a warrant.'

'Which old ones do you need?'

Dawn drew a slow, measured breath. Apparently, she delayed too long. Lisa's eyes opened wide.

'Back from when Tracey would have been there? I'm sure Jessica had something to prove Fraser didn't kill Tracey, but the P & C?'

'I'm not sure yet, but how did you know Tracey was involved with the P & C?'

'I had a vague idea. I remember Mum talking to Dad about her. Back before she disappeared.'

'Mum mentioned Tracey? I never heard her.'

'It was only the one time, I think.'

'What did she say?'

'Not much. Just that she was at the meetings, but you've not answered my question. Are you sure the P & C are the link?'

'Maybe.'

Lisa glared at her.

'Yes. I think so, but I've got no proof yet. I need the minutes to confirm.'

Dawn's phone buzzed in her pocket. She plucked it out and glanced at the screen.

The number wasn't familiar, but with everything going on, she needed to answer it.

Dawn slid the answer bar over, and Lisa nodded towards the table, indicating she'd join Abby.

'Detective Grave speaking.'

'Yowie. Glad I got you.' Ronnie's use of her nickname surprised her.

'Ronnie, what's up?'

'Just wanted to check Lisa was okay.'

Ronnie's tone was strange, and Dawn wondered why she was calling. She knew Lisa was home safe.

'She's fine. So is Abby.'

Lisa stopped walking and turned at the mention of Abby's name. Dawn wondered why Ronnie hadn't called Lisa herself. They were obviously friends. Ronnie babysat Abby often enough. Heck, Abby called her Auntie Ronnie.

'I'm so glad.'

Silence hung between them a moment.

'Ronnie. I have to go. I'm in the middle of lunch with them now.'

'Oh, sorry.'

Dawn was about to hang up but stopped as Ronnie blurted out her next sentence.

'Did Lisa say anything?'

Dawn watched her sister's worried frown.

'About what Ronnie?'

Dawn heard a door open, then slam. A muffled voice, the sound of fabric on the speaker, then a deep voice too hard to understand grew louder, angrier.

The next sound was unmistakable. Dawn didn't need to be in the room to recognise flesh hitting flesh. A whimper filtered down the line, then the phone went dead.

Lisa stepped closer. 'What's up?'

Dawn's stomach tossed and turned. Should she rush over to make sure Ronnie was alright? Of course she should, but Martin had warned her away from the Summersets. Still, Ronnie was an old friend.

'Have you ever seen any indication of Brad abusing Ronnie?'

'No. Brad is harmless enough. A bit opinionated at times, but he'd never hurt Ronnie.'

'Well, someone just did.'

Dawn stormed across the room towards the table where Ryan and Michael now sat opposite one another, Abby keeping them smiling.

'Sorry to break up the party, Abby, but I need to take Detective Ryan with me.'

Ryan rose, eyes alert. 'Where are we going?'

'I'll tell you on the way.'

Lisa grabbed her forearm and squeezed. 'Dawn. Be careful.'

She pointed her finger at her sister. 'You be careful. Don't leave this pub. You got me?'

Michael half stood—his eyes searched out Dawn's. 'I'll keep an eye on them.'

'Thanks, Michael.'

She wanted to say more. She wanted to tell him he didn't need to take time off work to protect Abby and Lisa, but deep down she was thankful he was.

As they walked out the front door, Ryan pulled the keys from his pocket and turned to her.

'Where are we going?'

'Ronnie got smacked around by someone. Lisa says Brad wouldn't do it.'

'But you think someone did?'

'I heard it myself. Over the phone. She didn't hang up right away. Someone hit her, I'm sure of it.'

'Let's go then.'

Chapter 34

A cool breeze ruffled Dawn's hair as she stepped out of the passenger's side. Despite the breeze, her hands were sweating as she pulled her weapon from her handbag.

Ryan lifted an eyebrow but said nothing as he drew his own gun and led the way up the winding driveway.

Holding her gun in both hands, Dawn peered in the driver's side window of a black Audi parked at the top of the driveway. She tested the door as she passed by. It was locked, no keys in the ignition.

Ryan waited. She lifted her right hand and pointed for him to go on.

The house was quiet. No yelling or screaming. The only sound was gum leaves swaying in the wind.

Ryan stepped onto the porch and stopped. Dawn took another step, but Ryan pointed for her to press back against the front of the house.

Taking two more steps, he studied the front door, then turned to face Dawn and wave her towards him.

She scurried closer, keeping her head ducked down instinctively.

'The door's open,' Ryan whispered.

She nodded for him to go in.

He stepped up, peered in, then scampered to the other side of the door. Dawn was ready by the time he got into position. She waited for the signal.

Tactical police did this type of work back in Adelaide. She wondered if they should be calling someone in, but this was likely a domestic case. Not exactly a terrorist or organised crime raid.

Ryan nodded. Dawn pushed the door the rest of the way open and stepped into the foyer to the left.

'Police!'

Ryan entered a fraction of a second behind her, heading to the right, weapon first.

'Police!' he called, but silence greeted them.

Dawn's heart thudded in her chest as she scanned Brad's office.

'Clear.'

She heard Ryan call out from the other side of the hall and joined him back in the foyer.

'Ronnie! You home?'

Dawn pressed herself against the left wall and stalked her way up the stairs and into the kitchen and family room area.

Her breath caught in her throat. She turned to see if Ryan was seeing what she was.

He nodded, his eyes darting to the blood smear on the white marble floor.

A sound from behind them made them spin round, guns raised.

'Whoa up!'

Brad's face went white as his hands shot up into the air, keys dangling from his right thumb, eyes wide.

Dawn lowered her gun. Ryan didn't move.

'Brad. Where's Ronnie?'

'What?' He frowned at Ryan, then Dawn.

'You need to step out. Now!'

Dawn ushered him back outside.

'I've got to get the kids out of the car. What is going on?'

'Outside Brad, *now*!'

Dawn's adrenalin was on high alert as she turned him around and shoved him out the door.

'And don't touch anything.'

'What is going on? I need to get the kids inside.'

'The kids need to stay where they are.'

'But they're tired.'

'I don't have time to explain. I will, though. But I need to clear the house with Ryan first.'

She guided him towards the car, trying to back her partner up at the same time.

'Clear the … what is going on. Where's Ronnie?'

'Brad. Just do what I'm telling you to do. Take the kids, drive into town and I'll get Ross to call you when we're done.'

'Done?'

Brad seemed to suddenly realise what was going on.

'Ronnie!' He tried to push past Dawn.

'Brad. Stop! Your kids.'

Dawn heard the little girl's cries and saw something click in Brad's eyes. He stopped trying to push past Dawn.

'I promise. I'll let you know as soon as I do.'

She watched as he hurried to the driver's side of his car, slid behind the wheel and with shaking hands, put his key in the ignition.

Turning, he soothed his daughter and backed out of the driveway.

Dawn hurried back through the door to find Ryan standing in the kitchen, staring at the floor. Her heart thudded as acid rose in her throat, but as she rounded the long white stone bench, she let out a breath with relief.

On the floor wasn't the body of her friend like she'd been expecting. Instead, it was Ronnie's mobile phone, screen smashed. Blood spots dotted the floor, but not enough to be lethal.

'Let's clear the house and call the sergeant.'

Ryan stalked his way towards the hallway, while Dawn crossed the family room to what she thought could be the laundry. All the time her head was spinning with the same questions, over and over again.

Why Ronnie? Why now? And most of all, how was this connected to Jessica and Tracey's murders?

Chapter 35

Constables Reynolds and Jamison sat on the edge of the same desk but jumped to attention when Sergeant Martin entered the room.

The senior constable studied Dawn, eyes squinting as Martin began the briefing.

'Okay. A forensic team is on the way from Cairns. Detectives Ryan and Grave have done a preliminary search of the Summerset residence and found Veronica Summerset's phone, broken on the kitchen floor, a blood trail leading to the back door, but no sign of Veronica. Her vehicle was in the driveway, locked.

'Her husband, Brad, was collecting the kids from school, so he's in the clear, but Detective Grave was on the phone to Veronica when she was assaulted. Talk us through what you know, Grave.'

Dawn pushed off the desk and opened her mouth, but was cut off before she could speak.

'What the hell is she doing here?'

Ryan puffed his chest out, ready to start an argument. 'Her job.'

The senior constable joined Ryan in the middle of the room.

'I'm here in a consultative role, but we've already been over this Senior.'

'She's right, Rick. Sit your arse down unless you have something constructive to add to the investigation.'

Martin stuck a picture of Veronica on the whiteboard, to the right of Jessica's pictures.

'Carry on, Grave.'

'Thank you, sir. Ronnie, Veronica to you, was one of my closest friends when I lived here. She looks after my sister's daughter, Abby, and was with her the night Jessica was killed and Lisa witnessed her body being dumped.'

Reynolds scribbled in her notepad, eyes scanning the whiteboard, bright and alert. 'So you think the cases are related?'

'I think Ronnie knows something. It was in the way she asked about Lisa during the phone call. She knew Lisa was alright, so why ring? But then she asked specifically if Lisa had said anything.'

'That's weird.' Jamison said what she'd been thinking at the time.

'I thought so, Jamison. Then, straight after she asked about Lisa, I heard a door slam, then the sound of a male voice, yelling, then a hard slap, likely across Ronnie's face. She must have put the phone down and not cut the call off, but then someone smashed her phone and the call ended.'

Dawn watched the senior constable closely. His arms were crossed over his chest, jaw set firmly closed, brow creased.

'Ryan and I have discussed this with the sergeant, but I think it's time to put it out there. I'm going to stick my neck out and say Jessica's case is also related to the death of Tracey Warren.'

'Your brother was charged with her murder.'

Ryan lurched towards the senior constable, but Dawn put her hand on his chest. Every fibre of her wanted to bury her fist in the constable's face, but her brain was telling her he wasn't worth it. But, more importantly, why was he baiting her?

'You seem to have intimate knowledge of the Tracey Warren case, but I don't recall you being on the local force then?' Dawn glanced over at Sergeant Martin for confirmation. He gave it with a nod. 'My brother wasn't charged at all, Senior. He was a suspect, yes, but his untimely death put an end to the investigation.'

'His suicide note said he did it.'

'Still, no charges were laid. But you've raised a very good point, Senior.'

His eyebrows rose. 'Which is?'

'If my brother didn't commit suicide, and let's be clear, I've never believed Fraser would hang himself, then we should probably put his photo on the board too.'

She pointed at the whiteboard, but her eyes drilled into the senior constable's.

'Exactly why you shouldn't be on this case.'

He turned and strode towards the exit. 'And I'm not staying while she is here. I'm putting in for stress leave.'

He didn't wait for a reply. Instead, he continued out the door.

'Should I go after him?' Jamison was already walking as he spoke.

'Leave him Scott. He'll cool down.'

Martin turned back to the whiteboard, opened a file in his hand and retrieved the photo Dawn had seen on his desk the day before.

'Why is he so upset about linking Tracey Warren's death to Jessica's?' Ryan scanned the room, looking for an answer from anyone.

Sergeant Martin pressed her brother's suicide photo to the whiteboard. 'Because Tracey was his niece.'

Dawn's mind raced. 'And he said *I'm* too close to the case. He wasn't a cop when she died though, was he?'

'No. He joined shortly after she was buried. You have more in common with him than you think.'

Martin added another photo of Fraser to the whiteboard with Blu-Tack and Dawn's stomach knotted for more than one reason.

Ryan broke through her tension. 'So, where are we at with suspects? Do we have the land records for the Summersets yet?'

'Reynolds, chase that up,' Sergeant Martin pointed, and Reynolds started typing. 'Ryan, take another run at Brad. Now his wife is missing, maybe you can poke a hole in Fairweather's alibi. Find out who might want to hurt Veronica while you're at it.'

'Will do, where is he now?'

'At the Top Pub.'

Martin didn't wait for Ryan's reply. Pointing at Jamison, he gave out orders.

'You take Reynolds when she's done and head to the swimming pool. Fairweather will be there, but leave him for now. Let's wait and see what Brad has to say.

'Reynolds, I want you to focus on the female swimmers. See if any of them have anything to say about inappropriate behaviour from Fairweather. Jamison, you see if any of the other trainers have anything interesting to say.'

'Yes, sir.'

'Lisa is at the Top Pub. I need to take care of Abby so she can get the P & C minutes and audited books for us this afternoon, before the staff leave. I'll tag along with Ryan, if it's okay with you.'

'Fine by me. When you get the minutes, bring them in here. I'll go over them and get Reynolds and Jamison to help when they get back. You two are on overtime for this one.' He pointed to the two constables. 'Until Veronica is found, no one knocks off.'

'Except the senior, apparently,' Reynolds whispered as Dawn headed towards the exit with Ryan.

Chapter 36

The wind was gone. A blanket of oppressive, moist air settled over the town as the late afternoon sun tried to peek out through thick clouds. The hum of cicadas grew louder as the setting sun reflected a myriad of rainbow colours through the skyline.

'What do you make of the senior?' Ryan asked, as he rounded the bonnet of his vehicle to join Dawn on the pavement outside the pub.

'I had no idea Tracey was his niece. You'd think he'd have even more reason to want the truth, not settle for making my brother the scapegoat.'

'Unless he had something to do with her death.'

'If he did, there's no obvious connection between him and Jessica. And why grab Ronnie?'

'Maybe they aren't related. Maybe Jessica's murder was a copycat killing?'

'Then the whole P & C and swimming connection goes out the window.'

Ryan shrugged. 'Just saying.'

He pushed the glass door open. Dawn drew in the cool air, but knew it wasn't going to last long. There was no air-conditioning around the bar and courtyard dining area.

'They should be out back. I texted Lisa we were coming down to talk to Brad and she said he was with her. The kids were playing together earlier in the park over the road.'

'Handy.'

'Maybe. She'll keep the kids busy while we question Brad about Fairweather.'

Ryan studied her as they stepped into the courtyard's sauna-like atmosphere.

'How are you handling all this?'

'This. What?'

'Fairweather, the guy who, you know, back when you were a kid … and now, he's your niece's dad.'

'It is what it is. I can't change any of it, but if I can prove Fairweather has been sneaking around with under-age girls, and has anything to do with our victims' deaths, he'll wish he was never born.'

'What will you do to him?'

Dawn grinned as images of slow torture filled her head, but she knew she wouldn't do anything so cruel. Despite what he'd put her through.

'For a start, I'll make sure he never sees his daughter again.'

Brad sat next to Lisa, trying to keep a brave face as the three children laughed and played like nothing was amiss.

'Brad. Can we have a minute?'

Ryan crooked his finger conspiratorially. Brad glanced at Lisa, who smiled, patted his hand and offered to watch the children.

'We won't be long,' Dawn promised, as she led Brad away from the table, around the corner towards the front entrance.

'Have you got any news?'

'Nothing yet. The forensic team will be on scene by now. We should know more soon, but do you know anyone who would want to hurt Ronnie?'

Brad's eyes were wide, like Dawn had asked him to kill his firstborn child, but he smoothed his features quickly.

'No one would want to hurt Veronica.'

Brad kept his eyes on his shoes.

'No one? You're sure about that?'

Dawn wanted to rattle him. Still, he wouldn't look her in the eye.

He knows something.

It was time to push on about Fairweather's alibi.

'You said you were drinking with David Fairweather on Friday night—while Ronnie watched Abby. Are you sticking with your statement?'

Brad licked his lips and nodded.

Ryan took over, with a voice of pure doubt no one could mistake. 'Are you sure mate?'

'David wouldn't do this.'

'You know him that well, hey?'

Dawn let Ryan carry on. Brad was always a man's man, looking up to whoever was the most popular guy in school. Ryan had an alpha streak Brad seemed to be responding to.

She could have gotten all upset about the chauvinism, but she learnt long ago that not every suspect, or even witness, responded to her interview technique. When she first started working as a detective, one of the station's most decorated and respected detectives told her to play to her strengths and utilise the skills of those around her. She never forgot it.

'Your wife is missing, mate. And we've got two dead young women.'

'Two?'

Brad finally met Ryan's piercing gaze. Dawn could see the cogs turning as panic set in.

'Who?'

'We have reason to believe this latest victim was murdered by the same person who killed Tracey Warren back in ninety-five.'

'And David Fairweather is a prime suspect in both murders.'

Dawn couldn't help herself. She needed to make Brad aware of exactly what Fairweather was capable of.

'No way. David is a good bloke. Top sportsman. Great teacher.'

'Would you say that if he molested your daughter?'

'What the hell?'

'Careful Grave,' Ryan warned.

'Look, we have strong evidence to suggest David Fairweather has been abusing young women. And we can link him to both Tracey and Jessica.'

It wasn't entirely true. So far, Tracey's involvement with Fairweather was only hearsay, and Dawn was the only one alive to back that up. And there was no physical evidence to support Jessica having an affair with him. No phone calls.

Phone calls.

They needed Jessica's phone records. They'd requested them days ago.

'No way. It's just girls idolising him. He's a champion swimmer.'

Something in the way Brad spoke made Dawn think he was reciting David word for word.

'He's told you that?'

Brad pressed his lips together.

'Brad, if you're covering for Fairweather, and he turns out to be our killer, you are going away as an accessory to murder. Do you understand what that means?'

Ryan waited. Brad said nothing, his eyes back on the ground.

'No access to your kids.'

'David would never hurt Veronica.'

'Even if she knew you didn't have drinks with him on Friday night? Even if he thought she might tell her old friend Detective Grave here?'

Ryan pointed to Dawn. Brad's eyes followed his finger.

'Alright. Alright!'

'Was David Fairweather with you Friday night?'

'No.'

'Do you know where he was?'

Brad glanced from Dawn to Ryan and back. His shoulders sagged.

'He's been cheating on his wife for years. That's why she left him. But not with under-age girls.'

'You know that for a fact?' Dawn met his gaze, eyes blazing. She knew Fairweather slept with her own sister, but she also knew he liked young girls.

'Do you know who the woman was he was with?'

Ryan drew his attention. Dawn's heart pounded, forcing blood to rush loudly through her ears.

'The school receptionist. What's her name?'

'Rhianna?' Dawn was floored.

'That's her.'

'How fortunate I'm heading to the school with Lisa shortly.'

'What?' Brad looked confused. 'What for?'

'That's none of your concern.'

She turned to leave, Ryan a step behind, but he caught up quickly.

'Don't expect me to babysit Abby,' Ryan groaned, but something about the protest seemed forced.

'Wouldn't dream of it. Michael's coming over.'

'Of course he is.'

'What's that supposed to mean?'

'Nothing.'

Chapter 37

Michael was sitting in the pub courtyard with Lisa and the children when Dawn returned, alone. Ryan left as soon as they finished talking to Brad, giving her some excuse about following up on some leads, but she knew he was avoiding Michael.

Maybe there was something to Lisa's observations.

No!

She forced the thought away. The last thing she needed right now was a fling, or… Michael's soft brown eyes twinkled as he smiled.

Definitely not a romantic interlude.

She was going home to Adelaide as soon as she solved this murder case and found Ronnie. This was all getting way too personal. And now it might all link to Tracey and Fraser, she was even more determined to stay focussed on work.

Michael stood as she approached.

'Hey.'

'Sorry to do this to you.'

'Abby is no problem.'

'He's taking her home for me. This hanging around at the pub is not good for her.'

Lisa pointed to her daughter, sitting on the front bar once more, chatting the ear off anyone willing to listen.

She remembered being in that very same spot many years before. Her dad used to take her down to the pub after swim training.

He'd have a beer. She'd have a pink lemonade and a packet of chicken-flavoured chips. She must have been four, maybe five.

Lisa was too young for training, but Fraser would be there, too. Not on the counter like her. Not chatting to Ben and Mari like she loved to do. Fraser would be out with the local boys, across the road, playing footy or cricket.

'Hello!' Lisa waved a hand in front of her face. 'I expected you to go ballistic when I said we're going home.'

Dawn shook her head, bringing herself back to the present.

'And you were right. That's nuts.'

Memories of her encounter the night of the storm made Dawn shiver. Fairweather had turned up unannounced and she'd not even heard him. Someone could come through the scrub from any direction.

'You're armed. I know nothing of any interest.'

'I think you do. Ronnie asked if you'd said anything. Then she was cut off.'

'Really?'

'Really. You must know something.'

'I have no idea what. But if I do, and someone comes looking for me, you'll be able to kick their arse and then all of this will be over.'

'Your confidence in me, while very welcome, is terribly misplaced. I'm not setting you up as bait and I can't be awake, gun in hand, twenty-four seven.'

'I can help.'

Michael's eyes twinkled with excitement. 'I have a rifle, and a licence.'

'Oh my God. You two watch way too much television.' Dawn rolled her eyes. 'Wait here until we get back, Michael. Take Abby across the road to the park or something, but don't go back to the house without me.'

'I'm not hopeless you know.' He stepped over the bench seat and strode to the bar to collect Abby.

'You shouldn't emasculate him. He might be a softy on the outside, but Michael endured a horrid childhood.'

Dawn wondered how her sister knew about Michael's childhood but shook the thought away. Now wasn't the time to deal with Michael.

'Let's go. We need to pick up the minutes before the staff leave for the day and I need to question the receptionist.'

Dawn started walking without waiting for Lisa. Her sister caught up and asked the last question Dawn wanted to answer right now. But knew she'd have to.

'Why are you questioning the receptionist?'

'Because apparently, she's been carrying on an affair with Fairweather for a while. Long enough for his wife to find out and leave him.'

Her sister's silence was exactly what she'd expected. The father of her gorgeous daughter didn't only cheat on his wife with her. He was a repeat offender. A serial cheat. And with under-age girls. And she was going to prove it.

'I need to send the sergeant an update. And I want to chase up some phone records. Can you drive?'

'Drive?' Lisa gawked, her tone calm, but her eyes raging. 'You can't drop a bombshell like that and keep on working.'

'Can we argue in the car? We'll miss the staff if we don't move.'

Lisa's mouth was still open. She closed it in a way that reminded Dawn of their childhood. Lisa rarely blew up about anything. Always the peacekeeper. Always keeping things bottled up and close to her chest. A true Cancerian, if you believed in that sort of thing—and Lisa did.

Dawn handed over the keys to the hire van. Lisa snatched them, spun and strode to the car. Dawn pulled her phone from her pocket and texted Ryan and Sergeant Martin to see if they could organise a warrant for Ronnie's phone records.

As she put her belt on, a reply pinged on her phone. Glancing at it, she didn't need to see the caller ID to know it was from Ryan.

'Der!'

Of course he'd be following up on Ronnie's disappearance. She'd read too much into his comment about following leads. He was genuinely following up on the case.

She glanced at Lisa, eyes fixed on the road in front of her, body rigid.

'I'm sorry about Fairweather.'

'You warned me back when we were kids. I always found him so handsome, so charming.'

Dawn's heart rate kicked up a notch.

'Lisa.' She waited for her sister to glance her way. 'Did Fairweather seduce you when you were in school?'

Her sister's body shuddered.

'Pull over. Let me drive.'

Tears rolled down Lisa's cheek as the van backfired and rattled to the edge of the road. 'I should have told you.'

She wanted to scream at Lisa, but she didn't. She had no right to judge her sister for not telling anyone. She'd kept her own secret all these years. If she'd told her sister everything, maybe she wouldn't have been another one of his victims.

There they were trying to link Fairweather to other abuse cases and her sister was one of them. The difference between Dawn and Lisa seemed to be that Lisa was still infatuated with the man.

Chapter 38

The car park was nearly empty as Dawn steered the van into a spot right in front of the main office entrance.

Glancing over, she saw Lisa wiping her face and checking herself in the rear-view mirror. Was she doing the right thing, getting her sister involved like this?

'I'm sorry to ask you to do this.'

'It's okay. If the P & C are the link in your case, then you need the paperwork.'

'You don't have to hang around while I question Rhianna, though.'

'My bubble was burst years ago. Time to put my big-girl pants on and face reality. Even if David was somehow interested in me permanently, I realise now that's not a good thing.'

The realisation she and Lisa were chalk and cheese when it came to men hit home harder than ever. Dawn had never needed a man in her life, but in being so independent, she often pushed them away when they tried to get close.

While Lisa clung to any man who would have her. And they usually weren't worth it. Losing their mother during those teenage years seemed to have stuffed them both up beyond any help.

She reached for Lisa's hand and squeezed. They needed to stick together. But how? She lived in Adelaide. They were thousands of kilometres away from one another.

She opened her door and stepped out. It was a problem she wasn't going to solve today.

Lisa straightened her loose-fitting floral dress, pulled her shoulders back and planted her usual smile on her lips. 'Let's do this.'

As she followed her sister towards the office, Dawn couldn't help but wonder how many times Lisa had put a fake smile in place over the years. Probably too many.

Lisa held the door open. Cool air wafted from the doorway as Dawn reached it.

Rhianna hurried behind the counter, packing up files and collecting her bag. She glanced up, her expression a mix of suspicion and annoyance.

They were almost too late.

'Sorry to bother you Rhianna. We know it's late, but I have a few questions to ask you. And my sister here needs to collect the P & C archives.'

'Questions? Official ones? The principal has finished for the day.'

Excellent! Maybe it's my lucky day after all.

'That's not an issue. My questions are for you and of a private nature.'

Rhianna's perfectly waxed eyebrows knitted together.

'But if you can point me in the direction of the P & C archives, I can get them out while you chat.' Lisa's smile was plastered in place.

'I don't know. I should check with the principal or the P & C chair first.'

'I'm on the committee and I have every right to access the records of a publicly incorporated body.' Lisa's tone was pleasant, but there was no doubt she knew she had access.

'Of course. Follow me.'

Rhianna collected a set of keys from a cabinet behind the reception desk and tottered on her bright green high heels down the carpeted hallway.

She guided the key into a storeroom door lock and turned, opening it to reveal a large room, with a dark grey compactus shelving system.

'How far back do they go?'

'No idea.'

She shrugged, removed the key and stepped back into the hallway.

'Pull it shut when you're done.'

The receptionist tottered away. Dawn peered into the room.

'I'll call Ryan. I think we need help with all these.'

'Thanks. I'll find them and put them in the hallway for someone to pick up.'

'Okay. See you soon.'

Dawn dialled and put the phone to her ear as she followed Rhianna down the hall to the reception area.

'Ryan. We've got the records but need a hand to load them.'

'On my way.'

'Thanks.'

She hung up as she reached the front counter.

'I don't think they're allowed off the premises.'

'We'll look after them.' Dawn launched straight into her questions, hoping to distract the receptionist. 'What's your relationship with David Fairweather?'

'What?'

'We have a witness statement stating you were with David Fairweather last Friday night.'

Rhianna's mouth opened, but no words came out. Instead, her face rolled through a myriad of emotions, landing on suspicion.

'What's this about?'

She was smarter than Dawn expected.

'The murder of Jessica Mills.'

The woman's expression was identical to the day Dawn told her they'd identified the body at Archer Point as Jessica's.

'Were you with him Friday night?'

Rhianna cleared her throat. 'It's frowned upon.'

'What? Sleeping with a staff member or a married man?'

'His marriage has been a sham for years.'

'They all say that. Were you with him or not?'

'Yes.'

She bit the word off like it was red hot.

'All night? From when to when?'

'All night. We had quite a night. Do you want details?

Dawn resisted the urge to cringe and decided to take another tack.

'You know Fairweather has been accused of having sex with under-age girls.'

Rhianna didn't flinch.

'You know where this is going. If you are covering for him, you'll be charged.'

Rhianna pressed her lips together.

'So, you've never fielded a complaint from any of your high school students?'

Silence hung in the air until the front door opened.

Ryan stepped in. Dawn turned and pointed down the hall. He strode past without a second look.

'Hang on. What's going on? Isn't he the detective?'

'He's just here helping a friend.'

'I need to make a call. This isn't right.'

Rhianna picked up the phone on the desk and dialled. Dawn watched the numbers being punched and realised she wasn't calling the principal.

'We'll be gone by the time they get here. Tell whoever you're calling they can find the records at the police station.'

'But!'

Dawn rushed down the hallway, as Rhianna started talking down the phone.

'Let's get these out. Larry Summerset is on the way.'

'Summerset?' Ryan grabbed three boxes. Dawn lifted two.

'I guess it makes sense. He's the chairman,' Lisa reasoned as she collected two boxes and followed.

'Did you get them all?'

'They only went back seven years. The rest are either gone or archived elsewhere.'

'Damn.'

Ryan pushed the door open with his back and held it for Dawn and Lisa. 'It will have to do.'

'You can't take those,' Rhianna rushed around the counter.

'I most certainly can, and I have,' Lisa huffed. 'If anyone has an issue, they can take it up with P & Cs Queensland.'

All seven boxes were loaded into the back of Dawn's van. She slammed the side door as a black Mercedes scrambled into the driveway.

'Time to go.'

Ryan ushered them into the car. Dawn didn't argue. Ryan stepped back as she reversed out of the parking spot.

The last thing she saw in the rear-view mirror was Larry stepping out of the car, hands waving, Ryan standing legs splayed, arms firmly folded across his chest.

She smiled.

The chairman wasn't getting anywhere with Ryan. The detective was going to stonewall him at every turn.

Chapter 39

Lisa dropped the last box of paperwork on the kitchen table as Dawn licked sweat from her top lip.

Glancing around, she realised there was no air-conditioner to simply flick on. Sighing, she crossed to the kitchen sink and opened the casement window to allow some airflow.

'I can't believe you don't have air-con yet. How on earth do you survive up here without it?'

'You've acclimatised to Adelaide.'

'Or it's hotter up here than when we were kids.'

Lisa smiled but said nothing as she lifted the lid on the box marked *2015*. 'Are you sure bringing the paperwork here is a good idea?' She glanced at Dawn and then peered inside the box.

'It was our only choice. You saw Larry. Give him another five minutes and I guarantee he'll be on the phone to the sergeant trying to get the minutes back. If they are here, he can't touch them without stepping onto private property.'

The screen door hit the wall with a loud bang as Abby tore into the kitchen.

'Where's Michael?' Dawn asked, then peered past the panting girl and grinned.

Michael gave a breathless wave, hunched over and sucked in a deep breath. 'You two might have grown up swimming, but this one,' he took a breath, 'can run like the wind.'

Michael stepped inside the kitchen and scanned the room. 'I see you got what you were looking for.'

Dawn's phone rang as the front screen door creaked open. She answered and rushed down the hallway, concerned

Larry might actually come to get the minutes anyway, but stopped when she saw Ryan stroll in.

The smug grin on his face said he'd fobbed the P & C chairman off, but the voice on the end of the line told her it might not last long.

'I've just had a call from Larry Summerset and, as you can imagine, he's not happy. Spouted on about getting his son to get the minutes returned and to press charges, but I advised him I knew nothing about any illegal procurement of paperwork.'

'Thanks Ross. That's why I brought them ...'

'I don't know anything Grave.'

'Of course.'

'I've never heard Larry so upset.'

'He definitely didn't seem happy when we saw him in the parking lot. It's got to make you wonder.'

'It certainly does. He's usually a smiling, happy, relaxed kind of guy.'

Dawn remembered Larry from her swimming days. Always a cheery smile. Always happy to help kids in need of new swimmers or anything to help them compete. This was all so out of character for him.

'Have we heard back on the land settlement? Is there a mortgage on the properties, or for the original development?'

'Land title searches didn't show any registered mortgages against the land Larry purchased.'

'Interesting. Ronnie is missing. Larry is in a tizz about the P & C minutes being under scrutiny. And there is no mortgage registered on the land.'

'And we still don't know where the money for his development came from back in ninety-five.'

'Exactly. I'll dig through the minutes tonight. Any luck with Ronnie's phone records?'

‘Got them. Nothing out of the ordinary. Calls between her and Brad. A few incoming from Larry. The last call she made to you. And a couple of calls to the school earlier in the week.’

‘We’re missing something. Did we find a syndicate, anything about a land trust to help Larry buy the land?’

‘Not yet. I’ll keep digging into it. You’ve turned out to be one hell of a detective, Grave.’

‘Would never have happened without your encouragement Ross.’

‘That’s Sergeant Martin to you.’

Dawn smiled as she hung up and returned to the kitchen.

Ryan glanced up as he filled the kettle and put it on to boil. ‘What’s so funny?’

‘Nothing.’ She turned to her sister. ‘Found anything?’

‘I’ve barely started.’ Lisa flicked through a pile of paperwork. ‘All that I’ve found so far is …’ Lisa frowned at the page of minutes in front of her.

Dawn rounded the kitchen table to peer over her shoulder. ‘What is it?’

‘I wasn’t at this meeting.’

Lisa pointed to a Q and A under a particular item of discussion on the minutes.

‘Who’s the treasurer?’

‘Fairweather.’

‘I still think it’s unusual having a teacher on the committee. Especially an office bearer.’

‘He’s got a son at the school. I guess he’s entitled to be on the committee if he wants to, and, let’s face it, finding volunteers for this type of thing is like drawing blood from a stone these days.’

'So Jessica was querying the allocation of grant funding?'

'Looks like it.'

'So, who's secretary?

Lisa didn't need to scan through the minutes to know the answer. 'Ronnie.'

'I think we might be on to something. I need to check on a few things. Are auditor reports here?'

'The 2015 won't be audited yet, maybe check 2014 to find the auditors details.' Michael opened the lid on another box marked *2014*. 'Here it is.'

Dawn accepted the file Michael handed her. 'You know a lot about committee stuff.'

Michael's eyes twinkled.

'The Yuku Baja Muliku Rangers are an incorporated body, and partly a volunteer organisation. We have to keep all this stuff too. You should come and meet the kids one day. They love telling white fellas all about the bush.'

'Can I come?'

Abby's crystal blue eyes grew round. Her killer Shirley Temple smile could win anyone over.

'You can come if your Auntie Dawn comes.'

Ryan poured his cup of tea. 'Blackmail.'

Dawn interrupted him before he got carried away. 'Thanks, Ryan. Strong, dash of milk, no sugar.'

Dawn opened the auditor's report. 'Okay. Let's see what we have here.'

A cup of sickly white, half-brewed tea appeared in front of her. She shook her head but returned her focus to the paperwork.

'Talk about keeping it in the family.'

'What?'

Ryan leant over her shoulder, peering into the file. His chest touched her shoulder, his breath warm on her neck.

Michael appeared at the other shoulder.

Dawn glanced sideways to see her sister chewing her lip, trying unsuccessfully not to smirk.

Dawn popped up. Both men stepped back so hastily, they nearly knocked into one another.

'Brad Summerset is the P & C's auditor.'

'Is that even legal?'

Michael ran his fingers through his thick, motley coloured hair.

'It's a small town. We only have one accounting firm. Brad bought out the former owner's wife when old man McInnes died.'

Lisa didn't seem at all alarmed, but Dawn's head was spinning.

'Larry is Chair, Ronnie is Secretary, Brad is the auditor and Fairweather, a teacher, is the treasurer.'

Dawn glanced at Ryan.

'Are you thinking what I'm thinking?'

'Most definitely. We need to check all the grant money issued to the school and P & C in the past few years.'

'And make sure it was acquitted appropriately with the grants department.'

'I'll call Sergeant Martin back.'

Chapter 40

Dawn jolted awake to the sound of a kookaburra laughing outside her window. He was quickly joined by another, then another, until a chorus of birds laughed at her horrible lack of sleep.

They'd scoured through the P & C minutes for hours, finally deciding to snatch some sleep before starting again early. But between the breezeless, hot, sticky night and vivid, unrelenting dreams of drowning in paperwork, she'd barely managed a few hours' sleep.

Stretching, she fought her way out from under the mosquito net, being careful not to catch it and tear the whole thing down from the ceiling.

She dressed in a white tank top and loose-fitting shorts with a muted floral pattern. Crossing to the dressing table mirror, she scrutinised the dark puffy shadows beneath her eyes. Her brunette hair was showing the slightest bit of grey at the roots, and thin, uncontrolled frizzy ends stuck out at all angles.

She combed it back against her head, willing it to behave until she could get it trimmed.

Coffee.

She desperately needed a cappuccino, but Lisa didn't have a machine and she didn't have the energy to drive or walk to the main street.

Deciding on another cup of tea, she pressed the kettle button down and unlocked the screen door, hoping to find a cool breeze blowing outside.

Nothing but the scent of stale, rotting vegetation greeted her.

Stepping out, she crossed to the balcony, stretched and opened her arms wide to the sunrise, then jumped as something caught her eye across the deck.

Spinning, she frantically searched for her weapon, but realised she wasn't wearing it.

'Hey. Wait up.' Michael held his hands up, despite her not pointing a gun in his face.

'What the hell are you doing out here?'

She glanced down both sides of the long, wide veranda, wondering where he came from, then realised he had a pillow on the outdoor lounge, pushed to one end, a double-barrel shotgun pressed up against the wall next to it.

'Just keeping a promise.'

'What promise?'

'To myself. Lisa insisted on coming back to the house. Until you catch Jessica's murderer, I'll camp out here.'

'There's no need.'

'Maybe not. I'm sure you can take care of yourself. But maybe you can consider me your backup. You seem to like having a partner.'

'Ryan? He's not my partner. I don't even work in Queensland.'

Michael shrugged like he wasn't buying it.

Do I consider Ryan my partner? I guess he is, on this case, sort of.

'What's the plan today then?' Michael deftly changed the subject. Dawn didn't change it back.

'The plan today is for you to go back to work. Before your Elders, or your boss or whoever it is you answer to, get stroppy with me.'

'I told you, I've taken leave.'

'Michael, as much as I appreciate the help, this could get dangerous, and I can't be responsible …'

'You're not.'

Lisa stepped out onto the veranda, hands holding her head like it might fall from her shoulders any second. Her dark blonde hair was tangled and matted, but she still looked amazing.

'What the hell! Your voices are loud enough to wake the dead,' she hissed.

'Sorry,' they said in unison.

'Since you've woken me up, I might as well cook breakfast.'

'I thought you'd be an early bird these days, with all the yoga and meditation stuff you do.'

'There is absolutely nothing I'll get up at the crack of dawn for, except Abby, or an early flight to an exotic destination. And since Abby doesn't wake up early, ever, and I'm not expecting to win the lotto anytime soon, I'm usually blissfully asleep at this hour.'

'Well, the sun comes up so freakin' early here. The birds woke me.'

'Wear earplugs and one of those mask thingies.' Lisa waved her hand in front of her face.

Dawn glanced at her watch. 'I need to get to the station anyway.'

'Do you need help?' Michael puffed the pillow out and put it back where it belonged on the outdoor lounge, picked up his gun and turned to face Dawn expectantly.

'Actually. Staying right here with Abby and Lisa is good, if you are okay with that?'

'Here? I'm taking Abby to school and then I've got work to do.'

'School? Abby can't go to school when we are investigating the P & C and the Summersets, and you helped take the minutes from the school.'

Lisa dismissed Dawn with the wave of her hand and strolled away towards the kitchen door.

Dawn followed. 'Don't ignore me, Lisa. I'm serious.'

'What are they going to do? Kidnap me in broad daylight?'

'Possibly.'

'Abby will be with teachers all day. And I'll be seeing clients at work. No one has tried to come after me so far. I don't know anything, and I can't stay cooped up here all day. We finished going through the P & C paperwork. I'm done.'

Lisa disappeared inside. Dawn sighed.

'I'll keep an eye on her.'

'Thanks. I appreciate it. Two women are dead, Ronnie is missing, and somehow Lisa thinks she's immune.'

'Denial is easier for some people.' Michael's tone made Dawn turn to study him. Were they still talking about the murders?

'I have to go. I'll see you later today, or maybe tonight. If anything happens, let me know. Even if it seems inconsequential.'

'Inconsequential. Got it.' He saluted, a smile creeping across his lips.

'I'm sorry. Occupational habit.'

'It's fine. I like being told what to do. Clear communication makes life a lot simpler.' He stepped closer.

Definitely not talking about the case now.

'Gotta run.'

Now wasn't the time to think about relationships. She had her career ahead of her. A promotion on the radar.

As she brushed her teeth and packed her handbag, she couldn't stop thinking about the young constable in Coober Pedy—choosing to stay in the outback for love, over a budding career. As bad a decision as she thought it was at the time, she now wasn't so sure Jenny had it all wrong.

Chapter 41

Dawn rotated under the air-conditioning vent, thankful for the cool air despite the morning being less humid than earlier in the week.

'Did we get the CCTV footage from the school yet?

Constable Jamison was head down at a computer, but glanced up when she spoke. Then quickly resumed typing.

'Not yet.'

'What's the hold up? Can you chase it up?'

'On it.'

Jamison returned his attention to his screen as Reynolds hung up the desk phone and glanced up.

'That was Melody Smythe from the Indigenous Grants department. She said all the grants have been acquitted appropriately, but she's going to send over the receipts the P & C lodged so we can confirm things on our end. She'll go back to the first grant application back in nineteen ninety-five. But the old ones will take a while because they're not stored electronically.'

'If the grants are all acquitted appropriately, then we are back at square one.' Dawn slumped onto the corner of Reynold's desk.

'Not necessarily. Summerset is coming in here this morning, with his son, to try and get those P & C records back.' Sergeant Martin tapped his lip with the whiteboard marker.

'The ones you don't know anything about,' Dawn grinned.

'Yes, those ones. But while he's here,' he pointed the marker at Dawn, 'we can question him about the grant money.'

'And about how he acquired the land on the hill without a mortgage.'

'He'll have his lawyer with him though. I don't think you'll trip him up so easily.'

Ryan handed Dawn a cappuccino from the new café down the road. She sipped it, savouring the flavour as her mind raced.

'We need to question Fairweather again. Rhianna covered for him, but I don't know. I still think he's good for this.'

'Do we have enough for a warrant on his financials?'

Ryan drained his coffee and tossed the cup in the bin alongside Reynolds' desk. It landed perfectly and the young constable nodded approval. Ryan lapped it up with a Labrador grin.

'We do now.'

Dawn turned to see Sergeant Martin waving a piece of paper. 'Jessica's phone records have finally come through. Damn telecommunications companies take their time.'

Dawn crossed the room and snatched the paper. Martin grinned knowingly.

'I can't believe Ronnie's came through before … Fairweather. I knew it.'

'Could be she was speaking with the treasurer about her concerns? Don't jump to any conclusions Grave,' Ryan warned.

'I wouldn't trust him as far as I can throw him, but I'm open to hearing what he has to say. But you have to admit, his reputation, his direct link with the victim …'

'All circumstantial. We need evidence and your testimony from twenty-odd years ago, when you were fifteen, isn't enough.'

She thought about Lisa's testimony. Would it add any weight? Probably not. And her sister wasn't likely to stand up in court against her daughter's father.

'Is this link enough to get a warrant for Fairweather's bank records?'

Dawn scanned the sergeant's face, hopefully.

'I'll get onto it. I think I know a favourable judge who isn't one of Larry's best mates.'

A constable that Dawn hadn't officially met appeared by the main office hallway. It made her wonder where the senior was. He'd left pretty annoyed the day before, but surely, he was professional enough to turn up for work when they were desperately trying to find a killer and Ronnie's kidnapper.

'Sir, Mr Summerset and his lawyer are here.'

'Excellent. Thanks Sam. Reynolds, take them down to interview room number two. Ryan, with me.'

'Sir!'

'You're a consultant, not a detective here, Grave. You'll have to observe.'

Ryan nudged her as he strode past. 'Drink your coffee and take a chill pill. I'll channel a little feisty for you.'

Reynolds chuckled. Jamison rolled his lips. Dawn sipped her coffee, swallowing hard and followed behind reluctantly.

As she entered the adjoining room, she observed Larry and Brad's twin brother Trevor, seated on one side of the table, shoulder to shoulder in the tight space. Larry stood as Ryan and the sergeant entered.

'What's going on, Ross? Why am I in here?' Larry indicated the interview room with a wave of his hand.

'We just have a few questions, Larry.'

'That makes two of us. Where are the P & C minutes? What's this all about?'

'Take a seat.'

Sergeant Martin's tone was polite, but something in the way he studied Larry made the P & C chairman lower himself into the chair once more.

'I already told you, Larry. I have nothing to do with the P & C minutes. As far as I know, it's a committee matter between committee members, so we'll leave it to you to sort out.'

Trevor sat back, pen in hand, studying the sergeant suspiciously, but said nothing. There were no legal grounds to recall the minutes from Lisa's possession and he obviously knew it.

'But since you mentioned the P & C …'

Ryan dragged a chair out from under the table, sat and shuffled up against the edge to get as close as possible.

'I'm wondering how it works, legally speaking.' His eyes landed on Trevor. 'When a chairman, and secretary of a committee are related to the auditor. Is that strictly kosher?'

'The committee votes on who to approve as the auditor. I'm assuming there have been no objections?'

Trevor glanced at his father for confirmation. Larry nodded, but his eyes never left Ryan's face.

'You know Veronica is missing, right?' Ryan pushed on.

'Yes. Terrible. What are you doing about finding her?' Larry's eyes said he was worried, but his tone was calm.

'We are following a number of enquiries and waiting on the forensic report.'

Ryan leant back in his chair, which creaked under his weight. 'I am surprised that wasn't the first thing you asked when you came in, though.'

'Well …,' Larry stammered. 'I knew you'd be doing your best.'

'Really? Very uncommon attitude in this type of abduction. Usually, the family are pushing for answers. Offering to get in front of the camera, the local news. Anything to get their loved ones home quicker. Safely.'

Larry seemed caught off guard. His son intervened. 'There hasn't been a ransom demand, if that's what you're asking.'

'I wasn't. But that does bring us to our next question.'

'Look. We were only here to get the P & C minutes back. If you can't help us, then we'll be leaving.' Trevor rose, lifting his father by the arm.

'Come on, Dad.'

'Larry, we've been discussing something, which we think might help us find Veronica.'

Sergeant Martin eased his chair back and rose as Larry shuffled out from his seat with an unusual lack of coordination.

Dawn wasn't the only one to notice.

Trevor hadn't let go of his father's arm. 'Dad. You don't need to answer any more questions.' He now steered him towards the door.

'You purchased the land on the top of the hill in, what, ninety-five?'

Martin didn't wait for a reply.

'No mortgage, what was it, over 50k. Not much now, but a lot back then. Where did you get that sort of money?'

Larry frowned. Glanced at Trevor, then back at the sergeant. As he opened his mouth to respond, his son cut him off.

'It was an inheritance.' Trevor nudged his father through the door. 'Now, we are done gentlemen. If you need anything else from my family, any of us, you can call me.'

He thrust a card in Ryan's face. The detective snapped it up, studying it as the door slammed shut. 'Well, that went well.'

He waved the card at the sergeant.

'Inheritance, my arse. Larry was raised by a single mum, and she died penniless as far as I know.'

Dawn watched Martin and Ryan leave the interview room, thinking the exact same thing. Larry often talked about how he'd come from nothing. She needed to find a will or the executor or the legal firm who handled the estate.

Trevor was too young to have had anything to do with the estate. So who, if anyone, handled the money that gave Larry his big financial break?

Chapter 42

Dawn opened the door to meet them in the hallway. 'We need to bring Fairweather in for questioning over Jessica's phone records.'

She drew alongside Ryan in the wide walkway as another constable she didn't recognise wandered past.

'And find out who, if anyone, knows anything about Larry's inheritance.'

'The Supreme Court will have a record of whoever was granted probate.'

Martin opened the door at the end of the hallway and held it while Dawn and Ryan stepped through.

'I'll chase that up. You two bring Fairweather in, but Grave, make sure you don't ask any questions during the interview.'

'Good luck keeping her quiet, Sarge.'

'I can be quiet, when I need to be.'

'I've not seen any evidence of that.'

Ryan was baiting her, she knew he was, but still, it was hard to resist. Over the years, she'd learnt that lesson the hard way. Being female and being fast-tracked to detective came with a lot of ridicule. Thankfully, there were a few cops along the way who hadn't judged her by her gender.

'Just stick to what we know as fact,' Martin warned as he opened the side door leading directly to his office. Dawn and Ryan carried on towards reception.

'We don't know squat.' Ryan held the door.

'We know Fairweather was talking to Jessica. That's enough for me.'

'Let's see what excuse he comes up with, then.'

‘I’m concerned about Ronnie and I’m wondering why Larry isn’t. Yet Brad was beside himself.’

Dawn held the door handle of Ryan’s four-wheel drive and waited for him to unlock it. Heat radiated from the interior as she slid in and sweat broke out instantly.

‘Did you see the way the old guy stumbled when he got out of his seat?’

‘Yeah. And the way he frowned when you mentioned the money for the land.’

‘It was his lawyer who told us about the inheritance.’

Ryan started the car and backed out.

Dawn glanced at her watch. ‘Problem for Sergeant Martin to chase up. Let’s check the school and see if we can get Fairweather on break.’

‘On it.’

Dawn let her mind try to piece things together as they rode in silence, Ryan likely doing the same.

Ronnie asking her what Lisa had said, made no sense. Larry appearing not to care about Ronnie being missing, wasn’t entirely unexpected. The day they interviewed Brad, and Larry turned up, she noticed there was tension between Ronnie and Larry. But why? He was a sweet old guy who did so much for the community.

But now, his whole land deal was under scrutiny and Trevor was closing any access to the man she’d known all her life. And he seemed so frail. A little confused even.

Her heart told her there was no way Larry had anything to do with Jessica or Tracey’s murder and misappropriating grant money was even less up his alley. There were Indigenous kids on the swim team when she was there. Larry always tried his best to make sure they had what they needed.

‘Something isn’t adding up with all this.’

‘I agree.’

Ryan parked outside the school office, further away than last time as the parking lot was nearly full.

'My gut tells me Larry wouldn't do any of this.'

'Maybe your gut is too attached to the case? It looks a lot like the P & C have been doing something shady.'

'Yes, but Fairweather is the treasurer, and he's the one talking to Jessica after hours.'

'Possibly about the P & C stuff.'

'I doubt that. More likely he's been grooming her.'

They stepped out of the car in unison.

'You'll need more than your gut to make that stick. But let's ask the man himself.' Ryan pointed in the opposite direction to the main building, at Fairweather, hastily fumbling with his keys as he rushed across the grass towards the staff car park.

'He looks in a hurry.'

They picked up the pace. Ryan broke into a jog as Fairweather reached a late-model Toyota Prius. The lights flashed as it unlocked.

'Fairweather!' Ryan called.

The teacher turned, spotted Ryan, then turned back to his car, yanking the door open. Dawn pushed up her pace, but Ryan beat her. He casually placed his arm inside the door as Fairweather tried to close it.

'Sorry to bother you, but we need to get you down the station for a formal interview.'

'Why?' Fairweather's hand was still on the handle, trying to close the door against Ryan's hold.

'You'll find out when you get there.'

Ryan put both hands on the door, stepped around it and yanked it open all the way, ripping the handle from Fairweather's grip.

'What's *she* doing here?' Fairweather glared at Dawn.

'Consulting.'

'Yeah, right.'

He grudgingly got out of the car. Ryan slammed the door shut.

'You better lock that.'

'I'm supposed to be back at school in half an hour. I've got a class to teach.'

'Then we better hurry.'

Ryan waved his hand towards his vehicle. Fairweather sighed, locked his car, shoved his keys in his pocket and followed Ryan. Dawn stayed back a moment to observe. There was a wariness about the guy, making her wonder if he'd been expecting them. Either way, he seemed twitchy enough to take flight any second.

Chapter 43

The rigid interview room chair never felt so good. Dawn missed leading an investigation. She missed Adelaide and the less humid, often cooler spring days. She missed her team. Jack, Rickard, Max, even Johnnie.

But there was something about being back in Cooktown that felt right. As she glared at Fairweather over the interview table, she acknowledged that *something* definitely wasn't him.

She pressed *record* on the equipment and nodded for Ryan to get started.

'Friday, September twenty-fifth, twenty-fifteen.' He eyed the clock ticking loudly on the wall. 'One thirty-two p.m. Interview with David Fairweather. Detective Ryan and consulting Detective Grave present.'

'Why am I here?'

'Can you confirm you've been cautioned, Mr Fairweather?'

'I have. Why am I here?' he repeated, glancing from Ryan to Dawn and back, fingers drumming to an unheard beat on the table.

'You are aware we're investigating the death of Jessica Mills and the disappearance of Veronica Summerset.'

'Heard about Veronica. I hope she's alright.'

'We have Jessica Mills' phone records. They indicate you've had numerous conversations with the student, a minor, after hours.'

Ryan's tone left no doubt where the interview was heading.

Dawn nearly chuckled aloud at the look on Fairweather's face. Did he honestly think they wouldn't check a victim's phone records?

'What's *she* doing here?' He glared at Dawn.

Why did everyone keep asking that question?

'Detective Grave is consulting on this case for various reasons, none of which are of any concern to you. *I'm* running this interview, Mr Fairweather. Grave is here in an observational role only. Now answer the question.'

'Technically, you didn't ask one. But I'll humour you.' Fairweather sat back in his chair and crossed his arms firmly over his chest.

'I've been training Jessica for a few years. She was struggling a bit at school, with keeping up her grades, and was thinking of quitting. I was trying to convince her to keep competing, but she had too much on.'

'Like the student representative council and attending the P & C meetings?'

'Possibly.'

Fairweather's tone became cautious.

'So, Jessica didn't ring you about anomalies in the P & C's grant funding for Indigenous students?'

Ryan leant forward. Fairweather pulled back, rolling his lips, then licking them.

A knock on the door made Dawn and Ryan turn.

'Sorry to disturb you, sir, but Mr Fairweather's lawyer is here.'

Reynolds' expression reflected Dawn's.

'Thank you Constable.'

The door opened, and Trevor Summerset breezed into the already cramped interview room. While he looked like Brad, his hair was styled differently, shorter, off the collar and his eyes were smaller, making the colour hard to see and giving him a hawk-like appearance.

'Come on, David. You're done here.'

The chair scraped on the lino as David stood.

Ryan's chair nearly fell backwards as he bolted upright. 'We have more questions.'

'You're on a fishing expedition Detective.'

'How would you know? You only got here five seconds ago.'

Ryan blocked Fairweather's exit.

'Is my client under arrest?'

Trevor waved his arm towards Fairweather who was trying to wriggle past Ryan, but the detective splayed his legs, taking up most of the room between the interview desk and the wall.

Ryan didn't answer.

'Then we are going. Come on David.'

Dawn rose and turned to face Trevor. 'Interesting.'

'What?'

Trevor loomed over Dawn. She wasn't short, but she wasn't tall either. Trevor, like Brad, was a little over six foot.

'Actually. I'm wondering about a few things. How did you know David was here and why on earth are you his lawyer?'

Trevor's eyes blazed. He was fuming on the inside, but why? She hardly knew the guy.

'Just do your job and find Veronica.'

'Not my job. I'm only in a consulting role.'

She sat on the edge of the interview desk grinning, as Trevor Summerset and David Fairweather left without closing the door behind them.

She waited a second as Ryan tidied up the chairs compulsively, then asked, 'What do you make of that?'

'I think we hit a nerve.'

'Did someone tell him we were coming to interview him?'

'Who? How?'

'Trevor and Larry were here, trying to get the minutes back. When they failed, they either rang Fairweather because something in the minutes implicates him or there was something else about the minutes they needed to discuss with him.'

'So he was in a rush, but not to avoid our questions. So, to what?'

'To get to Lisa and the minutes!' Dawn jumped up from the table and rushed out the room, leaving Ryan frowning for a split second before running after her.

Chapter 44

Dawn was out the front door before she remembered her van was still at Lisa's and Ryan was her ride for the day. Impatiently she waited for him to unlock the car so she could get in.

'Isn't Michael still with her?'

'No. She's at work. Abby is at school. He said he would keep an eye on them though.'

'She went to work knowing whoever she saw dumping Jessica's body might still be looking for her?'

'I know. I tried to convince her to stay at home, with Michael, but she said they would have come after her already if they thought she knew anything and, according to her, she didn't. She never saw who dumped Jessica's body. They knew her, but she didn't recognise their voice when they called her name.'

'Where's her work?'

'She works at a holistic health clinic in Helen Street. Up the road from the library.'

'Okay. You check in with your sister, then we need to get back to the library. We never did go through the microfiche, and we might find something in there we missed in the minutes.'

'Okay. But I want to go straight back to Lisa's afterwards and rip those minutes apart. We are missing something. Something that ties this all together.'

'You know this might have nothing to do with Tracey Warren's murder.'

'I know, but my instincts and ten years on the job are telling me they are connected.'

Dawn pointed to a sage green and bluish grey weatherboard building with turned posts and traditional fretwork over the veranda.

'That's it.'

'What is she, a naturopath or something?'

'Lisa was always a free spirit, but she went full hippy on me the year Mum disappeared.'

'It must have been hard. Losing your mum like that.'

Dawn shrugged.

'Let's go.'

She opened the car door and stepped out, slamming it harder than intended. The last thing she wanted was to off-load on Ryan about a past she wanted to forget.

He joined her as she pushed the clinic door open. A tinkle of soft bells chimed above her head as the scent of musk and lavender wafted on the cool air.

Soft Indian temple-style music played in the background. A young woman with dreadlocks, emerald-green eyes and a nose ring glanced up and smiled.

'Welcome to Cooktown Wellness. How can we help you?'

'I'm here to see Lisa. It's quite urgent.'

'She's busy with a client right now. She's nearly done though.'

'We'll duck over to the library. If you could ask her to call Dawn as soon as she is done.'

'Dawn. Like her sister Dawn?'

The girl's business-like manner evaporated.

'The one and only.'

'No way.' The young woman hopped off her stool and ran around the desk, arms wide. 'I've heard so much about you. I'm Emily. Lisa never stops talking about you.'

She enveloped Dawn in a tight hug. Dawn sighed through it.

Why does everyone want to hug me?

'Oh, wow. You've got so much negative energy. I can sense it.'

The woman continued to squeeze. Dawn tried to wriggle free.

'A hug should last at least thirty seconds. We can share energy this way.'

'I'm not into sharing.'

Dawn pulled away. Emily studied her a moment, nodded like she read Dawn's mind, or chakra or whatever it was health gurus did and floated back to her desk,

'I'll tell Lisa as soon as Mrs Nelson is done.'

'Thanks. I'll be over the road.'

Ryan held the door open, a grin from ear to ear.

'Not a word.' She waved her finger in his face as she stepped back out into humidity. It was less oppressive, but still stickier than she cared for after so many years down south.

'Microfiche then.'

Ryan crossed the road as Dawn's phone rang.

'Detective Grave speaking.'

'Dawn. I've found something.'

'Michael?'

Ryan stopped outside the library, listening while Dawn put the phone on speaker.

'You're on speaker. Where are you?'

'After I dropped Lisa at work I came back to the house and started going over the minutes again. Thought I might find something we missed earlier.'

'Don't you have something to do?' Ryan teased.

'I'm on leave. But I found something.'

'So you said.'

Dawn slapped the detective on the arm. 'Shut up and let him talk Ryan.' His grin widened.

'What did you find Michael?'

'The principal attends a lot of these meetings, but there's one in particular, where Jessica is questioning the grant funding again, he's present and further down, during open questioning, your friend Ronnie has recorded a conversation discussing grants from years ago, when Tom Fletcher was actually secretary of the P & C.'

'Interesting. Did he have kids at the school?'

'I don't know. Like I said, when I went back to do Year 12, he was principal.'

'I'll get a background check done on him.'

'Okay. Not sure it's relevant but thought you might need to know.'

'Keep digging. Let me know if you find anything else interesting.'

'Will do.'

Dawn hung up and pointed to the library.

'Luckily we happen to know someone who can probably tell us why Tom Fletcher was on the P & C.'

'This time we check out the microfiche though. I'm not taking the old lady's word for it.'

'Deal.'

Chapter 45

Cool air greeted them as they entered the library. Ceiling-high bookcases lined the walls. The librarian sat at a large nest of tables, gathered together against a wall with high windows.

A mix of various shades of grey heads bobbed up and down, huddled together around the table. A quiet hum of low voices filtered across the room.

Sharon glanced up, a smile spreading from her lips to her eyes. Rising, she excused herself and scurried over, fussing with her hair and dress on the way.

'Detectives. What can I do for you today?'

She spoke loud enough to turn every head at the table their way. The whispers rose to an audible level.

Dawn understood a few comments.

'Sorry about that. It's the Murder Book Club and with everything going on … well.'

'We understand. We'd like to have a look through the microfiche we discussed the other day.'

'No worries at all, luv. Follow me.'

Sharon hurried towards the microfiche machine set up on a bench alongside two outdated computers with tiny screens and clunky keyboards.

Dawn could feel eyes on her back. Glancing over her shoulder, she watched Ryan waving to the book club like he was a superstar at a rock concert.

'Cut it out.'

Her scolding tone only made him wave more.

'Maybe you could speak to the club one day.' Shaz was looking at Dawn, not Ryan. The intense gaze made her squirm. But when the librarian didn't seem to want to let the question go, Dawn said something she knew she was going to regret.

'Maybe.'

'Wonderful.'

Shaz flicked a switch on the wall and the machine backlight turned on.

'Can we have the microfiche from mid ninety-five to late ninety-six?'

'Of course. Won't take a second.'

She scurried towards a tall cabinet, pulled out a drawer and rummaged through.

'We need to focus on the school. The principal. Grants. Any SRC events and anything to do with Larry Summerset's inheritance or the development.'

'Not my first dance Grave.'

'Sorry. Habit.'

Shaz returned with an armful of folders. Dawn frowned as the librarian dropped them with a thud onto the bench.

'Don't you use microfiche on rolls?'

'No luv. Way too fancy for us. I've been trying to get one of the new machines, but then the council complained all the records are on flat sheets, so a new machine would be useless.'

Dawn shrugged. It made sense. Especially since no one used microfiche anymore. Everything was stored in the cloud, in some databank across the other side of the world or in the case of evidence, in a basement somewhere.

'Thanks. This is going to be slow going.'

'Maybe you can tell me what you're looking for and I can point you in the right direction.'

Dawn glanced at Ryan who shrugged and made a face telling her he wasn't fussed.

'Okay. You said you were on the P & C, when my mum was.'

Shaz nodded.

'Do you know Tom Fletcher?'

'Oh yes. The school principal.'

'Yes, that's the one. I've been told he was on the P & C back when you and mum were. Is our information correct? Secretary or something? Did he have kids at all?'

'Well, I don't know about kids.' Shaz held her fist to her mouth a second. 'Maybe.'

'So why was he there?'

'If my memory serves me well, and it usually does,' Shaz tapped her temple, '—brain's still doing its thing for now—Tom was helping with the grant applications to start with. He was a lawyer back then. Very good one from all accounts, until that nasty incident. He might have become secretary afterwards. I think I finished up around that time.'

'Incident. What happened?'

'Oh, I don't know all the details, but he was disbarred as far as I know.'

'And he's now the principal?'

'Well, someone had to be, and the stuff that supposedly happened was all lies. He told me so himself.'

'Then it must be true.' Dawn kept her tone even, but as Shaz opened the first file to check dates, she turned and rolled her eyes at Ryan who looked as shocked as she was.

'I'll make a call.' He stepped away as Shaz handed Dawn the first wad of microfiche, bound in an elastic band, which was slowly disintegrating from the tropical climate.

Everything made of rubber or plastic fell apart in the humidity. Dawn once owned a pair of riding boots that she popped into the wardrobe, got them out a year later and felt like she was walking on rocks as bits of the soles broke away with every step.

'Oh, sorry about that. I hope it hasn't damaged the film at all.'

'It will be okay. Here, let me take a look. Your ladies over there are waiting for your help by the look of things.'

Shaz glanced at the table where the entire book club had ground to a halt to either watch Dawn, or Ryan as he held his phone to his ear and paced back and forth.

'If you're sure.'

'I'm positive.'

The last thing Dawn needed was a nosy librarian knowing what she found and leaking evidence to a possible suspect.

Shaz shuffled away as Ryan returned.

'I've got Martin looking into the disbarment.'

'We never found a syndicate behind Larry's land deal, did we?'

'No, only the Summerset Trust.'

'I think I'll send Reynolds a message and ask if she can jump on the ASIC site and find out who the trust members are.'

'It's likely only a family trust. Loads of businesspeople have them, to protect their assets from liability.'

Dawn retrieved her mobile as Ryan picked the first film from the top of the pile.

'True, but I've got a hunch.'

Chapter 46

Dawn's eyes were itching from dryness as she handed Ryan another film, filed the previous one and leant over his shoulder to watch as he slid the platform slowly across. Images whizzed by the screen.

They were focussed on the screen when a voice made them jump.

Lisa giggled. 'Sorry. Didn't mean to startle you. What are you doing?'

'Chasing down leads.'

'Any word on Ronnie?'

'No, but now you're here, I have a few questions about Ronnie.'

Dawn glanced at Ryan who nodded for her to go on while he continued the search.

'What is it?' Lisa asked as Dawn led her towards a quiet corner. The only spot far enough away from the Murder Club was two bright, lime-green beanbags set next to a children's bookcase with large picture books on display.

They huddled in the corner, but Dawn didn't bother to sit.

'You remember I said Ronnie asked me what you'd told me—before her phone was broken and the call dropped out?'

Lisa chewed her nails.

'You said you didn't know what she was talking about. You need to think Lisa.'

Her sister pulled her thumbnail from her mouth and bit her lip.

'But I don't know anything. Jessica never got the chance to tell me.'

'I don't think Ronnie was talking about Jessica. I think you and she talked about something else. Something she wants you to remember. It might mean nothing to you, but maybe I'll figure out something from it, or it will give us a lead.'

'When I got back to our place, Abby and Liam were watching *Peppa Pig* reruns. Sara, Ronnie's little one was asleep, and Ronnie was cutting flowers from the garden. But when I told Ronnie what I'd seen, she insisted on driving me to Hopevale.'

'Was Hopevale your idea or hers?'

Lisa clasped her chin with her thumb and forefinger.

'Well, I was thinking of staying at her house. It's huge, you know.'

Dawn nodded. It was more than huge—it was a mansion.

'Why didn't you?'

'Ronnie said it wasn't a good idea. That I should go to Hopevale where no one would find me easily.'

'Surely Brad would have protected you?'

'You'd think so, but now you mention it, Ronnie was pretty nervous when I told her I thought Jessica knew who killed Tracey and we could finally clear Fraser's name.'

'Nervous?

'That's the only way I can describe it. But I guess she would be—after I off-loaded about the body being dumped out at Archer.'

'Did she say anything on the trip to Hopevale?'

'We talked about old times. About Trevor and Brad's degrees. About our kids and how much we loved having them.'

'Nothing else?'

'Not that I can recall.'

Dawn sighed.

'I'm sorry.'

'It's okay. We'll figure it out.'

Dawn returned to Ryan. Lisa followed.

'I have to get back to my next client. I'll let you know if I think of anything else we talked about.'

'Okay. Thanks.'

'Check this out!' Ryan sounded more excited than Dawn had heard him all week. They needed a break in this case. They needed to find Ronnie before she was the next victim in whatever this was.

'What did you find?'

Dawn peered over Ryan's shoulder at the microfiche machine and smiled when she sensed Lisa hovering over her shoulder, peering into the wide, flat projector screen.

'Larry. At the opening of his development on the hill. You'll never guess who's with him.'

Dawn gaped at the screen. 'Tom Fletcher.'

'The disgraced lawyer.'

'Oh my God.' Lisa bolted to attention, fingers over her mouth. '*That's* what we talked about.'

'What?'

'Trevor used to work for Tom Fletcher, before he was disbarred. Trevor bought him out, but later relocated to the city.'

'When was this?'

'I don't know. But after Trevor graduated.'

'So, could Tom Fletcher have brokered the land deal and done the conveyancing?'

Dawn struggled not to jump up and down on the spot, while Ryan pulled out his phone and took a photo of the microfiche article.

'I'd say that's a very likely scenario.'

'Let's get back to the station and find out what Reynolds found from the ASIC search.'

Dawn dragged Lisa by the arm. Ryan was two steps behind her. As they passed the book club table, a collective of eyes traced every step, all the way out the door.

Chapter 47

The threesome crossed the quiet road to Lisa's clinic. Dawn ushered her sister inside.

'Don't leave this place until either Michael, Ryan or I come and get you.'

'What's going on?'

Emily rounded the counter with a worried expression. Dawn put her finger up to her lips to warn her sister to remain quiet, as a buzzing made her pocket vibrate.

'I need to take this.'

She answered without checking the caller ID and put the call on speaker. The voice shouting down the line wasn't Constable Reynolds getting back to her about the ASIC report.

'Dawn! You have to help me!'

'Ronnie?'

Lisa pointed Emily back to her stool and ushered Dawn into her office. Ryan closed the door behind them.

'Where the hell have you been?'

'I can't explain. Not now. You have to stop him Dawn.'

'Stop who?'

'Brad. He's got a gun!'

'A gun? Where is he?'

'At the school.'

'How do you know? Where are you Ronnie?'

'I just do. You need to hurry.' Ronnie was breathless.

'Why the school? What aren't you telling me?'

Dawn yanked the office door open. Ryan pulled his keys from his pocket and dialled a number on his phone. She could hear him talking to Sergeant Martin at the station as they jumped into the car.

Lisa yanked the back door open.

Dawn held her hand over the microphone. 'You can't come.'

'Abby is at the school.' Lisa glared. Dawn waved her hand submissively, dragging her seatbelt on and returning her focus to Ronnie.

'We're on our way, but you need to give me more to go on, Ronnie. Where have you been? Why is Brad taking a gun to school?'

'I don't know.'

'Is he going to hurt the kids?'

Ryan flicked a switch. Lights flashed as he backed away from Lisa's work.

'I don't think so.'

'Is this about Tom Fletcher? How does the principal fit into all this?'

'Not now, Dawn. Please. Brad hasn't been himself since …'

Dawn could hear the tears in her friend's voice.

'Since when Ronnie?'

'Get the kids, Dawn. Make sure they're safe and please, don't shoot Brad.'

'Shoot him! You don't seriously think he's going to hurt anyone?'

'Not now Dawn. Please!'

'We're on our way. Don't hang up on me.'

The sound of fabric over the phone muffled Ronnie's words. A deep voice growled in the background.

Is that the same voice I heard when Ronnie was attacked?

She didn't get a chance to contemplate for long.

'That's the guy I heard last Friday. Out at Archer.'

The blood drained from Lisa's face as she leant forward, trying to listen as the voice faded, and the sound of some sort of scuffle filled the phone.

'You're sure?'

Lisa nodded.

'Ronnie. Can you hear me?'

'I told you to let it go missy.'

The line went dead.

Ryan added the siren to the strobing lights.

Chapter 48

The car slid on the hot, moist bitumen as Ryan steered the vehicle into a parking spot. Dawn was out of her seatbelt before the vehicle came to a complete halt. As she flung the door open, the blaring of the lockdown siren sent tingles down her spine.

'He's here. But where?'

'How did Veronica know he was here?'

Ryan pulled his weapon from his shoulder holster. Dawn retrieved her handgun and tossed the bag back on the front seat … She didn't even recall slamming the door as she scanned the grass and pathways.

'She has to be around here.'

'Who was the guy?'

'I've got a pretty good idea, but I can't figure out how he managed to dump Jessica's body. He's too old and frail for that.'

'And why go after Ronnie?'

Dawn heard Lisa's door slam. 'You stay here!'

'Not on your life. I'm going to Abby's classroom.'

'The school is in lockdown. No one in or out.'

'I might look like a peace-loving hippy to you, but don't let my looks fool you. I'm getting Abby out of here.'

Dawn wanted to argue, but there was no point. Lisa wasn't confrontational, but she could certainly be pig-headed when she wanted to be.

'Stay away from the office. I've got an idea I know why Brad is here.'

Dawn held her gun low, in both hands and jogged towards the office entrance as the sound of emergency services sirens grew louder.

'Backup is on the way. We should wait.' Ryan was right behind her, despite his words of caution.

'I can talk Brad down.'

'You sound confident.'

'I'm not sure, but I've got an idea what's been going on. Once the grant paperwork comes through, we'll know for sure, but it wasn't until we saw those pictures, from the paper, and Michael mentioned the scrutiny Jessica was putting on the grant money, in particular the older grant funds, that it clicked.'

A scream stopped Dawn, as she reached out to open the office door.

Peering through the glass, she watched Rhianna being shoved down the hall—Brad's weapon pointed at the base of her skull.

'Let's go,' she whispered, then opened the glass door, listened a moment, then stepped inside. Hugging the left side of the foyer, she waited as Ryan shimmied up against her and tapped her on the shoulder.

Step by step, she inched her way to the corner, where the hallway intersected the foyer. Glancing around, she saw Rhianna and Brad disappear into Tom Fletcher's office.

'They've gone into the principal's office.'

'What now?'

'Now I try to call Brad.'

Dawn punched numbers on her mobile phone. Her finger hovered over the call button.

'You think he'll answer?'

'Worth a try? He's got two hostages, and I don't think Cooktown has a resident hostage negotiator handy.'

'You got that right, but you're not …'

'On this investigation. I know, but I know Brad.'

'You've not seen him for twenty years.'

'Nearly twenty-one, but who's counting.'

Dawn pressed the green call button. Her heart thudded in her throat. Body heat radiated from Ryan, who was pressed up against her, gun at the ready, eyes scanning behind him and down the hall in the opposite direction.

'Come on Brad. Pick up.'

The call rang out.

She pressed *call* again and waited ten rings, drew a deep breath and yelled at the top of her voice.

'Pick it up, Brad. Ronnie's in trouble!'

Ryan jumped.

The call connected.

'What the hell are you …'

'Shut up and listen Brad. Don't talk. Don't even grunt. Ronnie's life depends on it.'

For once in his life, Brad didn't have a smart-arse remark for her.

'Ned's got Ronnie. You've got Tom. I'm not exactly sure of the connection yet, but I know there is one and I think you know what it is.'

Dawn watched Ryan's eyes widen. He dug into his pocket, retrieved his phone and dialled. She heard him asking for a search. One she hoped would put the pieces together.

The sound of Rhianna sobbing, and Tom Fletcher calmly trying to talk his way out of the situation distracted Brad for a second.

'Shut up!' He yelled at his hostages, no doubt waving his loaded rifle for good effect.

'Brad. Listen to me. I'm still gathering evidence, but I think I know why you're there, after Tom.'

His breathing was ragged, but he was listening.

'You thought he had Ronnie. I guess in a way, he does now, but he didn't. She saw you coming in with the gun and called me.'

The lockdown siren continued to blare. Dawn put her finger in one ear to try and block it out.

'Brad. I can put him away. I'm waiting on a few grant reports to seal the deal, but I need your testimony to make sure he goes down for murder. Can you give me that?'

The desktop phone rang in the principal's office. The sound carried down Brad's phone.

She covered her phone mic.

'Get the bloody switchboard shut down,' she hissed at Ryan, who was still on the phone, waiting for an answer about why old man Ned was involved.

'We're trying. But you might want to know, Ned is Tom's stepfather.'

'There's our connection. The drunk old bastard didn't look like he could hurt a fly.'

She took her hand away to speak, but what she heard over the line sent a cold chill down her spine. Loud voices came over the phone and down the hall. Dawn advanced. Ryan tried to grab her arm but missed.

Cursing, he followed.

'Brad. What's going on?'

Dawn spoke into the phone as pieces of conversation echoed down the phone and through the door.

She was almost there.

'Let her go or I'll shoot you …'

'… the balls … get …'

Rhianna screamed. Dawn's blood ran cold, her heart rate jumped, and a thud hit the wall inside.

'I'm going in.'

Dawn put her hand on the door, hoping it wasn't locked. Relief washed over her as the knob turned in her hand. Another scream forced her to hurry. Thrusting the door open, she hit something, someone. Gun in hand, Ryan right behind.

'Police! Put your weapons down!'

Rhianna was huddled in the corner, tears streaking her mascara and running down her face. Brad was on the ground, scrounging for his gun. She stepped on the barrel. He tried to slide it free, but Ryan landed on top of him in a dive to rival her swimming career.

A grunt, then a crack made her cringe. Turning, she studied Tom Fletcher, reclined in his high-back chair like he'd just finished a board meeting.

His smarmy smile made her shiver.

'Thank you, Detective.'

He rose, circled around the table.

'Don't move. Hands where I can see them.'

'Surely you don't think I'm armed?'

'I can see you aren't, but tell me—is your stepfather?'

Tom Fletcher's eyes widened, then narrowed to slits as his lip curled in a half grin, half snarl.

Chapter 49

Dawn shoved Brad out the front door to a barrage of angry parents. But a hum of silence washed over them as Ryan nudged the principal forward with one hand on his shoulder, the other holding his cuffed hands at his back.

'Will someone turn that bloody siren off!' Sergeant Martin stormed up the path. 'And get these parents back.'

A chorus of voices called out to the sergeant.

'Where are the kids?'

'I want to pick up …'

He raised his hands, turned to the growing crowd and pressed his palms down a few times like he was patting heads.

'Give us a minute to ensure the threat is over, then we'll let the children out, one class at a time.'

He turned to Dawn as she held the rifle between thumb and forefinger by the barrel.

He pulled on a pair of gloves before taking it from her.

'I'll get the forensic team in.'

'Make sure they search the office thoroughly.'

'Will do.'

'Ned has Ronnie.'

'Ned!'

'Yes. Didn't the senior tell you?'

'No.'

'Ryan got him to run a search, and Ned is Tom Fletcher's stepfather. He grabbed Ronnie when she called to tell me Brad was here, with the gun. I think she managed to escape whoever tried to grab her from the house, but Ned tracked her down.'

'And you think he might still be around? Why Ronnie?'

'He's in this with Tom.'

'In what?'

'Chase those grant reports and do a financial check on Tom, Ned and Brad's accounts. We need to know who all the directors of the Summerset Trust are. Reynolds was getting the details. Not sure if they've come through yet.'

'Reynolds, Jamison. Grab these two bozos and take them to the station. Keep them apart. No visitors until we get there.'

'I want my lawyer,' Tom Fletcher piped up as Jamison took over from Ryan.

'I thought *you* were a lawyer.' She heard Jamison chuckling at his own joke as he led the school principal away.

'I'm guessing Trevor won't be representing him.'

Dawn glanced around, doing a slow circle, trying to get her bearings. Rhianna limped towards her with the aid of a paramedic.

'Where's Abby's class? Lisa should be here with her by now.'

Her stomach knotted.

Rhianna stopped. The paramedic held her arm firmly against her chest in a sling.

'If you go left of the office, she's in the third building on the right side.'

'Thanks Rhianna. I'm sorry you had to go through that. You did very well!'

'By well you mean I screamed my head off until I nearly passed out.'

Dawn smiled, tapped her good arm and squeezed.

'Better than getting in the way.'

Rhianna shrugged, pursed her lips and nodded, seemingly happy with the backhanded compliment.

'Let's check on Abby and Lisa.'

Dawn strode down the concrete path towards the schoolrooms. Passing the first one, she saw the class teacher opening the door.

'Everyone, line up along the veranda. I'm going to do a head count, then we can get you on the way home.'

'Maybe the teacher didn't let Lisa in the classroom. That would make sense during a lockdown.' Dawn hoped that was true.

'Maybe.' Ryan didn't sound very sure.

Butterflies flitted in Dawn's stomach as they approached the third building. It was deadly quiet for a class of grade one children.

As Dawn stepped onto the veranda, she caught a glimpse through the window, which explained everything.

She stepped back, but it was too late. The occupants had already seen her. Silently, she kept her hand at her side, below the window height and directed Ryan around the back of the building.

Tugging her earlobe, she indicated he needed to listen in. Ryan hesitated a moment. She waved her hand more frantically. Finally, he nodded and disappeared around the side of the classroom, a heartbeat before a familiar figure stepped out under the shade of the veranda.

His eyes were narrowed, but bright. Nothing like the last time she saw him, leaning against the bar, barely able to stand.

Was it an act?

She hadn't realised it at the time, but now she thought about it, Ned showed an unusual interest in Abby and Lisa at the front bar during lunch.

Did he hear Ronnie's call?

'Ned. What's going on?'

Her voice was calm. Her insides writhed.

'You are a smart little missy, aren't you?'

'I like to think so.'

Dawn studied Lisa, whose eyes were wide, but despite the knife Ned pressed against her chest, her sister appeared composed.

She stepped forward. 'What now?'

'That's far enough.'

Ned tapped the knife against Lisa's breastbone.

'Brad's under arrest. I'm not sure why you've grabbed Ronnie, though. Maybe you'd like to put down the knife and tell me all about it?'

Dawn glanced through the classroom window, but quickly looked back to Ned. She'd seen Ronnie inside, unconscious on the floor. At least she hoped she was only unconscious. Abby and Liam were crouched alongside her. The class teacher hovered over Ronnie.

'You need to let Tom go.'

'We will, after he's given his statement. We can't hold Brad long without his witness statement.'

'Don't play dumb with me missy. I know you. You're exactly like your mum. Can't keep your pointy nose out of it.'

The investigation was closing in, but it wasn't blown open when he tried to grab Ronnie. It was a brazen move. Or maybe a desperate one.

The lightbulb flicked on. Ronnie was a witness. So was Brad. Without witnesses, it was only white-collar crime, not murder. And even then, a good lawyer could possibly get them off. The evidence was still so slim.

Her reply was on the tip of her tongue, but then Ned's comment about her mother sank in. She blinked as her brain digested the information. It was the second time he'd mentioned her mum being nosy.

Ben told her Ned used to drink with her dad. Did her dad tell Ned of her mum's suspicions about the grant money? Or was it the possible affair they talked about?

'Why don't you put the knife down and we can talk about this.'

'I can't let this one live. She's seen too much.'

'It was dark. I didn't see anything.'

'Lisa. Shut up.'

Her sister gaped at her a moment, then pressed her lips together firmly. Dawn risked a glance inside the classroom. It was a mistake. Ryan was leaning through the rear fire-exit, waving for the children to come out.

Ned followed her gaze, then shoved Lisa towards the doorway. Dawn needed to think fast.

'Ned. There is only one good way out of this. You need to stop.'

'You should have stayed in the city.'

Ned dragged Lisa through the door, slammed it closed with his foot and locked it. Panic erupted inside.

The teacher scampered back from Ronnie and Ryan made a last-ditch effort to grab a child under each arm and run for it. Dawn saw two more children scurry away in front of him.

'Sit down! Shut up!' Ned screamed.

Chairs slid across the floor, as children squealed and scampered back under the tables on their hands and knees. They huddled together in small groups, eyes wide, faces streaked with tears. The teacher softly cooed to them.

Abby, who hadn't left Ronnie's side, jumped to her feet, and threw her hands on her hips. Her flushed cheeks and blonde ringlets were out of place amongst the mayhem.

A voice behind Dawn made her jump.

Michael grabbed her arm and pulled her away from the windows. 'I've got an idea.'

Chapter 50

Sergeant Martin appeared from the rear of the building, a little girl on either side, squeezing the life out of his huge hands.

Ryan was right behind him, carrying the two children he'd helped through the fire exit before Ned rushed back inside.

Dawn gawked at Michael. 'You can't be serious!'

'Hear me out.'

A petite, auburn-haired paramedic stepped up and pried one of the children from Ryan's grip. 'Come on sweetheart. I'm going to check you over and then mummy is waiting in the car park for you. That's it.'

The little girl sniffed away tears, wiped her face with the back of her hand and held her arms out to the freedom offered by the ambulance officer.

'Grant is going to help you out, mate,' she promised the boy on Ryan's left hip. He nodded and shimmied down as another paramedic asked him his name.

Dawn turned back to Michael as he finished laying out his plan.

'You should consider a different career there, mate.' Sergeant Martin nodded he liked the plan.

'It's risky. What if he doesn't let anyone out? They could all choke on the smoke.'

'When the visibility gets to a dangerous level, the sprinkler system will activate,' Michael assured her.

'Can we get a sniper here, just in case? That's my sister in there at knifepoint and I think Ronnie is already seriously injured.'

'We don't have a sniper. Tactical are too far away.'

Martin rubbed his chin but turned at an unexpected voice.

'I'll do it.' The senior constable stepped forward. An assault rifle with a laser scope was slung over his shoulder.

'Got this out when I heard the second call on the radio.'

'Are you any good with that?' Ryan's tone wasn't mocking. They all wanted to be sure no one else but Ned was going to get hurt if the plan went awry.

'He'll do alright,' the sergeant assured them.

'Okay. Get into position Senior.'

Dawn waited for him to move.

The senior chewed the inside of his lip. 'Did one of these guys actually kill Jessica?'

'Yes, and probably, most likely …' Dawn considered how to break this to the girl's uncle, '… Tracey too.'

The senior stopped chewing, changed to biting his lip, but said nothing. Turning, he jogged away to find a position where he could get a shot off if needed.

'Okay. Everyone clear what they're doing?' Dawn scanned the faces. Ryan grinned. She wasn't sure if it was because she was giving the orders, or nervous tension. It didn't matter. She wasn't letting anyone else run a rescue operation when her sister's and niece's lives were at risk.

'Let's get this corroboree started then.' She nodded for Michael to take up position. Her palms sweated as she waited for him to appear on the other side of the building.

Waving his firesticks in the air, he smiled, ducked down and made his way up onto the veranda unseen.

Dropping to his haunches in front of the door, he put one stick on the concrete veranda, the other on top with a wad of coconut fibre scrunched on top.

Dawn watched him rub the two sticks together, the coconut fibre in between. Within seconds the rough hair-like material began to smoke. At first, she was afraid he'd set the whole building alight, but as she watched the tendrils of smoke find their way under the door, she sighed with relief.

Ned placed Lisa between him and the door, in case they breached. She was the first to start coughing.

Ned was a canny old bastard and certainly seemed comfortable using the bowie knife he held at Lisa's throat. She wondered if he might be military trained.

The children remained cowering under the tables, as smoke slowly drifted inside and rose to the ceiling.

Dawn peeked around the corner of the building, catching a glimpse of Ned as he strode across the room, grabbed Lisa and pulled her away from the door. Holding her to his chest, he screamed for Dawn to show herself.

'You are as big a pain in my butt as your mother was.'

'What's he talking about?' Sergeant Martin hissed from behind her.

'I don't think my mum ran out on us, Ross.'

The sergeant sucked in a breath. 'Triple homicide?'

'Maybe my brother too.'

Michael fanned the smouldering coconut husk and added a handful of gum leaves. Under different circumstances, the scent would have been soothing.

'You'll kill all these kids,' Ned coughed.

'You need to come out, Ned. I told you, there's only one good way out of this alive.'

Dawn turned to Sergeant Martin and whispered, 'Everyone ready?'

He nodded.

She scanned over his shoulder to see Ryan stalking towards the fire-exit. The sergeant unclipped the gun at his waist and retrieved his Taser from the front of his utility vest.

'Let's do this.'

Dawn turned to Michael and gave him a thumbs-up signal.

The ranger fanned the fire, kicking up another batch of smoke that filtered under the front door and rose instantly to create a thick blanket across the ceiling.

'What the hell are you doing?' Ned's voice was growing raspy.

Dawn could hear children beginning to cough and hoped the paramedics were ready. They could have tried to shoot Ned, but this way was better for the kids. They didn't need to see a man's head blown off right in front of them.

Another puff of smoke entered the room. Visibility was almost gone in the top half of the room now. The alarm made everyone jump. The sound of sirens in the distance wasn't unexpected. They'd been called earlier, parked nearby, and were ready to deploy as soon as the fire detectors activated.

It was the next phase everyone held their breath for. Dawn stepped up onto the veranda. Hunched down low, below the windows, she couldn't be seen. Sergeant Martin followed along behind her.

Michael stamped the fire out. Dawn waved him away. He hesitated, but stepped back like they planned.

She couldn't explain why, but the guy was growing on her and the last thing she wanted was to see him get hurt.

Screams erupted from inside as the sprinkler system activated. Water began streaming from under the door in seconds. Now was their chance.

Sergeant Martin stepped back, lifted the battering ram he carried and swung. The door crashed open, thudding against the wall and bouncing back. As wood splintered in all directions, Dawn scurried in.

The room was chaotic. Ronnie lay on the floor, Abby and Liam by her side. Ryan entered through the fire exit—gun drawn.

'Put your weapon down!' Dawn yelled.

'Police. Get down on the ground.'

Sergeant Martin went left, gun in hand as he rounded on Ned. Dawn's heart leapt to her throat when she saw Lisa on her knees, a handful of hair in Ned's hand. He dragged her to her feet. She screamed, holding her hair with her hands as she scrambled to her feet.

Ryan and the teacher rounded up the children and hurried them out through the fire-exit. Dawn turned to see Abby and Liam unmoving by Ronnie.

'Abby. Get your butt outside.'

The little girl's eyes weren't wide with fear. They were squinted, her brow furrowed.

'Let my mummy go.' She jumped to her feet, dragging Liam with her.

'Abby. Not now, sweetheart. You need to go with Detective Ryan.'

'Do what Auntie Dawn says, baby.' Lisa begged, until the knife touched her throat.

'Ned. What's the plan? You wanted to eliminate a witness, but now you've got three, four, maybe more in her place. This isn't going to help.'

Dawn focussed down the line of her weapon as she spoke. She had a shot, but then Lisa shifted. She couldn't risk hitting her sister. She also didn't want to kill Ned in front of Abby.

Sergeant Martin glanced over his shoulder, and she knew what he was thinking.

Did the senior constable have a shot?

'You should have stayed in the city.'

'This would have come out eventually, Ned. Nothing stays secret forever. Who killed Jessica? You, or Tom?'

The children were all gone, except Abby and Liam who remained at Ronnie's side. Dawn avoided looking past Ned. Instead, she forced herself to fix her gaze on his.

His eyes watched her like a hawk.

'That money wasn't theirs.'

'What money? The grant money?'

'Bloody waste. They sniff it or piss it up the wall.'

'You're talking about the Indigenous grants.'

'Bloody politically correct bullshit.'

'Jessica was a smart kid. She wasn't going to waste any grant money. It wasn't wasted on her.' Dawn suppressed the rage rising through her body. 'You're just making up a crap excuse, trying to justify your theft.'

'I've paid taxes all my life. That money is my money, not theirs.'

Dawn thought the only tax Ned ever paid was alcohol tax, but now wasn't the time to goad him.

'So, you killed a girl to get to the money?'

Ned's lips curled. Lisa wriggled, but the old man tightened his grip on her hair. She winced. Dawn watched the sergeant out the corner of her eye. He stepped forward, drawing Ned's attention.

'You stay right there, Ross.'

The tip of the Bowie knife prodded into Lisa's neck, nicking the skin. A trickle of blood ran down her neck.

The sound of sobbing caught Dawn by surprise. She risked a glance behind her, expecting Abby to be the cause, but the tears were Liam's.

Abby hugged her friend. Dawn's heart nearly exploded. She turned back, catching a glimpse of Ryan coming back into the room through the fire-exit.

Her eyes rested on him too long. Ned turned.

'Stay right where you are. No heroics today. This little lady and me are heading out that door and you are all going to stay right where you are.'

'Ned. I promise you, if anything happens to my sister, you're going to wish you were dead.'

Ned grinned, like he enjoyed the challenge. None of this was making any sense. Was he trying to get himself killed?

Then it hit her. That's exactly what he was doing.

'You're covering for Tom. Right? But why? He's only your step-kid. Not your flesh and blood.'

'I'm not covering for anyone. I wanted the money. Those bitches were going to blow the deal.'

'But you aren't the only one who got the money.'

'I'm not talking anymore. You two, get over there.'

Ned nodded from Ryan to Sergeant Martin, to the corner of the room behind Dawn.

'I'm going out the back. Don't follow. I'll let your sister go when I'm out of town.'

A flicker of khaki flashed past the fire-exit. Dawn focussed on Ned as he backed out the door, dragging Lisa with him.

As his back cleared the fire-exit, his grip on Lisa loosened. She darted away, as the knife hit the ground, a microsecond before Ned.

Ryan and Martin rushed forward. Dawn met Lisa, gripping her in a tight hug as Michael appeared in the fire-exit doorway, grinning from ear to ear, his firestick in hand.

Chapter 51

Cars of all shapes, colours and sizes lined the school road as far as the eye could see. A news helicopter circled overhead as Dawn carried Abby to Ryan's car. Lines of children from outlying areas were being loaded into school buses.

Ahead, Sergeant Martin drove a police four-wheel drive, escorting them through the traffic, lights flashing, no sirens. Dawn knew Ned was in the rear of the same vehicle. She'd put the cuffs on him herself, not bothering to be gentle.

From the back seat, she watched Ryan and Michael in the front—stern faced and pensive. Lisa held Abby. Dawn held Lisa, fussing over the trickle of blood at her neck.

'Is Auntie Ronnie going to be okay?' Abby asked, her eyes brimming with unshed tears.

'The paramedic said she will be fine Abby, but we'll go with Liam's nana and visit her tomorrow. Okay?'

The little girl nodded, then peered up at her mother.

'Mummy is going to be okay too, Abby. I promise.' Dawn was going to make sure of it.

Ryan glanced over his shoulder, as if reading her mind.

'None of this makes sense, Ryan. Ned is an old man. He didn't …' she glanced at Abby. '… commit this crime.'

'I heard his voice.'

Lisa shook herself, as though she'd woken from a deep sleep. Dawn knew it was shock setting in.

'You should have gone to the hospital.'

She rubbed her sister's shoulders, trying to warm her despite the heat.

'He was there Dawn.'

'I believe you. But he wasn't alone. Ryan, we need those company records. The grant paperwork.'

'Reynolds has it. We'll go over it, then *I'll* interview Summerset, Clements and Fletcher.'

Dawn rolled her eyes as Ryan glanced back.

'Don't give me that look. You can't do the interviews. The last thing we want is a judge overturning the case on a technicality.'

Dawn caught Ryan's eye in the rear-view mirror and sighed. He was right. But they were all going to lawyer up and so far, all the evidence was circumstantial. Even if the financials or grant records implicated them in dodgy deals and ripping off the government, nothing was going to tie them to the murders.

'I've got an idea.'

'I can tell I'm not going to like it already.'

Ryan fixed his gaze on the road ahead as Dawn outlined her plan.

'That could work.' Michael nodded and smiled.

Ryan scoffed. 'You're a park ranger, not a cop and there are so many things that could go wrong with it.'

Michael said nothing. Dawn forged on.

'But Trevor and Brad didn't hurt anyone. I'm sure of it.'

'What makes you say that?'

'Because I grew up with them. They were Fraser's friends and there's been something off with Brad since I got here. Ronnie said it herself. I think he actually believed Fraser was responsible for Tracey, until he found out who actually did it.'

Dawn was careful with her language. Aware Abby was listening to every word, despite her eyes being closed. The little girl was a livewire and never missed anything going on around her.

'Brad always had a crush on Tracey. If he thought Fraser didn't do it, for all these years, he would have told me. I think he only found out recently.' Lisa stroked Abby's hair as the six-year-old dribbled on her shoulder. Maybe she was asleep after all.

It was an eventful afternoon. Dawn was thankful her niece wasn't waking in a cold sweat after what they'd been through. Still, there was tonight to get through.

'Alright. Run it by Martin first. It's not my station.'

'It's your investigation Ryan.'

Ryan parked outside the police station and turned to Lisa. 'Maybe Michael can take you home, with my car.'

He scanned Michael's face.

'On it.'

Michael hopped out of the passenger's seat and was outside Ryan's door before Lisa could protest.

Dawn reached for her hand and squeezed.

'All the likely suspects are in jail, but Michael will stay. Won't you?'

Dawn glanced into Michael's eyes and saw a tenderness there.

'Of course. I won't let anything happen to you, Lisa. And Abby looks like she's done for the day. I can carry her upstairs.'

'Thanks. All of you.' Lisa studied her hands, wrapped around her daughter tightly.

'When I decided to meet with Jessica, out at Archer Point, I was sure it would clear Fraser. Jessica suggested as much. But it all went so horribly wrong.'

'Why did Jessica want to meet out there? She had to drive illegally to make the trip. Why Archer?'

'I honestly don't know. Maybe she thought I'd remember something about Tracey's death?'

'No. I don't think so. I think there is something else. Jessica was a junior ranger. Maybe she found something out there?'

'We found the piece of fabric on the beach. It can't have been there all those years,' Michael reminded her as he slipped into the driver's seat and Ryan stepped aside, closing the door.

'You're right. How did it get there? And why?'

'Let's get going. Maybe one of our suspects can shed some light.' Ryan rounded the bonnet and waited outside Dawn's door. She kissed her sister on the cheek, touched her finger to her lips and gently dabbed Abby's cheek, then turned to find the door open.

'When did you get chivalrous?'

She slipped out. Ryan didn't step back. 'Don't get used to it.' He held her gaze a moment.

'Let's see if we can get a plea deal for the twins, in exchange for the truth about who's behind all this.'

Chapter 52

Dawn opened the door to the first interview room. Trevor jumped up, then slowly sank back down into his chair, alongside his brother. Brad's eyes were fixed on his hands, clasped together on the table, knuckles white.

'What are you doing here?' Trevor didn't hide his distaste.

'I'm not here as a cop.'

'Because you have no jurisdiction here.'

'True. I'm a consultant, but I've got sway. I'm here to make you an offer.'

'No deals. Brad didn't do anything wrong.'

'What about you?'

'Are you charging my client?'

Dawn laughed aloud. 'I told you. I'm not here to charge anyone. I'm here to make sure Brad doesn't do a life sentence for murder.'

'Murder!'

Trevor lifted his nose into the air. 'He's on a mental health directive. He waved a gun around. I'll get him off with a psychiatric reference in a heartbeat.'

'We're … Detective Ryan and the sergeant are still gathering evidence, but they have enough to charge you both with financial fraud.'

Trevor sat back, exhaled, ran his hand through his hair and pressed his lips together.

'Here's what I know.'

'Is this being taped?'

'No. I'm here as a friend. I told you already. We're after a murderer. In exchange for Brad's testimony, we'll do all we can to minimise the fraud charges. I'm guessing you started ripping off the grant money back when you were at school. A judge will take that into consideration. You were only kids. I don't think you masterminded this.'

Brad finally glanced up, meeting her eyes.

'I didn't kill anyone.'

'Be quiet, Brad. I'll do the talking.' Trevor interrupted, then glanced at his brother. Wrapping an arm around Brad's shoulder, he squeezed. A tear rolled down Brad's face.

'I believe you. You thought Fraser killed Tracey, until you found out about Jessica.'

Dawn watched Trevor closely, trying to read exactly how much he knew about the whole scheme.

'How *did* you find out about Jessica?' Dawn held Brad's gaze as he opened his mouth to speak.

'Don't answer that.' Trevor was quick and focussed. Still the lawyer, despite the circumstances. Dawn was mildly impressed.

'This all sounds like a fishing expedition. If you had any real evidence, you'd be charging my client.'

'Oh, I'm not authorised to charge anyone, as I've told you. But have no doubt, Brad is facing charges. Assault. Unlawful use of a firearm. I'm sure Detective Ryan will think of something else to add and it won't take long for all the paperwork to come through about the fraud charges. Brad is the auditor. He must have known.'

Trevor bit his lip. Brad sat back in his chair, pulled his shoulders back, appearing to rally.

'I'd like to see Veronica now. Is she alright?'

'She's recovering. But she's still unconscious. I'm sure I can arrange a visit soon, but you're still being held for questioning for now.'

Dawn knew Trevor wouldn't complain. Time was on his side. The fact Brad hadn't been charged yet was a good thing, and the lawyer knew it.

'You'll get one shot to roll on whoever is driving this train. I'll give you a bit of time to consider it.'

Dawn slowly rose, then stopped.

'You've got young children Brad. Ask yourself when you'll see them again, if you keep quiet.'

Dawn opened the interview door, hesitating, hoping Brad would speak up. When he didn't, she stepped through and closed the door behind her.

Ryan met her in the hallway. Sergeant Martin a step behind. 'I thought you had him for a second.'

'So did I.'

They made their way back down the hallway to the main office area. Sergeant Martin strode down the centre to the whiteboard, turned and pointed at Reynolds.

'ASIC report.'

'Yes, sir.'

'Who are the directors of the Summerset Trust?'

Reynolds wore a grin from ear to ear as she rolled her chair back and strutted towards the sergeant and plucked a whiteboard marker off the shelf below the board.

'Larry, Trevor and Brad Summerset. And you'll never guess who else?'

'Tom Fletcher,' Dawn offered.

'How did you know?'

'Call it instinct. Do we have Fairweather's bank records yet?'

'Here.' Constable Jamison held a wad of paperwork in his left hand. Ryan was closest. Stepping forward, he reached for it and began scanning.

Dawn watched as a smile crept across his face.

'I knew that new-model Prius was outside his pay grade.'

Dawn scooted around behind him. 'That's a lot of money.'

'And it's every month.'

Ryan shuffled through the paperwork, then tossed it down on Jamison's desk.

'Let's get Fairweather back in here, and I need someone going through Tom Fletcher's financials with a fine-tooth comb.' Sergeant Martin snatched the whiteboard marker from Reynolds' hand and used it as a pointer.

'We need to charge Fletcher or take his statement about Brad's attack and let him go very soon, so let's get cracking, people. I'll get a warrant for Fletcher's phone records. Reynolds, I need you and Jamison going over the receipts for the grant money. Anything weird, I want to know about it.'

The room exploded into action.

'I want the CCTV footage from the school. Where the hell is it?' Dawn scanned the faces in the room.

'It arrived this morning, before all hell broke loose.' Reynolds started typing on her computer, then slipped out of the chair. 'Here. I've queued it up for you.'

Dawn slid into the seat, adjusted the height, checked the time stamp on the footage and set it running.

'Don't you want to come with me to get Fairweather?'

Dawn glanced up as Ryan hovered over her shoulder. 'I want to see this footage first. I've got a hunch it is going to help put all this information together.'

'I'll wait then.'

She wasn't sure if it was the adrenalin of seeing the investigation coming together or if it was Ryan's body heat, but a flush hit her system like a hot iron.

Shaking it free, she upped the playback speed and watched the stream of children leaving school until the school resembled a ghost town.

Her heart rate kicked up a notch as a white Prius pulled into the parking lot.

'That's Fairweather's car.' Ryan said.

She checked the time stamp.

'Three forty-five. Well after school finished.'

They watched the footage continue. Sergeant Martin's phone pinged in his pocket. He glanced at it as Dawn looked up.

'Warrant is in. I'll pull the financials. Keep me in the loop.'

He rushed to his office. Dawn's eyes returned to the screen to see Jessica get into the vehicle.

Ryan patted her shoulder.

'Let's go pick him up.'

Chapter 53

The interview room was brightly lit. Dawn paced inside the adjoining room, her heart rate quickening as she watched Ryan enter and read Fairweather his rights.

'I want my lawyer.'

'Let me guess. Trevor Summerset is your lawyer.'

'You know he is.'

'How convenient. He's already here with …'

Ryan glanced at Sergeant Martin like he genuinely needed a reminder. The sergeant grinned.

'Sorry. There are so many suspects here. I can't recall exactly who's representing who.'

'Trevor is representing all of them.' Martin answered the question with the answer Ryan knew was coming.

'Really? That's got to be some sort of conflict of interest, doesn't it?'

Martin shrugged. 'It's a small town.'

'What are you talking about?' Fairweather looked ready to implode. His cheeks were flushed. Sweat ran down his forehead like a marathon runner.

'This is all Dawn Grave's doing. That bitch has had it in for me for years.'

Ryan and Martin turned their gaze on Fairweather. Dawn felt the chill in the room, despite the glass between her and them.

'This is about Jessica Mills, Mr Fairweather.' Ryan's voice was deadly calm.

'And Tracey Warren,' Martin added.

Fairweather's mouth dropped open. 'What?'

'We have camera footage from outside the school showing you picking up Jessica after school on the Friday she died.'

Fairweather sat a moment, stunned.

Did he not know the cameras were there?

'I want my lawyer.'

He sat back, crossed his arms over his chest and huffed.

'Trevor is busy with Brad Summerset, Tom Fletcher and Ned Clements,' Ryan offered with a grin.

'Trevor's a busy boy. You're in deep for picking up Jessica after school, but we've received some financials to link you to a huge fraud racket. Maybe I should organise a court-appointed lawyer for you? You're going to need one.' Sergeant Martin leant in close. His features almost fatherly. Even Dawn was convinced.

Fairweather's face paled. 'What financials?'

'Money, deposited into your account from the Summerset Trust. We're still digging, but does government fraud ring a bell for you?'

Fairweather started to speak, but Ryan cut him off.

'I think you get more jail time for ripping off the government than murder these days anyway. Don't you?' Ryan glanced at the sergeant who nodded.

'Then there's the sexual assault charges. You know, when they hit the media, I'm sure we'll get a few more young girls coming forward and everyone knows how much inmates love child molesters.'

Ryan was bluffing, but Fairweather didn't know they couldn't yet prove he'd molested Jessica. Still, Dawn would be pressing her own charges soon and then hopefully more women *would* come forward.

A stab of guilt hit Dawn in the chest. Maybe if she'd come forward twenty years ago, Jessica would still be alive.

She shook her head. Fairweather didn't kill Jessica. She was sure of it, or there'd be a trail of bodies to find.

No other missing cases fit his MO. They'd checked and come up empty.

'I never killed anyone.'

'That's what Brad said, too.'

Ryan nodded at the sergeant's statement. 'You're right. He did.'

Dawn watched Ryan study Fairweather closely, looking for any micro-expression that would tell him he'd hit the right suspect.

'Or maybe it was Clements who killed Jessica?'

Ryan waited a second. Nothing.

'I'm thinking Fletcher?' Sergeant Martin added.

Fairweather's eyelashes flickered.

'You get one chance at avoiding a murder charge and life in prison Fairweather. This is it.'

Ryan shoved a pad and pen across the interview desk. Fairweather blinked at it, biting his lip so hard Dawn thought he might draw blood. As he picked up the pen, she let out a breath so hard, her cheeks hurt.

They'd need more than his testimony to nail Tom Fletcher for Jessica's death. They could hold him now, if Fairweather's statement implicated him like she suspected, but he'd wriggle out of it without evidence to back it up.

She could hear the smarmy bastard already. Telling them it was his word against a sexual predator. There was no doubt in Dawn's mind that Fletcher knew Fairweather's weakness. No doubt he'd exploited it all these years.

Her hands were shaking by the time Fairweather handed the pad back to Ryan and the detective studied the statement.

'We'll be remanding you in custody for now.'

Fairweather opened his mouth to protest.

'You're up to your neck in this. Don't push me. I'd be happy to see you hang for preying on young women like you do, but unfortunately we don't have the death penalty anymore.'

Ryan slid his chair back. Dawn shuddered as the metal legs scraped on the commercial lino floor.

Sergeant Martin followed Ryan out the door. Dawn met them in the hallway.

'Let's go pin the bastard to the wall.'

Ryan waved the statement in his hand.

'We can't. He'll lawyer up and claim Fairweather is scum and can't be trusted. I can see it already.'

Dawn grabbed the statement and read.

'This doesn't say he witnessed the murder.'

'You want to let him walk?' Ryan glanced at the sergeant.

'Dawn's right. We need to make sure when we charge Fletcher, we have enough to overwhelm him.'

'And how do you propose we do that?'

'Ned Clements.'

'His stepfather, what about him?'

'Lisa identified Ned as the voice she heard out at the Archer. But he had to have an accomplice. There is no way he carried Jessica's body to the water.'

'You think Fletcher was with him?'

'According to Fairweather's statement, he left Jessica with Fletcher after he …'

'Raped her.' Ryan filled the gap.

Rape wasn't what Fairweather called it, but that's what it was. She suppressed a shiver.

'We need to prove Fletcher was with Jessica. We need proof he drowned her, and Ned is the weak link. Have we matched the water in Jessica's lungs to the pool water?'

'I'll check. But we don't have a motive. Why would Fletcher kill her? It can't be to protect Fairweather.'

'No. This is all about the money, as Ryan said.'

'Sir.' Reynolds met them in the hallway.

'What is it?'

'I have something weird in the grant receipts. You said to bring it to you.'

'I did. What have you got?' He ushered the constable straight into his office.

'It's these receipts for tutoring fees, sir. Grants were issued to various local Indigenous students, including Jessica. The fees were paid into the P & C bank account and distributed to various tutors.'

'That makes sense.'

'Yes, but these people don't exist.'

'What do you mean?'

'They are not teachers at the school. They don't belong to any of the tutoring agencies in town. I checked.'

'That's it.' Dawn almost punched the air.

'We need the report on why Fletcher was disbarred. He was a lawyer before he became a teacher. I think he defrauded the government. He's been bleeding these grants dry for years. Then he faked an inheritance for Larry so he could use the old guy as a front for a development syndicate.'

'We can't prove he was behind this.'

'No. But I know someone who can. And I think I know how to catch him out. But we need to let him go to make this work.'

Chapter 54

Dawn's adrenalin kicked in as she paced back and forth in Sergeant Martin's office. Ryan's expression was pensive, as she outlined her plan. But as a slow grin crossed his face, she knew he was on board.

'I like it.'

'I don't.' Martin flopped back in his chair.

'What's our other option? Keep digging into paperwork and find more circumstantial evidence? We know Ned didn't carry Jessica's body on his own. We know Fairweather has an alibi. Brad is a mess. I don't think he was helping anyone dispose of a body.

'That leaves Fletcher. We could get a search warrant, based on Fairweather's statement, to search Fletcher's car, but he's clever. I doubt he used his own vehicle.

'I think Ned was mopping up for him. His car might turn up something, but that doesn't nail Fletcher. Ned will be staying in custody, which means Fletcher will have to do his own dirty work.'

'It's a solid plan,' Ryan offered.

'Yes, but I don't like baiting a suspect. It's too risky.'

The sergeant was still on the fence. Dawn needed to get him on side. She was desperate to clear Fraser's name. Desperate to get her sister's life back to normal.

'I'll be there, in the room. He won't know I'm there. Nothing is going to happen. But I need an hour to organise everything. You interview Fletcher, get his statement about the incident with Brad. Ask him if he knows why Ned would have grabbed Ronnie.

'Then tell him he's free to go for now, but make it clear he's not out of the woods yet. He'll know he needs to get rid of the only person likely to roll over on him, and I'll be waiting.'

'An hour?'

Martin glanced at Ryan who nodded he was good with the plan.

'Okay. Ryan, you're with me. Grave, you have no jurisdiction to arrest anyone here.'

'No, but I trust Reynolds. I'll have her nearby, in plain clothes. She can make the arrest and hold him until you get there.'

Sergeant Martin rose from his high-backed office chair.

'Okay. Let's do this.'

Ryan opened the office door leading to the hallway. Dawn stepped out. Sergeant Martin followed.

'An hour.'

'An hour.'

Dawn strode down the hall, a lightness in her step.

'Dawn.' Ryan's use of her first name caught her off guard. She turned.

'You've got your gun in your purse still. Right?'

She patted the handbag slung across her chest.

'Of course.'

'If Fletcher is our man, he's a ruthless bastard. Two women, held underwater until they stopped moving.'

'I've got this. Thanks.'

She smiled and carried on down the hallway, out the front door and into her van, phone in hand dialling to make the necessary arrangements.

If all of this went to plan, she'd be able to clear Fraser's name and get the case into his death reopened.

Something Ned said popped into her head. Was her mother's disappearance linked to the fraud? The old man told her to keep out of it. To let sleeping dogs lie. That her mother hadn't done that.

She shook her head. Now wasn't the time to try and figure out where her mum disappeared to. Now was time to catch a killer and find out if he was connected to Fraser's death.

Now all she needed to do was make sure the bait she had in mind was on board.

****

The room was pitch black. Dawn stretched her legs, trying to ignore the cold tile floor beneath her. Through the vent in the door, she could see the entire room. A dim nightlight above the bed cast an eerie glow around the sterile room.

A creak of hinges made Dawn hold her breath. Was this it, or only another check-in by staff? The door quietly clicked shut. Dawn watched, heart thumping in her chest, as a figure drew nearer to the bed.

The face was covered by the edges of a hooded top. No one wore a hoodie this time of year in Cooktown. Her gut told her this was it. Sweat beaded between her shoulder blades and ran down her back as she palmed her Derringer .22 cal.

The figure loomed, studying the woman in the bed. Dawn needed him to do more than come in after hours. She needed him to incriminate himself. She expected him to put a pillow over the victim and suffocate her, but what happened next took it to a whole new level.

He pressed his hand over Ronnie's mouth. Her friend opened her eyes and struggled. Dawn couldn't move. She desperately wanted to, but this was common assault, not attempted murder.

She knew the sergeant would reprimand her once he found out. But she also knew they needed enough to make it impossible for Fletcher to walk away.

'You've been a busy girl, Veronica. I thought I'd made it perfectly clear what I'd do to your kids and Brad if you spoke to anyone. Have you spoken to anyone, Veronica?'

Ronnie shook her head.

'That's a good little girl.'

He pulled the second pillow out from under Ronnie's head. She saw it from the corner of her eye. Kicking and bucking, she violently tried to break free. Her fingernails scratched at Fletcher's hand.

They had everything they needed. DNA under her fingernails. Her statement. Dawn's statement.

Dawn jumped up, flinging the door open with a thud.

'Hand's up, Fletcher.'

He kept the pillow over Ronnie's face and turned to face Dawn with a sneer.

'You've got nothing without a witness.'

Ronnie's feet kicked, but there was less effort now.

'Let her go, Fletcher. Or I *will* shoot you.'

'I don't think you will. Your mother said the same thing. But she couldn't do it either.'

Dawn froze. He was admitting her mum knew about the fraud. But more than that …

'You killed my mother?'

'It was a shame, because she was so good in the sack, and I thought the money would have been more than enough to keep her quiet.'

Dawn's mind drifted. She began to watch the scene like she'd died, and her spirit was floating on the ceiling.

Ronnie's hand fell away from the pillow. Dawn blinked—her stomach knotted. What had she done?

'Ronnie!'

She didn't want to shoot Fletcher. She wanted him to rot in prison for all the women he'd killed. Crossing the room, she rammed her gun into the back of her pants.

'You're right. I'm not going to shoot you.'

She rushed closer but pulled up short.

'Reynolds!'

Fletcher turned as the door burst open. Dawn's fist collided with his jaw, knocking him to the right. Reynolds held her gun on him as Dawn grabbed his wrist and spun him around. Reynolds threw her cuffs, Dawn caught them deftly.

As she squeezed the first one on his right wrist, she didn't hold back. Fletcher grunted. Dawn shoved him against the wall.

'Check Ronnie!'

Reynolds holstered her weapon as Dawn pressed the second cuff in place.

'Mrs Summerset? Veronica? Are you okay?'

Dawn glanced over her shoulder, hoping against all hope her loss of concentration hadn't been too long. Fletcher watched over his left shoulder as Ronnie opened her eyes and half-smiled.

Dawn puffed the air out from her lungs.

'Reynolds. He's all yours. I'll message Ryan and Sergeant Martin.'

The young constable patted Ronnie's hand, turned, grabbed Fletcher by the cuffed arms and led him to the other side of the room, ordering him to sit.

Dawn pressed *send* on the prepared message and crossed the room to sit on the edge of her friend's bed.

'He won't be hurting you anymore, Ronnie.'

Her friend reached for her hand. Dawn pulled it away.

'I'll give you a hug later. We need to get all the evidence first. Sorry.'

'No, I'm sorry. Sorry about how Brad treated you when you first got to town. Sorry I didn't tell you where Lisa was.'

'It's okay, Ronnie. I know you were only protecting your family. I get why you didn't say anything about Lisa. Thanks for taking her to safety. You probably saved her life.'

Ronnie tried to sit up. Dawn wanted to put the pillow back behind her friend's head and let her finally sleep soundly, but the pillow was evidence.

'Rest here a minute. We'll get you into a fresh room while we process the scene. There's a few someones waiting to see you.'

'The kids? Brad? Is he going to jail?'

'Probably. He was involved in the fraud. I'm sure the judge will be lenient with the sentence, but there's a lot to get through before we work out all the details.'

The door burst open. Ryan appeared, huffing and puffing like he'd run up a dozen flights of stairs. As soon as he saw Dawn, sitting on the edge of the bed, he sucked in a deep, steadying breath.

'It's all under control, Detective,' she smiled.

'I can see.'

He crossed the room and dragged Fletcher to his feet, before shoving him towards the door, one hand on his cuffs, the other at the scruff of his neck.

'Let's go over your interview again, hey sunshine. I think you might like to redo your statement.'

'I want my lawyer.'

'Oh. Didn't Detective Grave tell you? Trevor Summerset won't be taking your case. He's kind of busy making sure his brother and he come out smelling like roses.'

Dawn chuckled as Reynolds pulled the door closed behind them.

'He's a good catch, that one.'

'He's not mine to catch.'

'Oh, I think he is.'

An orderly stuck his head inside the door. 'You ready now, Detective?'

'Yes. I'll oversee the transfer. Don't touch anything without gloves on.'

'Yes, ma'am.' He held up his gloved hands.

Dawn stepped back, a lightness in her heart she'd not experienced for over twenty years. She needed to see Lisa and Abby, as soon as she finished up here. There was something she wanted to tell them. Something she never thought she'd ever say again in her life.

Chapter 55

Lightning crackled across the sky as Dawn sipped her glass of wine.

'I think you've earned a celebratory drink.'

Michael raised his beer from the worn cane lounge on the veranda – Abby curled up asleep in his lap, Lisa resting against his shoulder.

'It was a tricky one, for sure. Especially since I wasn't supposed to interview any suspects.'

'Control freak much,' Lisa teased as she sat up and reached for her drink from the Kauri coffee table, in need of a fresh coat of varnish.

'Possibly. But I'm good at my job. I've got to tell you something Lisa. Not sure if you're going to like it though.'

Dawn leant forward in her chair.

'You've been gone for twenty years Dawn. I don't think you can offend me anymore.'

Lisa grinned as she sipped her drink.

'I'm sorry Lisa.' Dawn studied her glass, reminding herself to make it last.

'It's okay. I get it.'

Michael handed his beer to Lisa and lifted Abby.

'I'll pop her to bed. Give you two a few minutes.'

'Thanks Michael.'

Lisa kissed his cheek as he rose.

They sat in silence until Michael disappeared inside.

'When did that happen?' Dawn nodded to Michael as the screen door closed behind him.

Lisa sipped her drink a moment, eyes glazing over. Finally, she spoke.

'At first, I thought Michael had tabs on you, but after the hostage situation, he said it was me he was sticking around for. The way he was trying to impress you confused me. But I think he wanted you to like him, because you're my sister.'

'You two are good together.'

'You don't mind?'

'Why would I mind? He's a nice guy. Too nice for me, if I'm totally honest.'

'What does that mean?'

Dawn studied the wine in her glass a moment, trying to formulate how to explain her disastrous love life.

'You assumed I've not been in a relationship. Well, that's not exactly the case.' She forced herself not to drain her wine, because if she did, she knew she'd be straight on to the next one. Staring out into the night sky, she sighed as another lightning strike lit the darkness.

Silence hung in the air. Lisa waited for more.

'My record with men is abysmal. It's a story for another time though. For now, I need to tell you about Fletcher. About Mum.'

Lisa shimmied forward on the lounge, drink in hand, eyes fixed on Dawn.

'He claims he was sleeping with Mum.'

'No. There's no way. She wouldn't have.'

Lisa put her drink down with a shaking hand.

'Cheat on Dad. Why not? He wasn't the most attentive husband. Always trying to live a lost youth through us, and that damned swimming club.'

'But cheating? Why not leave him?'

Lisa shook her head in disbelief.

'You know better than anyone how irresistible a charming man can be.'

Lisa sighed. 'There is that.'

'He started the grant fraud scam and roped Brad and Trevor in on it. It was their job to keep Larry in the dark and reap the rewards. I'm not sure Mum knew about it to start with, but once she figured out what was going on, she must have kicked up a stink.'

'And he killed her?'

Dawn reached for Lisa's hand and squeezed gently.

'Yes. It was Mum's top we found out at Archer Point when we were searching for you. It took a while to figure out, but it wasn't a school uniform. It was a P & C shirt, issued to members for special occasions.'

'How did it get out to Archer?'

'We think Jessica had it on her when she died.'

'So that's what she'd found out? What she wanted to show me?'

'We think so. But Fairweather was abusing her. Their relationship was corrosive, manipulative. She must have told him what she knew because after his last …' Dawn searched for the word, '… indiscretion with her, he called Fletcher. Fletcher drowned her, like he drowned Tracey all those years ago.'

'And Fraser?'

'He didn't own up to killing Fraser. He gloated about drowning Tracey and Jessica, but he said he didn't have anything to do with Fraser and I believe him.'

'Why?'

'Gut instinct. I don't know.'

The screen door creaked as Michael returned, a bottle of wine in one hand, a fresh beer in the other. Ryan right behind him.

Dawn rose and crossed the veranda to gaze out over the balcony. Taking a sip of her wine, she turned to watch Ryan as he joined her.

'When did you get here?'

'A few seconds ago.' He leant on the railing.

'All wrapped up then?' She didn't glance his way.

'For now. Brad is on a mental health directive, so we need to await his assessment before we can question him or lay charges.'

Dawn turned to face her sister. Ryan did the same. They both rested their elbows on the balcony railing.

'So, is he home with Ronnie and the kids?'

'He is for now, but he'll need to go into hospital in Cairns. Trevor gave us what we needed to bury Fletcher on fraud charges. Along with the financial records, we have enough to make sure he gets decent jail time. But the arrogant arse signed a statement, admitting to the murders of Jessica and Tracey. Forensics are going through everything now.'

'Did he admit to killing Mum?'

'He's holding out, but we have your statement, and we have a team,' he nodded to Michael, 'including the rangers, going through the national park out near Archer. If she's out there, we'll find her.'

Ryan's fingers touched hers on the railing. He wrapped his pinkie around hers. She smiled. Lisa's voice made him let go.

'Why there? What's so special about Archer Point?'

He focussed on Lisa.

'If Fletcher killed your mum out there, possibly during a rendezvous, and she was never discovered, maybe he thought he could do it again,' he shrugged.

'So, you think he kept dumping the bodies out there from habit?'

'It's possible. Hopefully the rangers or SES find something.'

'What about Ned?'

Dawn needed to change the subject. The thought of her mum's body, abandoned out in the bush, made her heart ache.

'Ned is going down as an accessory, but he won't last long.'

'Why?' Dawn frowned.

'Liver damage. He's had undiagnosed hep C for years. Doctors give him six months. He won't qualify for a transplant.'

'Maybe that's why he helped dispose of the body?'

'No. He helped dump Tracey's remains too.'

'Arsehole,' Michael said as he offered Ryan a beer, then sat down next to Lisa. She pecked his cheek. Ryan glanced at Dawn, a question in his eyes.

She lifted her glass of wine, promising herself not to accept a refill.

'I've got an announcement to make.'

All eyes turned to her as lightning cracked across the sky behind her.

'I've put in for long service leave.'

'What? Didn't you have a promotion on the horizon?'

Ryan took a swig of his beer, but his eyes didn't leave hers. Thunder rumbled in the distance, vibrating deep in her chest. She studied his eyes, trying to communicate with him all the reasons she was staying.

'I did. But I want to stick around and get Fraser's case reopened as a murder investigation. My friend Penny called me today. She and the handwriting expert are sure the suicide letter was written under duress.'

'Where are you going to live?'

Lisa's eyes were wide, with excitement or was it something else?

'Here. If it's okay with you. This place is a wreck. I can organise to do some renovation work while I work on the case.'

'But I don't have any money for renovations.'

Dawn shrugged. 'This place is still half mine, right?'

Lisa nodded.

'I've got some funds.'

'But I can't buy you out. What happens when you go back to Adelaide?'

Dawn glanced out over the balcony, drawing in the moist air, with the promise of more rain. The scent of the tropics filled her lungs as Ryan touched her elbow, fingers lingering a moment.

She turned to face him, then Lisa.

'I'm not sure I am.' Dawn glanced back at Ryan. A slow smile crept across his face.

'I thought the local police could do with a consultant.'

'I'll drink to that.' Ryan raised his beer. Dawn clinked her glass.

'Me too!' Lisa popped to her feet, rounding the coffee table as a crack of lightning lit the sky. Dawn was enveloped in a tight hug before the thunder rattled the old house.

'What's with all the hugs?'

'I'm so happy to have you home.'

Dawn sighed. Was she happy to be home?

Fairweather was facing multiple charges and more would likely surface once the news broke. Her mother's disappearance was finally being opened as a murder investigation, relieving more than two decades of abandonment issues.

Yes, Dawn was very happy to be home.

But there was one more thing she needed to do. Now she would prove Fraser didn't kill himself.

****

Join Dawn when a local murder case threatens to re-open old wounds in *Grave Intent*, book two in the new *Dawn Grave* Crime series available in November 2024.

Join my exclusive reader's club to stay up to date with all new releases, sales and up and coming events. Just visit my website www.fionatarr.com to join the team.

Thank You!

I hope you enjoyed reading this first book in the new *Dawn Grave* series.

If you did, why not tell your friends, or better still, leave a review with your favourite retailer so others can make an informed decision about buying into the series.

If you leave a review, I'd love to see a copy, but most of all, I'd like to thank you for reading my stories. You're awesome, really! Without you, I'd be a lot less motivated to get in front of my computer screen and dream up these crazy crime/mystery adventures. Without you, I'd have never bothered to publish. Thanks!

While you wait for my next release, you might like to read about Constable Jenny Williams as she searches for answers to a family mystery in the remote outback town of Coober Pedy.

Or if you've already read Jenny's adventures, you might like to read what happens when she takes that detective job in the city; the one we know she's born for.

Jenny joins the *Foxy Mysteries* series team in book 2, as Jack Cunningham's new partner. So if you don't mind skipping the 'how she got to Adelaide' bit (which I'll be writing next year), and enjoy a little sizzle with your mysteries, why not check out the whole *Foxy Mysteries Collection.*

I have so many books planned for the new *Dawn Grave* series, but I'll be writing more in the *Opal Fields* very soon.

I always love to hear what readers think, so if reviewing isn't your thing, I'm open to an email message or comment on my website. You'll find my books and my bio at www.fionatarr.com

Books by Fiona Tarr

Dawn Grave

Grave Doubt – a novella exclusive to the reader's club.

Grave Regret

Grave Intent

Opal Fields

Her Buried Bones

Her Broken Bones

Her Scorched Bones

Her Hidden Bones

Her Lonely Bones

Her Covered Bones

Foxy Mysteries

Death Beneath the Covers

Presumed Missing

Deadly Deceit

Twisted Vendetta

Dead Cold

Or the full collection

Foxy Mysteries Complete Collection

The Priestess Chronicles

Call of the Druids

Relic Seeker

Shiloh Rising

The Eternal Realm
The Jericho Prophecy
Delilah and the Dark God
Reign of Retribution

Covenant of Grace
Destiny of Kings
Seed of Hope
Legacy of Power
Heir of Vengeance
The Ehud Dagger - Prequel

Printed in Great Britain
by Amazon

62193007R20180